Helen J. Rolfe writes upliftin… fiction
with characters to relate to a…

Before she started writing …
in I.T. until she came to her se…
journalism and writing. She wrote articles fo…
Health & Fitness magazines as well as newsletter
content and media releases for a not-for-profit
organisation. In 2011 the fiction bug bit and Helen has
been writing fiction ever since.

Helen J Rolfe lives in Hertfordshire with her husband
and two children.

Find out more at www.helenjrolfe.com, and follow her
on Twitter @HJRolfe.

Also by Helen J. Rolfe

The Friendship Tree

Handle Me with Care

What Rosie Found Next

Helen J. Rolfe

Published by Fabrian Books

To all the volunteers with the CFA (Country Fire Authority) in Australia…you do an amazing job.

Chapter One

Rosie sat bolt upright and told herself the noises were all in her imagination. It had to be the unfamiliar surroundings of Magnolia Creek playing tricks on her in the middle of the night.

In an ideal world she wouldn't be doing this house-sit at all. She'd be happily settled with her boyfriend, Adam, in a home of their own. But their plans had been put on hold when he'd got a job overseas a year ago, and she started house-sitting in order to save as much money as possible. She was determined to realise the dream of having their own place one day, the security and stability she'd always wanted.

She reached out for the glass of water that had turned tepid in the November heat. The only sound she could hear now was the rustling of leaves on the trees outside her open window, and her heartbeat steadied. All the doors were locked. She'd triple checked them last night. There was no way anybody could get in to number twenty-seven Lakeside Lane, the luxurious six-bedroom home that was by far the biggest she'd ever looked after and its location the most remote. She was used to the sounds of the city – a car alarm in the middle of the night, bin men starting their early morning collections, the sound of passers-by returning home after a night on the tiles. The solitude of the Dandenong Ranges bordering Magnolia Creek in the state of Victoria was something else.

A scratching noise against the window sent her mind into overdrive and had her envisaging a pyromaniac in this bushfire-prone area, rubbing sticks together to get the first flames going. Fire had ruined her life once before. She couldn't let it happen again, not ever.

She shook her head at her own paranoia. This was ridiculous. The country was bound to sound totally different to the city and the suburbs of Melbourne. Of course it was.

She pulled the sheet over herself and relaxed her head into the plump pillow, but as she watched the shadows of the trees dance against the wall of the bedroom that would be hers for the next couple of months, there it was again … the same noise. And this time, she knew she hadn't imagined it. She knew exactly what it was. It was the garage door shutting.

The door creaked its way down and finished with a thud. And then, silence. Her breath caught in her throat as she reached for her phone on the bedside table before the intruder broke down the internal door to give them access to the house, access to her, all alone.

She froze. She could picture her phone – downstairs on the kitchen bench along with her iPad. Last night after the owners, Jane and Michael Harrison, left for the UK, she'd relaxed with her dinner and a glass of wine, buzzy sensations pervading her body at being part of this new world that wasn't really hers. She hadn't thought to find out where the landline was in the house, but now she really wished she had.

As calmly as she could, Rosie tiptoed over to her bedroom door and opened it slowly. Whoever was downstairs wasn't sneaking around at all. The internal door connecting the garage to the house clunked shut and heavy footsteps clomped down the hall towards the kitchen. She'd locked that door, so whoever was down there was either a professional burglar with their own tools to pick a lock, or they had a key.

She hovered against the doorjamb, afraid to move for fear the intruder would hear her, and when the kitchen lights flicked on, illuminating the hallway, her heart galloped as she shrunk away from the light.

It couldn't be the owners – they'd emailed from Singapore's Changi Airport when they realised they'd forgotten to give Rosie the vet's contact details should anything happen to George, the cat, who Rosie was in charge of for the eight week house-sit.

Whoever it was knew the place well and didn't care whether they woke anybody. Rosie's independent, determined streak kicked in. She wasn't about to hang around to find out whether the intruder would show mercy to an innocent twenty-something. She crept down the stairs one at a time, winding her way down to the wooden floor of the hallway below, praying she wouldn't find the creaky step this time. She wished she'd taken more notice of exactly where it had been last night.

She froze at the bottom, turned to the left and reached for her car keys from the hook on the wall. She removed them as carefully as if she was playing a game of Operation, anxious not to let the metal keys ting against each other and announce her presence. All she had to do was get out of the front door and leap into her car sitting down the side of the house. Perhaps if she'd parked it out front instead, it would've deterred whoever was in the house now. When she'd arrived yesterday, George the cat had been sprawled out on the driveway, basking in the sun, and she hadn't had the heart to make him move.

Rosie crept to the front door, but as she lifted her keys to the locked door that stood between her captivity and her freedom, she saw a figure in the corner of her eye.

She screamed, panicked, tried desperately to slot the key into the lock, but it was as though it'd grown ten sizes too big.

A man dressed in leathers and wearing a helmet filled the kitchen doorway. Rosie's whole body shook when he glared at her from behind his visor and boomed, 'Who the hell are you?'

She turned and with a last-ditch effort managed to push the key into the lock. She pulled the door open to the darkness of the night, but before she had a chance to make a run for it, a hand landed on the bare skin of her arm. She froze.

The man towered over her. 'Now where do you think you're going at this time of night, little lady?'

Chapter Two

'Let me go!' the girl screamed at him.

She didn't have a bag with the family jewels in it, she didn't even look like a thief. But the fact remained. She was an intruder. She kicked out her leg to make contact with his shins, but his reflexes were good and he jumped back, still holding her at arm's length.

'What do you want from me?' she yelled.

He flipped up his visor. 'I might ask you the same question.' Her attempts to hurt him as she struggled were laughable. He was way too strong and had no problem keeping a grip on her. 'What are you doing here in my parents' house?'

When she stopped wrestling he released her from his grip.

'Your parents' house?' she demanded.

The girl stepped back when he made no move to widen the gap between them.

'Yes, that's what I said. I'm Owen Harrison. Who the hell are you?'

She ignored him. 'You're not supposed to be here. This is my house-sit.' Her hands planted firmly on her hips and it made him smile all the more. She really didn't realise what good entertainment she was at four o'clock in the morning, did she?

‘I come and go all the time.’ He pulled off his helmet, turned and walked into the kitchen. This was his house more than hers. Where had his parents found this girl anyway? He tugged off his leather biker jacket and slung it on top of the kitchen bench.

‘Close to your parents, are you?’ She’d followed him into the kitchen.

‘What’s that supposed to mean?’

She snatched up her iPhone from its position on the bench. ‘If you were close to your parents, then you’d know they’ve gone to the UK and asked me to house-sit. We have a contract.’

He pulled a face. ‘Sounds formal.’

‘It is. I can show you if you need me to.’

Damn. He hadn’t expected his mum to find a bona fide house-sitter. He’d expected her to ask her best friend Bella to see to the cat. His mum had called him a couple of weeks ago when they’d had word from London to say his Auntie Sarah had died. His parents were heading over for the funeral and staying for a couple of months so they could sort out his Auntie’s affairs. Owen had considered going for the funeral, but he barely knew his mum’s sister. They’d only spoken at Christmases and birthdays, and Auntie Sarah had only visited Australia a couple of times since she’d emigrated when he was still a young boy.

When his mum had told him the news, he’d been knee-deep in renovation plans at his property on the Mornington Peninsula, preparing for tenants to move in, and he saw the opportunity for what it was: a time to search the house good and proper with his parents out of the country for a while.

He ran a hand across his jaw as he watched this girl. He wondered whether her hands were permanently glued to her hips or whether she actually thought her stance would scare him away. Well it wouldn't. He wasn't going anywhere. He needed to be here, he needed answers.

Ignoring the girl, he stood at the kitchen sink and pumped soap into the palm of his hand. Despite the shower before he'd come to the house, his fingernails were still grubby and he used the small brush kept beneath the sink to attack them some more. He took his time, amused by her reflection in the glass-fronted cabinet above the sink, arms now folded across her chest instead. He wondered how long he could keep her standing there like that.

He dried his hands and pulled open the fridge, parched. He pulled out a carton of apple juice and glugged it straight from the spout.

'I'm sorry, did you want some?' He offered her the carton but she was too stunned to say anything, and he glugged the rest before dumping the empty vessel beside the sink.

When he lolloped onto the sofa and locked his hands behind his head, he caught her looking at the tail of the tattoo poking out of the sleeve of his marl-grey T-shirt.

'Are you wondering whether I've got any more?' he asked.

'No,' she answered quickly, but he knew her mind was ticking, wondering where any others may be on his body. He watched her fidget beneath his gaze, her hands moving to an odd-looking necklace fastened around her neck.

'Is the pink car that glows in the dark yours?' He'd had enough of teasing her about checking out his tattoo. 'I saw it through the window in the laundry when the outside light came on. I'll bet you could see it from outer space it's so bright.' He laughed, but her mouth was set in the same hard line. 'Oh relax, I don't bite.'

She looked unsure.

'So come on, what's your name?' he asked. Whatever it was, he had no intention of moving on. He wasn't going to be the one to go. She could.

'Rosie.' She stayed behind the safety of the kitchen bench.

Pretty name. Pretty girl too, but she still had to leave. This was his place for the next eight weeks, and he needed that time to turn the house upside down.

He jumped up, suddenly ravenous, and went over to the pantry. He noticed Rosie edge away from him as he pulled out a loaf of bread followed by the butter from the fridge. Judging by her face, he was eating her food and she wasn't happy about it. He carried on and pushed two slices of bread into the toaster. Perhaps if he riled her enough, she'd run away from this house-sit and it would be at least one problem solved.

Her hands were back on her hips. 'You want me out of here, right?' he asked.

'As I said before, I have a contract to house-sit.'

He looked at the clock. Almost four thirty in the morning. He was bloody exhausted and all he wanted to do was eat his toast and crash out upstairs. Her leaving was preferable, but he wasn't enough of an arsehole to see a pretty young thing chucked out in the middle of the night.

'Look,' he said, 'my mugshot's on the wall over there and you know who I am, so would you mind if we sort this out in the morning?' His toast popped up and he buttered it roughly, too hungry to care. He tore a hole in it with his teeth.

‘You don’t expect me to sleep here with you in the house, do you?’

‘You’re free to leave any time.’

‘I’m not leaving,’ she said.

He tore off the corner of the second piece of toast. ‘Neither am I.’

She stood glaring at him for a minute or two. He was too tired to even try to give her the death stare back.

‘We’ll talk in the morning,’ she said. And with that she turned and took the stairs up a lot noisier than she’d come down them.

‘See you in the morning,’ he called when their eyes met briefly over the top of the bannisters.

Owen pushed a third slice of bread into the toaster. He hadn’t banked on anyone being here, at least not on a live-in basis. And as gorgeous as this girl was, he needed her to leave.

He pulled out his phone and checked his email again, and sure enough, when he reread the one from his mum he realised he’d been so preoccupied by the renovation project at the time that he hadn’t scrolled all the way to the bottom. The last paragraph told him not to worry about being unable to look after the house and the cat because she’d found someone to do it officially. It made sense; they were away for a while, and in bushfire season it was good to have the house occupied in case emergency procedures had to be implemented. His mum had even made a point of saying that he wouldn’t be able to come to the house like he usually did.

Owen scraped butter across the third slice of toast. He’d be back down to the Mornington Peninsula in a few days to finish the reno job by putting up the garden shed he’d promised his new tenants, then he’d collect his pickup he used to transport all his tools and usually the

Ducati. But right now, as soon as he'd answered his stomach's distress calls with this last slice of toast, he'd head up to bed before he fell asleep curled up on the floor.

When he heard a sound from upstairs, a dragging sound as though Rosie was rearranging her bedroom furniture, he hoped that by morning they could sort this mess out. He needed to take this opportunity to find out what was going on, what his parents were hiding, and having her in the house wasn't going to help. The conversation he'd overheard between his mum and dad was the reason he was here now, and the reason Rosie couldn't be.

About a month ago he'd been staying here at his parents' place for a stint, and one morning he pulled out one of the many travel books from the top bookshelf in the lounge area to read during breakfast. He'd picked a book about Europe and read up on London, a place he very much hoped to visit one day.

He finished his cereal and flicked the kettle on for a coffee, but as he returned the book to its place and took out another, this time on Italy, two pieces of paper floated down from the very same shelf, landing on the floor. He stooped to pick them up. This house was immaculate, always had been, so leaving loose pages around was never an option. But he'd only read the title of what seemed to be a magazine article before his mum appeared behind him and snatched the papers away.

'Hey, I was reading that,' he protested.

She balled up the pages. 'It's really old, I'll throw it.'

'But it was to do with property, I'm interested.'

Jane Harrison was already cutting through the kitchen towards the laundry.

‘It must’ve been from when we were looking to buy a holiday house. Old news now.’

Owen poured a cup of coffee. ‘So what was it doing up there?’ He heard the laundry door open, the bin lid lift, and then Jane was back in the house.

‘No idea,’ she said.

He shrugged and wondered why she’d turned the same white as the milk he’d just used to top up his coffee.

Enticed by the freshly baked cinnamon buns his mum pulled from the oven, Owen forgot all about the article, and with a second cinnamon bun, he sat at the kitchen table doing his accounts as his mum went out to tend those blessed rose bushes again. Owen and his brothers often joked she was more enamoured by those rose bushes than she was by them. And sometimes, Owen was inclined to think it was actually true.

He forgot all about the peculiar behaviour and his mum’s refusal to let him see the magazine pages he’d found, until the middle of the night. He woke around two a.m. thirsty as hell and crept downstairs for a glass of water. Back upstairs he stooped down to fuss George, curled up outside his parents’ bedroom, and he heard crying coming from the other side of the door. And then he heard voices.

‘Owen had the article right there in his hands, Michael.’

‘But he had no idea what it was.’ His dad’s voice was soothing.

Between sobs Jane said, ‘The internet is powerful. What if he’d searched the name, the business, and worked out who the article was about? Who knows what damage it could’ve done.’

'You know, he's stronger than you think. Maybe it's time we told him everything.'

Jane's voice rose an octave in the still of the night. 'My son's whole world would come crashing down if we told him the truth now! No, I can't let it happen. I won't let it happen. I've hidden everything and there's no way he'll find it. He must never know the truth.'

The sobs continued as Owen stole back to his room, heart pounding. He waited almost an hour and then he crept downstairs again, sure his parents were by now asleep. He opened the door which led from the laundry to the side of the house and in bare feet tiptoed outside and over to the recycling bin. He expected the magazine article to be lying right there on top but it wasn't. He went back into the laundry, grabbed a torch and then back outside he slowly but surely took everything out of the blue-topped wheelie bin until there was nothing left. He went through all the paper recycling as it came out and he went through it all as it went back in. But he found nothing.

He leant against the kitchen bench top now as he ate his toast. He was content moving from one place to another and dossing down in Magnolia Creek whenever it suited because he loved this town. Tonight's ninety minute journey, zigzagging his way to Lakeside Lane on his Ducati, revelling in the sense of freedom, had cleared his head and he'd felt ready to tackle the challenge of finding out exactly what it was his parents were keeping from him. He needed to know. He wanted answers. The time had come to get to the bottom of why he'd never felt good enough in his mother's eyes no matter what he did, how much he pushed himself, how successful he was.

He retrieved the key to the study from above the fuse box and pocketed it. Tomorrow, he'd have a good look through all the personal papers his parents kept in there.

He thought about the girl upstairs: the girl with the none-too-subtle pink car tucked down the side of the house; the girl with trusting brown eyes, a button nose and straight copper hair that grazed the middle of her back. He thought about the slight gap between her front teeth that made her look innocent and the odd necklace she wore that looked like a body with no head, legs astride, hands on hips. He knew he hadn't made a very good first impression with his rudeness, snatching supplies from the fridge and pantry she had most likely filled herself, but her presence had thrown him.

He climbed the stairs to head to the room at the farthest end of the house. At the top of the stairs, George was curled up neatly in his usual position against the bannisters, although instead of being outside Owen's room or his parents', he was outside Rosie's.

'So she's won you over already, has she?' He crouched down and stroked George from head to tail. 'Maybe you could let me in on your secret.' He rubbed his fingers beneath George's chin and the cat purred and dribbled contentedly.

In the morning they would sort this mess out. There was nothing else for it – she had to go. If he was going to turn this place upside down and find anything, then it was the only way. And if there was one thing Owen Harrison was used to overcoming, it was a challenge.

Chapter Three

When Rosie signed up for this house-sit, she envisaged waking every morning to the twittering sounds of birds performing their dawn chorus, enjoying a leisurely breakfast with only George the ginger cat for company and completely relaxing away from the city. So when she woke up to the deep, meaty pulsing of Owen's motorbike, she was bitterly disappointed.

'What time is it?' she said out loud, fumbling for her iPhone. When she noticed the time fast approaching ten o'clock her anger subsided a little. She'd slept much better than she'd anticipated given Owen's arrival in the middle of the night. After she'd left him in the kitchen, she'd gone up to her room and dragged the desk across her doorway to stop anyone coming in when she was asleep.

She yawned, stretched her arms up to the ceiling and padded over to the window where she pulled back the side of the curtain in time to see Owen's leather-clad figure astride the bike pulling out of the driveway.

When Owen had stood at the sink last night scrubbing filth from his hands, Rosie had looked over at the pictures dotted around the room and her eyes had settled on the family portrait on the kitchen wall. She'd immediately matched one of the boys to the man who stood before her, albeit a filled-out version of the lanky teenager from the photograph whose clothes had hung off him as though they were two sizes too big and whose hair had flopped in an unruly, childlike way. And as he'd pumped a second round of soap into his palm and scrubbed at his hands again, Rosie realised his green eyes were hereditary, the same shade as Jane Harrison's, the woman who had welcomed her to the house yesterday.

But Owen was so different to the woman who'd given birth to him. Jane, a quiet, no-nonsense woman with a flawlessly decorated house, was a woman with a together appearance – smart clothes, pleats down the front of her trousers, pearl-drop earrings – and a woman who seemed on edge, as though at any moment life could jump out of the closet and say 'boo'. It was hard to believe she could have a great oaf of a son like Owen who seemed to enjoy being as awkward as possible.

Rosie dragged the desk from its position across the bedroom door, back to its rightful place at the side of the room, and wondered whether Owen Harrison was coming back. Somewhere between the time Owen had arrived and when she'd woken up to the sounds of his motorbike, she'd become all the more determined that she wasn't going to be the one to leave. Her part-time job as a PR assistant at Magnolia House started in a few days, and it was the perfect opportunity to put her communications degree into practice. This house was in the perfect location to walk to work, and the house-sit had come up at exactly the right time given the lack of rental properties within commutable distance this side of Christmas.

It had taken confidence to take on a job in an area where the risk of bushfires was a part of everyday life, but Rosie had had plenty of challenges in the last eighteen months, and it was just another one to come her way. Jane Harrison had shown her the bushfire plan as casually as she'd shown her how to operate the washing machine and dishwasher; as calmly as she'd given her the rundown of the list of contacts that covered a gamut of possible emergencies from the pool water turning brown to a gas leak; as matter-of-factly as she'd told Rosie where the key to the study was should she need to use a printer. They'd talked about preparations during bushfire season, including clearing gutters and keeping the grass trimmed and watered, and Rosie had managed to dial down any panic derived from her personal history.

Downstairs, Rosie checked the kitchen for a note from Owen. Hopefully a note to say he'd gone for good. But there was nothing. When he still wasn't home by midday, she gave up waiting and went upstairs to unpack some more. She'd been too tired when she arrived yesterday and had instead enjoyed the first night in this lovely house by relaxing with dinner and a glass of wine. Once she got dressed and dried her hair, she would email Jane and raise the issue of her son. She didn't fancy being scared half to death again if he decided to come back, and she certainly wasn't going to be the one to leave Magnolia Creek.

She busied herself hanging clothes on rails, dumping electronic devices in a tangle of wires onto the desk, emptying her wash bags into wide drawers in the en suite. Her bedroom was no less luxurious than the rest of the home. A king-size bed stood in the middle of the light, airy room, and fluffy fawn cushions sat atop the crisp white linen. A gentle breeze rippled through the half open window that looked out to a view of the mountain ash trees and lush ferns standing tall at the front of the house and beyond.

After a long shower, Rosie hummed as the breeze through the open window fanned away the heat from the hairdryer. She tipped her head upside down to reach the strands beneath, and when she flicked her head back up she squealed at the figure standing in the doorway.

'Don't you ever knock?' she yelled, switching the hairdryer off and grabbing a T-shirt to hold across her chest. At least she'd already pulled on a pair of jeans and a bra.

Owen had the same smug look on his face as last night. 'Sorry,' he said. 'I shouted hello from downstairs and I knocked, twice.'

'Well if someone doesn't answer, it generally doesn't mean come in!'

'Oh okay, don't get your knickers in a twist.' The words played on his lips. 'Look, I know we got off on the wrong foot last night, and it was my fault, but I wanted to talk about … arrangements. I'll grab a coffee and a shower and then I'm all yours.'

Arrangements? Surely it was simple? He was leaving.

Lost for words, she waited for him to go and then pulled her T-shirt over her head.

Perhaps the desk should be a permanent fixture across her bedroom door.

*

Less than ten minutes later she joined Owen in the kitchen. She declined the offer of a coffee when he poured himself a cup.

'You were too quick for me,' he said, and at her confused expression, added, 'I haven't had a shower yet.' He nodded towards the deck. 'I was going to drink this outside first if it's okay with you.'

'It's fine.' She noticed the small scar that cut across his left eyebrow, and his dark messy hair covered the tops of his ears as though begging for a trim. When his eyes locked with hers, she scurried out onto the deck to where a newspaper sat on the table, the pages flapping gently in the wind. It was a warm afternoon with the garden now bathed in sunshine, and she'd been caught out by the changeable weather again. Melbourne's four-seasons-in-one-day reputation had her wondering whether she'd need to rethink her jeans in favour of a cotton dress.

When she heard Owen behind her, she stiffened, glad to feel George brush against her ankle. He'd be a good distraction while they talked. But when she noticed George happily curled up on the leather sofa inside, she looked down and saw a reptile skulking across the deck. She yelped and jumped up.

Owen slurped his coffee. 'No need to panic.'

'It's huge!'

'Rosie, meet Bertie.'

'Bertie?'

'Bertie the blue-tongue.'

Rosie eyed the lizard. It had to be well over a foot long. She shuddered thinking about how it had slithered against her bare skin.

'He won't hurt you,' Owen went on. 'Not unless you try to pick him up.' He tapped a foot near Bertie until the reptile turned and retreated towards the rockery at the side of the garden. Owen actually looked sympathetic rather than amused, but Rosie suspected he was trying to get on her good side so he could stay at the house a little longer.

She breathed a sigh of relief at the lizard's departure. 'I'm not likely to pick him up.'

'Probably a good idea, he'd more than likely bite you. They prefer to hide away from their predators.' He nodded towards the rocks where Bertie had found his sanctuary.

Rosie wasn't sure which unexpected guest had frightened her the most in the last twelve hours: Bertie or Owen.

Her heart rate returning to normal, she looked over at the pool where the cleaner was chugging away, stuck in a corner. 'Isn't that thing supposed to move around in the water?'

Owen frowned, took another gulp of coffee and then trotted down the steps towards the pool, calling over his shoulder, 'That *thing's* technical name is a Kreepy Krauly, and you'll get used to seeing it stuck in this corner.' He plunged his forearm into the water, wrestled with the hose for a minute or two and then headed back up to the deck as the Kreepy Krauly chugged merrily around the sides of the pool once more, sucking up all the debris along the tiles. 'Sometimes it needs a bit of encouragement to get moving.'

The Owen of last night would've laughed about Bertie the blue-tongue and how scared she'd been. The Owen of last night would've left her to fix the Kreepy Krauly. But this morning he was surprising her more and more.

He tipped his head back to get the dregs of coffee in his mug. 'If you think you can cope with the wildlife of Magnolia Creek, I'll take a shower and then we can talk.'

'Sure.' She stayed outside on the covered deck while Owen disappeared upstairs. She drew her legs up onto her chair, hugging them in close in case Bertie decided to take another wander, and only when she heard a strange buzzing coming from the kitchen did she move from her spot.

On top of the galaxy-black kitchen bench was a pager, doing a merry dance as it vibrated and tried to get her attention. She called up the stairs to Owen, but she had no idea whether he'd heard her or not. She wondered what kind of job relied on a pager, but she wasn't about to pry and see what it said.

She reread the bushfire escape plan and checked the FireReady app on her iPad that Jane had recommended for instant updates to Magnolia Creek and the surrounding areas. There was low fire danger for today, which was a relief, and the only incident was some twenty-five kilometres away. And rather than making her jittery about fires as she'd thought it would, the app reassured her that all was fine. Jane Harrison had also told her there hadn't been an incident here in more than twenty years. She was safe.

Seconds later Owen appeared in the kitchen and lifted up the pager. 'Was this buzzing?'

'Yes.' She tore her eyes away from the towel wrapped around the bottom part of his torso, but looking at his naked top half with droplets of water still snaking their way down his chest and back was no less distracting. She tried to lose herself in the FireReady app even though she'd seen as much as she needed to.

He charged out of the kitchen but not before she saw the full tattoo on his arm, the intricacy of the design a surprise. It was a rose, roughly the size of a baby's fist and almost like a ghost of the flower with a hint of red within the light and dark grey shading.

She was still thinking about the tattoo when Owen raced back down the stairs, yet again, wearing grey tracksuit pants and a black T-shirt with a loose hem at the bottom. 'Can our chat wait?'

He didn't leave her with much choice because he grabbed his keys and left. To where was anybody's guess, and now she was stuck in limbo again. She liked to know what was happening and when. She hated having to wait for things to unfold for her.

Perhaps she should call the house-sitting agency and let them sort this mess out. She went upstairs and pulled out her house-sitting contract and leafed through the pages, scanning for clauses in her favour, but as she got to the end of the paperwork she realised that in a peculiar way – discounting their introduction in the middle of the night – she'd enjoyed interacting with Owen today. Having another person in her living space was something she wasn't used to, hadn't been for a long time, but it was something she'd enjoyed. And she'd certainly appreciated him scaring away the lizard and fixing the pool cleaner.

She slotted her contract back into her file. As two grown adults, surely they could sort this out between themselves.

Chapter Four

Owen came and went the rest of the day as though the house were a youth hostel, and he was gone again the next morning. Rosie found it quite impossible to pin him down, and once again she was torn between chasing after him to force him to talk to her and phoning the agency to say she wanted out of this house-sit on the grounds that it had 'unreasonable complications'.

So much for the adult approach.

She'd thought about contacting Jane and Michael Harrison in London, but it would feel childish to do so. No, calling them had to be a last resort if she and Owen couldn't resolve this. Owen had certainly been pulling his weight around the house at least, feeding the cat before she'd had a chance this morning, emptying the dishwasher, replenishing juice and milk supplies – hopefully not drinking from the spout any more either.

She dragged the hose from the back of the house around to the front to water the shrubs and creepers that added to the English Tudor property's grandeur. She watered the dancing violet and yellow flowers in the hanging baskets positioned between the downstairs mullioned windows framed in dark wood, and she sprayed the foliage framing a front door made of the same wood with iron panels running across it. George sprawled out in the sunshine as she worked and brushed against her legs every time he decided it had been quite long enough since Rosie had paid him any attention.

She went to the kitchen to pour a glass of lemonade and took it to the back deck. She opened up her iPad and tapped Adam's name into the FaceTime app. It was early morning in Singapore, and if she was lucky she'd catch him before he got too busy. She couldn't wait to show him this place. They'd been together for four years now and often talked about getting a place of their own. She crossed her fingers that this house-sit could open his mind to living further away from a big city. She'd never given it much thought, not until this job opportunity had come up, but now she was actually here, it was addictive and she found herself wanting the peace and tranquillity more and more.

'Hello there.' Adam grinned when his face appeared on her screen. He ran a hand through cropped blond hair that formed a hint of a quiff at the front. 'I'm all yours for ten minutes and then I'm off to the first meeting of the day.'

With a roll of her eyes, Rosie smiled. Adam was fast climbing the corporate ladder, and the busier he was in his job as an investment banker, the happier he was.

'Are you missing me?' she asked.

'Of course I am. And I'm sorry we couldn't chat this past week, but it's been full on here. How was the drive up to … where are you?'

'Magnolia Creek. The drive was fine, less than three hours.'

'Not bad going from Geelong. How's your mum?' She'd spent three days with her mum in between house-sits.

'She's good. She's been taking Italian cooking lessons.'

‘Good on her.’

‘She fed me up with a lot of pasta when I was there.’

Adam drew in his breath. ‘Dangerous.’

‘I know. I’ll have to swim it off in the pool during this house-sit.’

‘You will.’ He laughed. ‘How are her plans going for renovating her house?’

‘Great. She’s all set to convert the attic space into a huge master bedroom with en suite, which obviously she can’t do until she gets rid of my things.’ Rosie knew construction wasn’t due to start for almost a year, but she needed to remind Adam that not having a permanent address wasn’t an arrangement she wanted to go on indefinitely. She wanted to feel settled, normal at last.

‘I’m sure you’re not imposing,’ he said. ‘So come on, what’s this grand house like?’

He’d changed the subject as usual, but Rosie was too relaxed today to get uptight about it. She flipped the camera on her iPad around so he could see the place for himself.

Framed by spectacular views of the fields and bushland that surrounded Magnolia Creek and stretched for miles, the garden was a real-life watercolour spread out before them. The smell was different too, although only she got to appreciate that right now. The freshly clipped lawn and floral notes pervaded Rosie’s senses and were far more powerful than any garden in the city or suburbs. She wished Adam could be here to feel the difference between a place this remote and the city.

‘You’ve certainly landed on your feet with this one,’ said Adam as she swept the iPad across the view beyond the rear of the garden, showcasing the Dandenong Ranges beyond, highlighted beneath the strength of the Australian sun. The rockery was dotted with a spray of yellow and vibrant red flowers, and in the middle of the lawn were various beds of roses. Some were pale-lemon with petals streaked with pink, others were ruby red, some an innocent white.

'You'll be gardening the whole time, won't you?' Adam laughed.

Rosie turned the camera back to her momentarily. 'Other than keeping the grass short, watered frequently and the flowerbeds tidy, it should be easy enough to maintain.'

She shifted the camera's focus to the pool now. The outside space, like the interior of the Harrisons' home, was beautifully cared for. Four pots stood at intervals beside the glass pool fence, and large creamy white Gardenias stood tall, nodding in the breeze as the sunlight caught their glossy green leaves. A leaf floated down from a tree above, into the crystal clear waters turned blue by the coloured tiles beneath. The solar heating showed off by disgorging its hot flush of water with a forceful glug, disturbing the surface, but it didn't look any less idyllic.

'Check out the gazebo.' She focused now on the structure at the far end of the pool past the row of baby-blue agapanthus. 'It's even got a beer fridge!' It would also be a great place to enjoy the shade and give her fair skin a much needed break from the summer sun.

'Nice. Have you been in the water yet?'

'No, but I will do, and soon.'

After a brief tour of the inside of the house, Rosie came full circle and sat at the outside table.

'How's the wildlife treating you?' Adam asked. 'Are there many snakes, spiders?' He'd never been one to step outside the city.

'It's not too bad, although I did meet Bertie.' She told him all about the lizard who'd taken her by surprise, neglecting to tell him about the other unexpected visitor. Owen would be gone soon enough, so there was no need to give Adam cause for worry about another man hanging around.

'Are you still planning on coming back for Christmas?' she asked as George jumped onto her lap and settled down, purring.

'I'll do my best.'

They'd discussed the possibility of her flying to Singapore for Christmas, but with the new job and now the house-sit, Rosie didn't want to leave Magnolia Creek.

'I wish you were here,' said Rosie.

Adam frowned. 'We've been over this.'

'I know, I know. You're there for work. This is the way it is for now.' She didn't mean to sound quite so whiny, but she rarely nagged him about working away and for some reason, in this gorgeous setting with nobody to share it with, it just got to her.

'I'd better go, Rosie. I love you.'

'I love you too.'

'It's not forever, I promise.'

Rosie's smile was weak and her voice small as she said goodbye.

She clicked out of FaceTime and reprimanded herself for sounding needy when she was perfectly able to look after herself.

In the kitchen she took out the eggs from the pantry and set about making a late breakfast. But as the water in the saucepan came to the boil, she realised she wasn't alone in the house any more when she heard footsteps in the hallway.

She hadn't heard Owen return.

Owen leaned around the doorjamb of the kitchen.

'Hey,' she said, quashing the temptation to ask, 'Have you found somewhere to go yet?' He swanned in as though he hadn't given it a moment's thought.

She carefully used a spoon to lower her eggs into the pan. She loaded two slices of bread into the toaster, but before she could ask him if he'd made alternative arrangements, he said, 'I'm sorry I haven't been around much.' He at least had the good grace to look sheepish now as he came over to inspect what she was doing. 'I'm not trying to avoid you. Give me five minutes to have a shower and I'll be back.' He took a bag into the laundry and she heard the washing machine whoosh into action, then he headed upstairs.

When the bread popped up, she buttered her toast soldiers and lifted out the soft-boiled eggs, placing one in the egg cup and the other on the plate. She sat at the kitchen bench to eat, and as she was tapping her spoon against the shell of the second egg to take the top off, Owen reappeared, hair glistening and still wet from the shower.

He leaned close to her. 'That looks awesome, I'm starving. Do you mind if I pinch a couple of eggs?' He pressed his palms together in a prayer position and Rosie couldn't say anything else but 'yes'.

As he moved around the kitchen preparing his own breakfast, she caught sight of the stem of his rose tattoo again and momentarily wondered whether he did have any others. She'd scanned his torso the other day when he'd answered the pager call wearing only a towel on his bottom half, but she hadn't spotted any. The thought of his body gave her an unexpected tingle through her own.

When his eggs were cooked and the toast buttered, Owen sat at the kitchen bench on the same side as Rosie. 'I haven't had this for years.' He dipped a soldier into the egg and yolk burst out of the top of the shell and ran down the sides of the china egg cup.

Rosie smiled and let him eat for a while before she said, 'Owen, I did expect the house to be empty when I signed the house-sitting agreement.'

'I know.' He finished his mouthful. 'And then I turn up, engines roaring, scaring the life out of you and stealing all your food.'

He must've been starving because he finished the eggs and toast in record time and then he was up, scouring the pantry for something else. She wondered where he put it all. He looked fit enough, muscular and didn't have an ounce of unwanted fat.

He found a banana but it had gone all squidgy so he threw it in the bin. He leant against the kitchen bench, opposite Rosie this time. 'I know this place works out well for you, Rosie, but the fact is I need to be here. Look, I'll pay the cost for you to rent somewhere else. How does that sound?'

She was too shocked to say what she really thought, which was that his suggestion was incredibly rude. 'You want to pay for a rental for me? Here, in Magnolia Creek?'

'Yes.'

'Why? Why are you so desperate to be here? Why would you want to pay for me to leave?'

'I don't have to answer to you.' He spoke matter-of-factly, but Rosie didn't miss the muscle in his jaw twinge.

'No, you don't.' She sipped from a glass of water. 'But the fact is there aren't any places to rent around here. I'm starting a new job at Magnolia House the day after tomorrow, and I don't want to face a big commute until I really have to.'

He puffed out his cheeks. Talk about stubborn.

'And even if there was somewhere else to rent,' she went on, 'I have a contract, a contract with your parents. I've been house-sitting for a while and I've got excellent references, something I don't want to jeopardise by abandoning this house. I have an obligation, Owen, to the house and to the pet-sitting part of the contract.'

'Right.'

She took her plate over to the sink. 'I'm not trying to be awkward.' Something in the way he looked at her made her feel sorry for him, but she wasn't going to back down. 'You can stay for a couple of nights until you've sorted something else out, but then you'll have to move on or I'll have no choice but to contact the agency.'

He sighed.

After she'd rinsed her plate and slotted it into the dishwasher she turned to him. 'I don't mean to be rude, but don't you have your own place?'

'What you mean is, do I really still live at home and rely on my parents at the ripe old age of thirty-three?'

'That wasn't what I said exactly.' She felt guilty. Despite his arrogance the night they'd first met, he didn't seem all bad now. It wasn't his fault he'd arrived not knowing about her arrangement with his mum.

'I was reading between the lines.' He grinned. 'I don't have my own place, at least not really. I'm what you might call nomadic. I'm only here on and off, and I pay for my keep when I am and help out around the place.'

Rosie nodded towards the photo of three boys, Owen on the right-hand side. 'Could you stay with either of your brothers?'

Owen shrugged. 'Ben is exploring Europe as we speak, but I guess Tom's a possibility.'

'Does he live nearby?'

'Near the city.'

She was relieved to hear he had possibilities and hoped he'd sort them out sooner rather than later. She looked over at the photograph again, the three siblings lined up to smile at the camera. As an only child she'd sometimes felt as though she was on the outside looking in when it came to the subject of sibling rivalry, the closeness of sisters and brothers, the adventures of childhood she suspected she'd missed out on. She scolded herself for feeling jealous of his intact family.

Shopping list in hand, Rosie left Owen scrolling through contacts on his iPhone and set off for the supermarket. Driving down Lakeside Lane she smiled at the sight of the road stretched out before her lined with purple-blue jacaranda trees in full bloom. In autumn she bet this road would become a carpet of soft blue when the trumpet-shaped flowers began to fall. She skilfully avoided the pothole she'd clunked in and out of when she'd first driven up to the house to meet Jane and Michael Harrison.

The sun shone brilliantly in the cloudless sky, highlighting the magic of spring in early November, and she couldn't resist parking at the end of the main street to take a look around Magnolia Creek. She walked past a veterinary practice with a lady sitting in the window with a cross-breed dog sitting on her lap. At a guess it was a Cavoodle, but there were so many breeds these days. She carried on past a florist which doubled as a garden centre and then came to a café with hanging baskets out front holding vibrant purply-pink blooms. It reminded her of those whitewashed Greek houses with their splashes of Bougainvillea outside that she'd only ever seen in pictures on the internet or in brochures.

Standing outside the café, she let the sun wash over her as she looked across the road at the white signpost pointing to bike trails, Clover Riding Stables, the lake and Magnolia House. She smiled. Her first job in the Public Relations industry started in two days, and she couldn't be more excited.

A voice came from the café behind her. 'We're open for coffee.' The voice grew louder and a woman with glossy black hair in looping curls appeared in the doorway and said, 'We've got scones and jam, homemade chutneys.'

The tall, slender woman held out her hand. 'I'm Bella, Bella Finnegan. My husband and I own the café.'

She shook the woman's hand. 'I'm Rosie Stevens. It's nice to meet you.'

'I thought it might be you. Jane told me to expect to see you out and about.'

Rosie smiled. She felt a part of the community already.

'Jane and I go way back,' explained Bella as she stacked coffee cups from a deserted table and deposited them on the far counter. 'Well come in,' she instructed as Rosie hovered in the doorway.

Bella's laugh was as welcoming as the smell of fresh baking in the café with its eight tables, small counter and cosy ambience. As Bella busied herself behind the counter, Rosie sat at a wooden table covered in a red and white gingham tablecloth topped with a holder stuffed full of serviettes and a small, laminated menu. Moments later a plate crammed with scones, jam and cream was put in front of her.

'It's quiet this afternoon so I've got time to chat.' Bella sat opposite Rosie. 'This is on the house, by the way. Call it a "Welcome to Magnolia Creek".'

'Thank you.' Rosie wasn't hungry after the eggs, but the scones smelled divine and she politely broke off a piece and spooned on some jam, then a dollop of cream.

'They're my speciality.' Bella winked. 'And getting you to sample them today is my little ploy to make sure you keep coming back for more.'

Rosie liked how honest Bella was, and she liked her cooking just as much, devouring the scones despite a lack of appetite as they chatted about Magnolia Creek and what it was like to grow up here.

'How do you know the Harrisons?' Rosie asked.

'We've known each other a long time now. Years ago, I was out on a hen night wearing crazy shoes—' she eyed her sensible lace ups '—seven-inch heels from what I remember, and before I'd even had my first cocktail I fell over, landing awkwardly on my arm.'

Rosie winced. 'Ouch.'

'I ended up in the emergency department for the rest of the evening, and Jane was the triage nurse. We got chatting, as you do when there are long waiting times, and we hit it off. I ended up telling her all about Magnolia Creek and how I'd grown up here and planned to one day open up a business with my boyfriend, Rodney – he's now my husband – and I think she was sold on the place. We swapped phone numbers and stayed in touch ever since.'

You could tell a lot about a woman by the friends she chose, and both Bella and Jane seemed down-to-earth women with genuine hearts.

'I'd love to live somewhere as beautiful as this,' said Rosie.

'So why don't you?'

'I think my other half would be bored stiff.'

'Nonsense. But then I'm biased.' Her silky-red lips broke into a grin. 'Are you planning on moving in together?'

'We are.'

'When's it all happening?'

That was the million dollar question.

'He's working overseas right now, but hopefully not too far in the future.'

'Well, I admire you.'

'Why?'

'The long-distance-relationship thing. It must be hard.'

'It's not so bad. I know it won't be forever.' Rosie wondered whether she was trying to convince Bella or herself.

'If you end up in Magnolia Creek, your other half can commute to the city. We've got a train station. Yes,' Bella nodded, noting Rosie's surprise, 'it's a small town and there are limited trains running, but nevertheless it's there. You'll find it past the fire station around the bend at the end of the street.'

Rosie had passed the fire station yesterday. She wondered whether she'd ever reach the point where seeing those fire engines wouldn't semi-paralyse her with sadness.

‘I saw Owen the other day,’ Bella went on. ‘I understand he took you by surprise when he turned up in town.’

‘I wasn’t exactly expecting him, or anyone else, to turn up in the middle of the night.’

‘I don’t suppose you were. But he’s harmless, a lovely guy with a heart of gold.’ Bella waved to a customer perusing the cakes. She patted Rosie’s hand. ‘More on him later, but for now I’d better get back to work before Rodney sees me slacking off. It’s been lovely to meet you.’

Rosie thanked Bella for the welcome-to-Magnolia-Creek scones and went on her way, glancing at her watch. There was no time to explore Magnolia House now. It would have to wait or she’d never get to the supermarket. She hurried towards her car, aware that if Owen had sorted another place to stay then she’d need to get back soon in order to say goodbye. He didn’t seem the type of guy to leave an explanatory note.

Two teenage girls sat on the bench at the side of the road. Sunglasses up on their heads, dolled up as though they were in the middle of the city on a night out, Rosie overheard one of them say, ‘I saw him in his leathers this morning. He’s gorgeous.’

At the mention of a motorbike she took a little longer to find her keys from the bottom of her bag.

‘You wait till he’s next at the pub,’ said the other girl. ‘He’s all mine. He very nearly was last time.’ She sighed theatrically. ‘I love a man in uniform, especially one who plays hard to get.’

What uniform did Owen wear besides jeans or tracksuit pants and scruffy T-shirts?

Rosie shut the car door and pulled on her seat belt, wondering how much truth was in the conversation she'd overheard. Those girls were barely teenagers beneath all that bling and make-up. Surely Owen couldn't be interested in them.

She drove on to the supermarket, reminded of how lucky she was to have Adam in her life. A man like Owen didn't appear to have many plans beyond getting up each day and doing whatever he felt like, but her thoughts didn't stop her from zipping around the supermarket and driving a little over the speed limit on the way back to the house, wondering whether she would see him one more time before he moved on.

Chapter Five

Owen puffed out his cheeks after Rosie said goodbye and headed to the supermarket. Finding somewhere to live at short notice was going to be tricky. He'd been determined to make Rosie leave, determined to find out what his parents were hiding, but for two reasons he had backed down and was in the process of sorting out alternative living accommodation. Firstly, he wasn't a complete dickhead, and secondly, Rosie had signed a contract. It was the thought of the contract that worried him the most. If she had a formal agreement and he refused to leave, this could all blow up in his face. His parents could head back sooner than he'd planned and he'd never get to the bottom of what they were hiding. And now he knew there was a secret, he was hungry to find out more.

He'd also seen the way Rosie had reacted to Bertie, and he'd seen she had no idea how to fix the pool cleaner. And he was going to use her femininity to his advantage. He'd let her stay and he'd find somewhere else, but he'd insist on visiting to clear out gutters, keep the gardens hosed down ready for bushfire season, and maintain the pool that had the potential to turn very expensive should the cleaner not do its job properly. He'd time his visits when she was working over at

Magnolia House and that way he could search the place and do the manual labour.

Owen dialled his brother Tom's number. Tom lived closer to the city and was married to Sadie, his childhood sweetheart, and he was fully domesticated at the tender age of twenty-six. He was also father to Ryan, Owen's ten-month-old nephew, and had bucked the trend by taking twelve month's leave from his job as a pharmacist in the city. Tom was the epitome of a family man to whom Owen didn't even try to measure up, but they were close and he knew his brother could help him out.

When Tom's voicemail kicked in, Owen left a message after the beep. He checked his pager, but it was all quiet today, thankfully. He could tell Rosie was desperate to ask him what the pager was for, and why he kept disappearing at odd hours of the day and night, but the mystery was a bit of a laugh and he got the feeling that once she found out, the fun and games would be over.

Using this window of opportunity before Rosie returned, Owen decided the study was as good a place as any to continue his search. He'd already rifled through his parents' bedroom – their wardrobes, bedside tables, chest of drawers – the day he'd walked in on Rosie drying her hair. He shook his head. This was no time to drift into a daydream about the girl who could be home any minute even though his mind flitted to her body in those figure-hugging jeans and lace bra. He retrieved the key from its hiding place in his bedside table upstairs. He'd kept it there so he could search the room without having to put it back to rights every time.

The large room with a long rectangular window at the end had an enormous walnut desk in the centre – the kind with a green leather top you'd expect to find in a big American bank – and on top of it sat a computer. One wall of the room was lined with shelves housing ornaments his parents had collected over the years. There was a set of thimbles that had belonged to his gran, a china jug in russet-red that his mum had picked out on a trip to Spain, photo frames filled with pictures of all three boys as babies.

He scratched his head as he looked at the two filing cabinets in the corner of the room and the eight drawers in the large desk. It was hard to know where to begin. Methodically, he opened the top drawer of the first filing cabinet and began to wade through the papers. He flipped through bank statements which showed nothing out of the ordinary, a file full of information about his dad's pension, a folder way at the back of the filing cabinet which contained homemade cards to his mum from him, Tom and Ben over the years. Funny, he'd never thought she was sentimental enough to keep anything like that. There was a card in bright yellow with a daffodil on the front that he remembered making at school and inside he'd written – in terrible handwriting – Happy Mother's Day. He ran his fingers over the words, but when he heard Rosie's car pull up outside he dumped the files on top of the desk, locked the study behind him and went outside to greet her.

She bustled into the hallway, plastic carrier bags looped over each arm. 'You're still here.'

'Yeah, sorry. Here, let me help you.' He took the bags through to the kitchen, calling over his shoulder, 'I'm on the case, should be out of your hair soon enough. Is there more in the car?' It paid to be nice to her if his plan was going to work out.

Rosie nodded and together they went outside to get the rest of the shopping in between them.

'This car is like a giant blob of Hubba Bubba,' he told her. The pink VW looked even brighter bathing beneath the sun.

'I'll take that as a compliment.'

'You should. The Hubba suits you.' His comment hung in the air when his phone chimed from the kitchen and he hot-footed it back inside with the bags he'd pulled out of the boot.

He took the call before it went through to voicemail. 'Tom! Great to hear from you.' It sounded like bedlam at his brother's place. He could barely hear Tom with all the background noise. 'What on earth's going on there?'

'We've got playgroup here this morning.'

Ah, that explained it.

'I got your message,' Tom bellowed. 'How are you?'

The posse in the background put pay to any further conversation until at last the noise became muffled.

'Have you shut yourself in a cupboard?' Owen quizzed.

'Don't laugh … this could be you one day.'

'As if.' His brother always did have a good sense of humour.

'So where are you?'

'I'm up at Mum and Dad's place.'

'I thought they had a house-sitter.'

'They did. Or, they do. I didn't realise, so I'm trying to arrange somewhere else to stay as I'm without any forwarding address at the moment.'

Tom laughed. 'Well, you're welcome here any time. As long as you don't mind the coffee mornings, sofas that have seen regurgitated baby milk for the best part of ten months, and the early morning wake-up calls.'

'Sadie told me Ryan is up for a good play at … what was it? Five a.m.?'

'Better. Four o'clock is his favourite time now.'

Owen shuddered. He didn't mind early, but he wasn't sure he wanted to be woken by a child leaping all over him each day. Then again, what choice did he have? 'It won't be for long, I promise. I'll try to spread myself around.'

'Stay as long as you need.'

The posse sounded as though they'd found Tom's hiding place, so Owen said, 'I'll drive over to you later. And Tom?'

'Yep?'

'Don't mention to Mum or Dad that I was here.'

'Not a problem.'

Tom knew the deal. He knew the tension that existed between Owen and his mum.

Rosie was busy unpacking the shopping, taking eggs from their cardboard box and slotting them into the plastic container with its special holes. He leaned past her to find a can of Sprite lurking at the back of the fridge.

'Tom says I can move in with him for a while until I get myself sorted.' He cracked open the can. 'What?'

'Nothing,' she said, turning to slot a box of porridge sachets into the pantry. 'It sounded manic, that's all. I could hear the yelling from over here.'

'Yes, apparently my nephew didn't use his lungs enough in the first ten months of his life, so he's making up for it now, along with his mates.'

'A ten-month-old has mates?'

He swigged from his can. 'They start early these days.'

She paused, a bottle of milk hooked onto her fingers. 'Can I ask you a question?'

'You just did.'

'Funny.' She leaned against the bench. 'No, I wanted to ask what you do for work. Do you work?'

He smiled. She thought she had him all figured out. 'You think I live off my parents' money, don't you?'

He loved it when she blushed, but he didn't want to wind her up any more than he already had. 'I'm a property investor. I buy apartments, units, sometimes houses. I do them up, and then I rent them out. Sometimes I sell them if it'll turn a quick profit, but usually it makes more sense to keep hold of them.'

She unpacked the last bag and stowed the dishwashing tablets beneath the sink.

He downed the rest of his can. 'I'll head upstairs, pack a bag. I'll be out of your hair in the next hour or so.'

Halfway up the stairs Owen stopped at the sound of Rosie's voice.

'I've been thinking.' She looked up at him from the hallway, her hand toying with her necklace.

He leaned against the bannisters. 'Sounds dangerous.'

Her wide eyes flicked to the floor and then back up again. 'This is an enormous house, so if you need to stay for a bit longer, then …'

She was in his way, no doubt about it. If she wasn't here he'd have turned the entire place upside down – not just the study – morning, noon and night until he found what he was looking for. But since the first night when he'd found her there at the house, he'd started to enjoy her company and he was pretty sure the feeling wasn't entirely one-sided.

'Are you asking me to stay here, with you?' He was enjoying this.

'Not *with* me.' She blushed. 'I meant—'

'Relax, I'm trying to make you feel uncomfortable. It's an irritating habit I have fun with.' He smiled down at her. 'But thank you. Staying here is a whole lot better than being woken up by a toddler sitting on my head or sticking his finger up my nose at four in the morning.'

Her laughter wrapped effortlessly around his ears.

'Do you have a boyfriend, Rosie?'

His sudden question took her by surprise.

'Yes. Why do you ask?'

'Because if I had a girlfriend I wouldn't be too happy about her sharing a house with another man.'

Rosie bent down to make a fuss of George as he weaved in and out between her ankles. Without looking at Owen she said, 'It's not a problem. You can stay here as long as you need and I won't mention to anyone that you're here.' She scooped George into her arms.

'I'll stay on one condition.'

She looked up at him again. 'What?'

'You let me cook dinner for you tonight.'

*

She hadn't intended to ask him to stay. Rosie blamed her over-romanticising the coming home to someone – anyone – and the dream of being part of a real family again. It felt so long since she'd had anything resembling the norm. She also blamed the low feeling she'd felt in the supermarket as she raced around stocking up on food for solo meals with only a cat for company. She blamed her girly instincts last night when she'd heard something on the roof – most likely a possum – and wished Owen could've roared up on his motorbike at that very moment.

She lay on her tummy on the bed, picked up her iPad and clicked on Adam's name. She knew she had to tell him about Owen, about sharing a house with another man.

'This is a nice surprise.' Adam grinned into the camera.

'I'm not disturbing you, am I?'

'No. I've finished meetings for the day, so I'm all yours.' His smile faded. 'What's up? You're frowning.'

Rosie recounted the whole story: Owen turning up in the middle of the night, how he had nowhere else to go, how the house was big enough for two.

'Do you really think this is wise?' It was his turn to frown.

'It'll be fine, really.'

'What does your contract say?'

'It doesn't matter about the contract.'

'Like hell it doesn't. There's a reason why you draw one up in this sort of situation. It means everyone knows where they stand, on either side.'

'I know. But—'

'No "buts", Rosie. You need to call the agency.'

Was it wrong to be enjoying how possessive Adam was being now? He wasn't the jealous type, never had been, but this had unsettled him good and proper.

'I'll pay for you to rent a place in Magnolia Creek,' he went on. 'Then you can still take the job.'

She turned onto her back and rested her legs against the wall. 'We've talked about this. There isn't much to rent at the moment. And you saw this place on the iPad. It's massive. I think Owen will be out so much I'll barely even see him. He's a property developer and constantly moving around.'

A sigh came all the way from Singapore.

She continued her justification for the new house guest. 'It's also good to have someone around in case there's a bushfire emergency.'

Knowing her personal history, Adam's voice softened. 'Fires are highly unlikely, surely?'

'You never know.' Life could be a game of risk and she knew from painful experience that sometimes you could lose.

'Just don't let him take advantage of you,' said Adam.

She smiled. 'Of course I won't.'

'Don't let him make you cook and clean up after him.'

She giggled. 'I won't.' Her insides buzzed naughtily when she thought of Owen's offer to cook tonight. This was a new feeling for her. It was living dangerously given how by-the-book her life was. Usually she knew exactly what was around each and every corner.

'He'll have me to answer to if he puts one foot wrong,' said Adam firmly before steering the subject onto safer ground. 'So, tell me, have you been reading up on all your notes, ready to wow them at your new job?'

She'd finally managed to use the desk in her room as it was intended rather than as a barricade across her door. 'I have. I think it's making me more nervous though.'

'It'll be good to put all that theory into practice.'

She smiled back at him. It was five o'clock in Australia, but Singapore was a few hours behind and

Adam still had a way to go to finish his day, so they chatted more about her mounting excitement at starting the new job and didn't mention Owen again.

By the time Rosie finished her call and descended the stairs, the smell of garlic and something rich and meaty wafted towards her and pulled her into the kitchen to where Owen stood at the cooker. She was about to greet him with a cheerful 'hello' but froze when she recognised the tune playing through the speakers.

He held up a wine glass when he caught sight of her lingering in the doorway. 'Is red okay?'

The sounds of the cello coming from the iPod docking station on the sideboard fell over her like a magic spell. She held her breath, torn between closing her eyes and losing herself in 'The Swan' by Saint-Saëns or running far away from the speakers that brought back so many memories.

'Rosie?' Owen stood proffering the glass.

'Yes, please, I'll have a glass.' She pointed outside, eager to escape. 'But I'll water the garden first.'

He left the glass on the table and returned to his culinary tasks. 'I cleared the gutters earlier,' he said, scraping mushrooms into the pan on the stovetop, his back to her now as he stirred the sizzling mixture. 'No need to call the handyman in when I'm here.'

'Right.' She floated outside, well away from the music, and unwound the hose from its holder on the fence near the pool. She turned the tap using all her strength, determined not to ask for any help right now, and started with the largest rose bush, bursting with ruby red flowers. As she sprayed it she watched droplets settle on the silken leaves and run down to the thorns before plummeting into the soil beneath. She moved on to the orange roses, the bush standing at hip height with cupped, pale flowers with hints of peach, thirsty and ready to be taken care of.

The smell of a home-cooked meal snaked down the garden and attacked Rosie's stomach as she turned the hose to the lawn. Starting at the back fence, she worked her way backwards towards the rear of the house and the pool. Watering down the grass and cleaning out the gutters were paramount in bushfire season, and she was glad to have Owen pitching in to look after the place.

When she reached the deck he was waiting for her. He pushed the glass of red into her hand. 'Here, you take this and let me put the hose away.'

Without argument, she took the glass and with her other hand wiped her brow, hot from the manual labour even though the sun had eased off in the early evening.

'What type of bird is that?' Rosie nodded towards the fence behind the rockery as the creature landed.

'He's our resident lyrebird.' Owen chuckled. 'He often stops by for a bit of a chirp and then he'll be off, back into the bush.'

The bird stood proudly, black eyes rounded, his beak snapping open and shut as he released a song that sounded like a kookaburra at first and then a car alarm, which, in all honesty, sounded more familiar to Rosie than the sounds of nature all around her now.

'That damn song will have you looking out the window to see whose alarm is going off. I swear he's doing it for a laugh at our expense.' Owen wound the hose onto its reel. 'Come on, almost time to eat.'

He led the way inside and called over his shoulder, 'I've changed the music too. I got the impression you weren't keen.'

Rosie didn't offer any further explanation on that front. She simply sat at the rectangular pine dining table and sipped her wine as Miley Cyrus belted out 'Wrecking Ball'. She gazed out the glass doors, over to the bush behind the back garden. The tranquillity of the countryside held as much magic in the fading sun as it did during the best parts of the day.

Owen cut into her thoughts. 'I hope you like lasagne.'

'As a matter of fact, it's my favourite.'

He topped up both glasses of wine and put the finishing touches to a salad, scattering thin slices of red peppers, red onion and crumbled feta across the top of spinach leaves, rocket and tomatoes.

'You seem to know your way around a kitchen,' Rosie observed.

'I've always enjoyed cooking.' He poked a knife into the lasagne to check the pasta was soft and then slotted the dish back into the oven. 'This is one of the more complex dishes I make. Stir fries, meat and two veg, a quick pasta and sauce are usually what I settle on.'

He brought the bottle of red over to the dining table that ran parallel to the kitchen bench, and sat opposite Rosie. 'Sorry, am I ruining your view? Should I move?'

'Don't be daft, it's fine.'

'Have you ever house-sat this far out of the city?' He took a sip of the smooth red.

'This is the first time.'

'And do you approve?'

'It's beautiful.'

His lips curled into a knowing smile and a strong hand extended over the base of his wine glass. 'Have you had much chance to explore?'

'Not as much as I'd have liked. But I've been to the main street now and got chatting with Bella from Finnegan's café.'

His face lit up. ‘She’s great, isn’t she? I bet you didn’t have a chance to escape either. Not before she cornered you for a chat.’

Rosie giggled. ‘We talked for ages. She thinks a lot of you.’

‘Well … what can I say?’ When Rosie rolled her eyes, he asked, ‘So why don’t you have a place of your own?’

‘We haven’t got around to buying anywhere yet.’

‘We?’

‘Me and my boyfriend.’

‘Does this boyfriend of yours have a name?’

‘Adam.’

‘Sorry, I’m being nosey, aren’t I? My usual company in a house is a sleeping bag, an airbed and the smell of renovations. I’m not really fit for human contact.’

He was better than he realised. ‘House-sitting suits me while Adam is working overseas,’ she explained. ‘He’s an investment banker. A part-time job as a PR assistant came up at Magnolia House, and it’s ideal for me following my communications degree.’

‘Aren’t you a bit old to just be finishing Uni?’ he asked. ‘God, I’m sorry. That didn’t quite come out the way I meant it.’

He looked so embarrassed all Rosie could do was smile. ‘It’s fine. I’m twenty-seven, and communications was my second degree.’

‘Your second? Why?’

She gulped her wine. ‘I originally did a degree in music.’ When he raised his eyebrows she added, ‘I did it because I loved music, but I had no desire to teach or be in any sort of band. So, I decided I needed to study something I enjoyed but something that would get me a job too.' She hoped her answer would suffice and breathed a sigh of relief when it did and Owen changed tack.

'So when's the boyfriend coming home?'

'Soon, I hope.'

Before he could fire any more questions her way, the oven timer pinged. Rosie brought the salad over to the table while Owen served the lasagne.

'This looks amazing,' she said. 'You can stay here a bit longer if you cook like this every night.'

As soon as the words were out she knew she shouldn't have said them. It was flirty and the wine was partly to blame, but she was also enjoying his company and felt a freedom she didn't usually feel in her well-structured life. But most of all she was enjoying these moments of normality: sitting down for a meal, talking over the day, discussing future plans. These simple things made her feel alive and present and stopped her obsessing about what was going to happen next.

Her eyes lingered on the tail of the rose tattoo as it moved with the tendons in his arm when he scooped out a second serving of lasagne, and she thought about how different this man was to Adam. Adam was grounded, had focus and knew what he wanted in life, but Owen seemed unpredictable, freer.

'I'll be heading down to Mornington Peninsula first thing tomorrow,' he said, laying the serving spoon down again. 'I'm putting up a garden shed for my tenants and I'll bring the bike back on my truck. I'll be home pretty late. You don't mind if I leave the truck in the garage, do you?'

'Of course not, I'm happy having my car on the driveway. It brightens up the place.'

‘It certainly does.’ He grinned. ‘Can I ask what happens between house-sits, when you have nowhere else lined up?’

‘I usually head down to my mum’s in Geelong.’

‘Ah, so in a way we’re quite similar.’ When she looked at him quizzically, he added, ‘We both rely on a base in between: I come here, you go to Geelong.’

She wasn’t sure how to answer that.

He sat back, swilled the remains of red wine in his glass. ‘You’re looking forward to Magnolia House, I take it?’

‘Yes, I can’t wait.’

They chatted about her job and what it would entail, and as they talked Owen topped up both glasses of wine. ‘The owners of Magnolia House have been there for a while,’ he said. ‘There’s never been a bad report about the place. I’m sure you’ll settle in quickly.’

Rosie cradled her glass as the inky night sky overpowered the pale blue of the day. Soon the view of the Dandenong Ranges would fade into complete darkness.

He sipped his wine. ‘Did you try Bella’s scones?’

‘I don’t think she’d have let me leave unless I did. Freebies can’t be good for business though.’

‘Ah,’ said Owen, finger hovering mid-air. ‘She’s an astute businesswoman. I bet now you’ve tasted them, and now you’re on a first name basis with her, you’ll go back without a moment’s hesitation.’

She let out a laugh. ‘Okay, so it was a shrewd business move then.’

‘I think so. We don’t want the roaring tourist trade here in Magnolia Creek, because we like things how they are, but we need to attract at least some custom to keep local businesses running. Rumour has it that a chocolate shop is opening up some time in the New Year.'

Rosie nodded, impressed, and as they chatted she realised that despite being nomadic, Owen was incredibly proud of his home town. In fact, he seemed more grounded than he was willing to let on. She longed for the same confidence, the same feeling of belonging.

She stood to take the dishes over to the sink, but Owen's hand wrapped around her arm. 'Sit down, there's no rush, and we can do them together.'

The sound of the word 'together' rolling off his tongue made her heart quicken, but his pager broke the moment.

He shook his head and muttered 'not tonight, sweetheart' before looking at Rosie. 'Sorry, I'll make a quick phone call and then come right back.'

'Take your time,' she called after him as she took the dishes to the sink and he went to use the phone.

Who was the 'sweetheart' he was referring to? The pager wasn't work-related, obviously. Rosie's mind drifted to those two girls sitting on the bench in town and the conversation she'd overheard about the man in the leathers and how he'd been playing hard to get. Owen was twice their age, at least, but had the pleasant man she'd shared dinner with managed to fool her into thinking he was more decent than the bikie who'd roared into Magnolia Creek in the middle of the night and scared her half to death?

Perhaps Adam was right. Perhaps this was a bad idea. After all, how well did she really know Owen Harrison?

'Sorry about that.' Owen joined her at the sink. 'It was just—'

She held up a hand to stop him. She'd let herself get carried away in the moment, relaxed in his company, had one too many glasses of wine. 'There's no need to explain.' She pulled out some plastic containers. 'I'll put the leftovers in here and then put them in the freezer.'

He frowned. 'Rosie, let me wash up. Please, you could've seen me out on the streets or shopped me to my parents and you did neither.'

She relented and let a yawn escape. 'Thank you for dinner. I'd better call it a night and give Adam a call before he thinks I've forgotten about him.'

If Owen had turned down 'sweetheart's' offer for the promise of something better here in this house, then he was about to be bitterly disappointed.

Chapter Six

Two days later, Rosie started the morning on her hands and knees in the garden. She'd found an old kneeling mat in the shed along with secateurs and a pair of gardening gloves that dwarfed her hands. After deadheading the roses and watering the bushes from underneath, as Jane had suggested to discourage spider mites which could attack the flowers, she now only had the lawn to mow.

The kneeling mat had saved her from being too uncomfortable, but she'd smothered herself in sunscreen before tackling the garden, and it was a magnet for anything grubby. Her shorts were clean but her legs were covered. She did her best to brush the worst off her knees. It would soon be time to clean herself up and head to Magnolia House for her first shift. The shift pattern suited her already as she hadn't had to leap out of bed this morning, and she'd been able to work outside in the coolest part of the day.

She returned the tools to the shed and wrestled the lawn mower out from between a set of shelves and a collection of spades and a garden fork. She pulled it out through the narrow doorway to the shed.

'Here, let me,' Owen called out from the deck. She was surprised he was awake considering she didn't hear his truck roll up to the house until around three this morning.

'I'm perfectly capable.' She refused to let go and his fingers touched hers on the handle of the lawnmower.

He didn't break her stare. 'I don't doubt it. But while I'm here, I'll do the lawns and you can whip the vacuum around.'

He sure knew how to wind her up. 'That's sexist and you know it.' There was no way she'd let go now.

'I prefer to call it "practical".'

'Yeah, well I'm happy to do the lawn.'

'Come on, no need to be—'

Rosie used her body to block him and pushed the lawnmower away and onto the grass.

'You're a determined little thing, aren't you?' His voice mocked her as he leaned against the shed, watching.

The heat rose in her cheeks. Of course she could do this herself without any help. If there was anything Rosie Stevens was, it was capable.

Owen thrust his hands into the pockets of his faded denims. 'I'll tell you what. If you can start the mower then she's all yours. But if not, you forfeit and I get the lawn, you get the vacuuming.'

'Ha! You're on.' It couldn't be that hard to start the blessed thing, could it?

When she'd circled the lawnmower a few times looking for any obvious buttons, Owen, a smile still in place, said, 'Let me do it, will you.'

'No way.' She'd seen a mower like this before and reached down to the cord that would make it leap into action.

She pulled the cord once. Okay, not hard enough. She braced herself, legs sturdy, and pulled again. Nothing. She pulled again, and then again in case she wasn't pulling it at the right angle.

'Stop having so much pride, woman, and let me help.'

She glared at him as he stepped forwards.

'I'll give you a hint,' he offered.

'Go on,' she huffed.

'Open the petrol cap on the top and check it's filled to the right level.'

She did as suggested. 'It's full.'

'Right, now, let me give you another hint before you put your shoulder out trying to start the thing.' He crouched down in front of the lawnmower and motioned for Rosie to join him. 'See that red button there?'

She leaned closer to see what he was talking about.

'Push the button four times,' he instructed. 'That'll get the petrol flowing. Then, see the lever on the handle? Push it as far forwards as it'll go – that's the throttle. Then give that cord a big pull and away you go.'

It sounded simple enough. She went through the motions and gave the cord a big tug again, but nothing.

'There must be something wrong with it,' she insisted, blowing at the corner of her mouth to get her hair out of her face.

Owen moved forwards and this time she stood aside. Eyes locked with hers, he grinned, raised his eyebrows and pulled the cord. He didn't need to say anything else as the engine purred into action.

'I guess I'll get the vacuum out,' she shouted over the noise and turned to walk towards the deck.

'Oh relax.' He pulled her back, his hand on her wrist. 'Here you go, I was winding you up. The lawn is all yours if you want it. I just thought it'd be fun to see you start the mower. Mum can never do it either.'

The mower drowned out any further conversation, and Rosie found therapy for her frustration by going up and down the garden in strips. She wondered how you made those defined stripes like they did on sports fields and wished she could give the garden the same kind of professional touch.

When she'd finished and walked up the steps to the deck, Owen had a rucksack on his back, his helmet and keys in hand. 'I need to head off,' he said. 'I just got a call to say my rental property up near Albury was broken into. I'm meeting the insurance assessor up there.'

'Aren't you taking your truck?' she asked.

'No, it sounds like the damage is to the glass panel of the back door and the rear windows, so I won't be needing my tools. I'll arrange a glazier and check the whole place over.'

He pushed his helmet on and Rosie said goodbye before heading upstairs for a shower. But even the 'good luck on your first day' message from Adam on her iPad did little to lift her spirits in a once-again empty house.

*

Magnolia House was a gorgeous whitewashed structure with a veranda stretching across the front in a big smile. The property overlooked the lake glistening beneath the sun, and beyond the water were eight holiday cottages dotted between gum trees and bushes in the deepest of greens.

Rosie's first day flew by. The owner of Magnolia House, Rebecca Martin, oozed passion from her veins about anything and everything to do with weddings. She was one of those people, Rosie decided, who would never understand how anyone could stay still. She flitted from one task to the other and gave Rosie a heap of responsibilities from the start. In her short five-hour shift, Rosie got to know the layout of the main house, she saw the interior of those beautiful whitewashed cottages and she selected photographs for a flyer to pass to jewellers all over Victoria in the hope they could capture the bride and groom's attention the moment they selected that special ring. Rosie finished her day by scheduling two viewings of the venue for couples who wanted to marry at the end of the following year.

When she left to walk home, her spirits and passion for the town were as fierce as the sun in the sky. In fact, she'd never loved Magnolia Creek more. She felt a sense of belonging, she was making friends, establishing herself. She was fitting in.

The feeling of euphoria certainly didn't fade when Rosie turned into Lakeside Lane and took in the always-beautiful sight of the jacaranda trees stretching all the way towards the end where number twenty-seven sat. About to cross the lane towards the driveway, Rosie decided to lengthen her walk and take a detour. She'd passed the opening for Daisy Lane before, but she'd never investigated where it lead. Daisy Lane was just wide enough for a single car, so as she listened for sounds of approaching vehicles, she made her way all the way to the end, eager to investigate every inch of this town that was beginning to feel more like home than it probably should.

At the end of the lane was a single cottage. It looked as though it had been abandoned for years. The window pane to the right of the front door remained, but the window on the other side was boarded up. The wooden railing on the small yet cute veranda was rotten and needed replacing, and the floor was part ripped up, exposing dirt and stones below. A For Sale board stood lopsided at the front of the property and Rosie wondered how long it had been there. It would take a brave person to buy this place, she decided as she walked around the outside of the cottage. It was tiny – two bedrooms max, at a guess – and peering through the window at the back, she could see the kitchen was little more than a battered butler's sink and a decaying cooker. A yellowed net curtain obscured her view of another room, but she could make out stairs going up to the roof space. A few tins of paint were lined up along one wall, suggesting someone may have bought the place and tried to make it liveable before admitting the property was beyond help and relisting it for sale.

She stood for a while. It was quiet here, and she liked it. It was tucked away and private, yet only a short walk from the main street. She'd grown up in a small house attached to the family newsagency her mum had run for almost ten years. But this place? This was the sort of home she'd only ever been able to dream about.

She looked at the For Sale board once more before she sighed and turned to head back to the house. She wondered, as she walked, whether to mention it to Adam. Even in its dilapidated state it held a magical quality, and she knew deep down it could be transformed into a real home. They could fence off the garden, lay a lawn, even put in decking given the generous size of the plot.

It wasn't as if she was asking for the world; just a small slice of it to call her own.

*

Rosie enjoyed the next couple of days in the house alone – the way it should've been. She read a book, went out for long walks and worked another two shifts at

Magnolia House, enjoying her lunch beside the lake each day, unable to resist donating the final crusts of her sandwich to the swan that jumped from the water at the first sign of company. She even went to Finnegan's on her way home, stopping for a cold drink or a coffee and a good chat with Bella, who had confirmed the rumour about a chocolate shop opening up on the main street in the New Year.

She found a bike in the shed at the house and spent her free time cycling along the main street and along the bike trails, basking in the feeling of freedom. And in the evenings, as Magnolia Creek gradually fell asleep around her, Rosie found herself not listening for the sound of the Ducati in case it arrived to spoil her peace, but instead listening for it to signal the moment the house would come alive again with familiar chatter and laughter.

The Ducati finally made an appearance a couple of days later as Rosie was in her bedroom making her bed. But when the engine idled for longer than usual, she peeked through her curtains to see what Owen was up to.

He'd taken off his helmet and his hair held the sheen from the sun overhead. The rays kissed his tanned skin as he chatted with someone, and Rosie picked up on the sound of female laughter. It wasn't long before the girl in question moved away from the porch that had hidden her at first, and Rosie recognised her as one of the teenagers she'd seen the other day.

Rosie turned her attention back to her bed and pulled on the pillowcases, unable to stop thinking about Owen and that girl young enough to be his daughter. He wasn't hers to be possessive about, but she *was* allowed an opinion.

When the chatter from outside stopped and Rosie heard the front door shut followed by Owen's footfall on the stairs, she plumped up the last pillow and was unsurprised to hear a knock at her door.

'Come in.' She plumped up another pillow even though it had already been seen to.

Owen poked his head around the door. 'Did you miss me?'

'It's been quiet.' She couldn't help but smile at him. 'How did it go with the house, was there much damage?'

'It wasn't too bad. All sorted now.'

He filled the open doorway and leaned on his arm resting against the doorframe. Rosie was busy thinking about how he really did need an orderly short back and sides when he said, 'I'm heading to the pub later tonight, if you're interested.'

She thought about that girl again. 'I've got a bit of work to do.'

'They give part-timers work to take home?'

She shrugged. 'I don't mind.'

'Well if you change your mind, let me know. I'm taking the bike and I'll be on light beer, so I could give you a lift.'

'Light beer?' She raised an eyebrow. 'Why aren't you drinking?'

She heard a weird buzzing noise, and Owen pulled out his pager from his pocket. 'Because of this thing. I'll catch you later.' And with that he was off down the stairs, out of the door, and away on the Ducati.

Owen came back a couple of hours later, and even though Rosie had taken to lying on her bed to read from her Kindle, she positioned herself back at her desk with her iPad to create the illusion that she was doing something work-related, in case he came upstairs and asked her about the pub again. She planned to stay home this evening and FaceTime Adam and mention the cottage she'd found. She had nothing to lose after all.

When Owen bypassed her bedroom and she heard the pipes in the old house groan as he took a shower, she was strangely disappointed. Twenty minutes later and her stomach rumbled so loudly she knew she couldn't hide away any longer, and she went down to the kitchen.

She took out the chicken breast she'd marinated earlier and set about dicing an onion, peeling and slicing a carrot and cutting up a few florets of broccoli. She added these and a rainbow-selection of sliced peppers to the wok once the meat was sizzling, finishing the dish by throwing in udon noodles.

She tossed the ingredients together as Owen came downstairs to join her in the kitchen. His arm snaked over her shoulder and his hand snatched a piece of chicken from the pan.

'I'd have made you some if you'd asked,' she said.

'I didn't think I wanted anything until the smell crept up the stairs and found me.' He looked longingly at the stir fry as Rosie scraped it into the awaiting bowl.

She laughed at him practically salivating. 'No tasting!' She let the dish cool a bit while she arranged the roses she'd picked earlier into a vase. Jane had told her to pick them as often as she liked or the garden would be overrun with them.

She pushed a pale yellow rose in amongst the ruby reds and then another, and grabbed the stem of the last one.

'Ouch!' She dropped the rose and wrapped her opposite fist around her finger.

‘Did the thorns get you?’ Owen stopped pulling on his boots and instead led her over to the sink. ‘It looks deep, we’ll rinse it with water first.’

Rosie held out her finger while Owen turned on the tap. When the water ran clear and the bleeding subsided, he wrapped her finger in a piece of kitchen towel.

She winced.

‘Am I hurting you?’

Looking up into those green eyes, Rosie realised he still had hold of her hand. She looked away. ‘I need a plaster.’

Owen found one from the first-aid kit in the cupboard by the sink and expertly wrapped it around her finger.

‘Thank you.’

‘Are you sure you’ll survive if I abandon you and go to the pub?’

‘I think I’ll live.’

‘Well if you change your mind, you know where I am.’ He carefully put the rose in amongst the others before he left.

Rosie sat out on the deck to eat dinner and watched the countryside change colour as the sun faded to a saffron hue. When she’d finished and cleaned up, she picked up her iPad. Adam was a mere click away, FaceTime was ready to go, but instead she bashed out an email to him telling him about her work, the weather – although she knew their relationship had hit a new low if all she could talk about was climatic ebbs and flows – and exploring Magnolia Creek. She typed about the cottage she’d found but then deleted the paragraph, deciding she’d rather hear his reaction, gauge whether it could be a possibility for them.

When she signed off and found she was idly rubbing the plaster on her forefinger, she plucked her keys from the hook in the hallway and set off for the pub.

Chapter Seven

Fairy lights were strung between the trees in the beer garden at Magnolia Tavern. The evening was filled with chatter and laughter and the sound of glasses being chinked together as Rosie weaved her way between outside tables and into the pub.

Owen spotted her from his place at the bar.

'What can I get you?' he asked.

It was a warm evening and even warmer inside. 'I'll have a glass of Sauvignon Blanc, please.' She needed something cold and refreshing.

Dotted about the room were groups of people, probably locals, clustered around the wooden tables, along the curved mahogany bar, and over by the dart board.

'So what changed your mind?' Owen asked.

'Huh?'

'You were supposed to be working.'

'I only had a couple of things to do,' she lied.

He loaded his change back into his wallet. 'Where's it from?' he asked.

'What?'

'Your necklace.'

She was playing with it again, without thinking, a panacea to her awkwardness.

His eyes flickered from her face to the necklace and back again. 'I've been trying to work it out since the first day we met. Is it a body with no head, legs and arms open wide?'

Rosie replaced any awkward feelings with laughter.

'Am I right?' he asked.

'No!'

'Look at it from my point of view.' He gestured for her to turn the necklace the other way so she could see it the way he did. And then he moved closer and ran his fingers along the delicate silver shape, tracing the outline. 'These are the two legs, these are two arms, and up here you'd expect the head.'

'It's a cello bridge.' Her grin faded, and before he could delve further, she asked, 'Who owns this place?'

Owen told her who the owners were and the conversation shifted to business owners in Magnolia Creek, many of whom had been here for years.

Rosie twirled the stem of her glass between her fingers. 'I like it.'

'You like what?'

'I like that so many people have been here for a long time, that this town is their home.'

Owen crunched an ice cube that had been hiding beneath the juice in his glass. 'It was pretty cool growing up here, although I think I could've been anywhere with my brothers and we'd have had a ball.'

'Did all three of you go to school here?'

'Yes, there's a school up the hill beside the vet's surgery.'

She'd seen the hill but not ventured up it yet. 'It looks like a bit of a climb each day, especially in the heat.'

'Not to mention the backpack stuffed with books. But it's only fifty metres or so before it flattens out. It's a lovely little school, only forty children or so.'

‘That’s tiny.’

‘I don’t think it’s much bigger now, but they’ve got a lot more there than they had in my day. There’s a playground, monkey bars, a climbing frame and plenty of space to run around. In my day it was a couple of sand pits and a large log we used as a beam of sorts.’

‘It sounds great for kids.’

‘I’d like to send my kids to a country school one day,’ he said. ‘I love all the green space, and being a kid to me is about freedom – running everywhere.’

Rosie sipped her wine, surprised at his candid admission.

‘Why are you looking at me like that?’ he asked.

‘I’m not looking at you like anything.’

He seemed doubtful.

‘Come on,’ Owen picked up his drink and hers. ‘Let’s go outside with these, it’s too warm in here.’

As they moved towards the door, Rosie spotted the same blond who’d been on the driveway earlier. She beamed an electric smile Owen’s way as soon as she saw him and only turned down the wattage when Rosie came into view. She didn’t look about to let some newcomer to town claim all of Owen Harrison’s attention.

No danger of Rosie claiming the limelight; that low-cut top the girl was wearing ensured most eyes would be on her.

Rosie sat opposite Owen at the picnic bench farthest away from the door to the pub. ‘The blond has a thing for you.’

‘Who, Stephanie?’

‘I don’t know her name, but the young girl with the not-so-subtle dress sense.’

He smiled. ‘Stephanie’s harmless.’

‘Just be careful,’ she said.

‘Careful?’

‘Young girls get hung up on boys and take a long time to get over a crush … longer than it takes for you to burn away on your motorcycle anyway.’

He shook his head but didn’t seem annoyed at her comment. ‘That wine’s gone to your head.’

‘No it hasn’t.’

Rosie’s look told him otherwise.

As they sat chatting, Rosie tried to imagine a young girl being besotted with Adam. He attracted his fair share of women with his dark blond hair, well-cut suits and boyish charm, but she wasn’t sure he had the same magnetism with girls that Owen had in spades. Then again, Adam wasn’t a flirt, and flirting seemed to come naturally to the man who sat opposite her now.

‘How’s the finger?’ Owen asked when she picked up her water, finger extended away from its condensation. She hated it when plasters got all wet. They smelled and the skin beneath the material always shrivelled up like a prune.

‘Much better, thank you. Those thorns are vicious.’

‘The roses look good though. My last girlfriend said having flowers all over the house showed we must have money, that flowers were a luxury item.’

‘She really said that?’

‘She did.’

‘So what happened to her?’

‘She went in search of adventure. I think she liked the big house but not Magnolia Creek. She said small country towns suffocated her.’ He put his hands to his throat and made a mock-choking sound.

Rosie sniggered.

‘She was harmless enough,’ he said, ‘… apart from her name.’

'Oh go on, what was it?'

'Orphelia.'

Rosie's laughter mingled with Owen's in the heady evening air.

'So, is there anybody else on the scene now?' Rosie asked, not sure whether she wanted an honest answer.

He shrugged. 'I enjoy women and their company, but I'm not desperate to settle down.'

'You haven't brought anyone home to the house since I've been there.'

'I don't often do that.'

'What do you mean?'

'I move around too much, so I tend not to stay over with a girl or bring them home to my bed. It makes me feel awful when I have to leave again, and they've thought I'm more serious than I actually am.'

'Sounds like a cop out to me.' She stared into the crowds, the people laughing and chattering all around them outside, and her hands found her necklace.

'Surely it's worse to lead a girl on, to have her waiting at your beck and call.'

Rosie thought for a moment. 'Why do I get the feeling you're directing your comment my way?'

He hesitated. 'It's just that here you are, house-sitting for my parents, while your so-called boyfriend is swanning around the world. The women I date know where they stand more than you do.'

'Rubbish!'

'Is it?'

'What makes you think you know anything about my relationship with my boyfriend?' She huffed.

'I heard you that day, out on the decking on FaceTime.'

'You were eavesdropping?'

‘No,’ he said calmly. ‘I came out to talk to you and realised you were chatting with someone and before I could creep away I heard enough.’

Rosie looked into the crowd rather than at Owen. In the eight days they’d been under the same roof – some of which they’d spent apart – he’d learnt enough to be able to summarise her whole relationship. He was right. Damn it, he was right. She had no idea where she stood and no idea when Adam was going to make the situation any clearer.

The truth hurt.

He rubbed a hand across his jaw. ‘I’m sorry, I shouldn’t have said anything.’

‘No, you shouldn’t.’

A smile played on his lips. ‘But you commented on my love life.’

She fiddled with the plaster on her finger. ‘Adam and I are serious even though, at the moment, we’re living apart.’

‘Okay.’

‘We almost bought a place together near the city a few months ago, you know.’

‘So what happened?’

‘We were outbid by some arsehole on the phone.’

‘That’s a bit harsh, isn’t it?’

‘We’d had our hearts set on the place and it was our only chance. Nothing else came up, so Adam went overseas to start the new job and I carried on house-sitting.’

‘So it’s the other bidder’s fault you missed out on setting up home with your boyfriend?’

‘Yes … well no … I mean, we thought we had it and the other bidder came in at the last minute. In my mind I’d already moved in and put my personal touch on the place. It was gut-wrenching to lose out when the buyer went over the price we were able to pay.'

'There'll be other places.'

Rosie's mind went to the derelict cottage on Daisy Lane, and she almost mentioned it.

'Adam is a good man, you know,' she said instead.

Owen toyed with the beer mat on the table, turned it over and then back again before he said, 'Right, enough analysing one another's love life. Tell me about the best and worse house-sits you've ever done.'

She almost wanted to hug him for being man enough to leave the subject of Adam alone. 'Your place is easily the best – and not because of the company.' She added the last bit before he could say the obvious.

He laughed. 'And the worst?'

'I once agreed to look after two puppies at a house in Glen Iris. They were six months old, and let's just say it's made me a bit wary of signing up for dog sitting again.'

'What happened?'

'The dogs were gorgeous in the daytime hours. But they were little buggers on the first night. One of them got out of the laundry where they sleep, and I woke up to find him in my open suitcase at the foot of the bed. It was cute he'd come to see me, but after I'd shut him back in the laundry and barricaded the door, I went back into the bedroom and I could smell something was off. It turned out he'd buried a bone in amongst my clothes and then peed all over everything.'

Owen couldn't keep a straight face. 'I'm sorry, but that's hilarious.'

'Not at three a.m. it wasn't!'

'You're a funny girl, Stevens.'

She gulped at the way her surname tumbled from his lips.

'And don't worry,' he said. 'George hasn't been known to pee anywhere other than outside or in his litter tray.'

'Glad to hear it.'

'You seemed so serious when I first met you,' he continued.

'What did you expect? I was terrified when you turned up in the middle of the night.'

'You're much more relaxed now, and you know what? I think we may even be friends.'

'Yeah, don't push it.' She smiled and looked up. 'Your admirer's back.' Stephanie stood two tables away with four or five friends now, flicking her hair over her shoulder and batting her eyelids when Owen looked her way.

'Wait here a minute.' He headed inside the pub and reappeared thirty seconds later wearing his leather jacket and helmet, and a second jacket and helmet were looped over his arm. He passed the spares to Rosie. 'I took the liberty of bringing these along tonight in case you changed your mind and joined me. I'm sorry it's not a great fit, it's a one-size-fits-all as the spare, but we're not going far.'

'Oh no, no way! You're not getting me on that bike of yours.' She held up her hands and refused to take the jacket and helmet from him.

'Well I'm not pushing it round the corner like some imbecile to walk you home.'

'I don't need walking home. I'm a big girl now.'

He leaned in and she got a waft of the crisp aftershave that reminded her of the house, where it lingered long after he'd showered and left. 'Where's your sense of adventure?' he whispered, wrapping the leather jacket around her shoulders. 'Let's give Stephanie something to gossip about and let her down gently that I'm only interested in being her friend.'

Rosie could see Stephanie ready to pounce should Owen move in her vicinity. She relented and shrugged on the jacket as they walked to his bike. 'You've got a lot to learn about women, Owen Harrison, if you think this is letting her down gently.'

She pulled on the helmet before she could talk herself out of it. 'Don't go too fast,' she wagged a finger at him. 'I don't have a death wish.'

He reached out and adjusted the chin strap on her helmet. She wondered whether he'd seen her gulp when his fingers grazed her neck. And when he flipped his visor down and climbed onto the bike, she realised she was more nervous about how close their bodies were about to be than how terrifying it might be on the back of a motorbike.

'Put your arms around my waist and lean with me on the corners,' he told her as she climbed on behind him.

Her voice competed with the rumble of the engine. 'I'm not sure about this!'

'You'll be fine.' He pulled away. 'Now give Stephanie a wave.'

Rosie didn't wave – she daren't let go of Owen – but she couldn't help but giggle as she watched Stephanie glower at them, bright red lips pursed as the Ducati manoeuvred its way out of the car park.

On the open road, the bike vibrated beneath her as her body pressed against Owen's. The wind lifted the strands of any hair not held down by the helmet, and the air cooled with the speed as they headed back to the house.

Owen's height made him look skinnier than he actually was. With her arms wrapped round his waist, her mind flitted back to the day she'd seen him wearing only a towel, and she was pretty sure Adam had never made her tummy flip like this, even when they'd first dated. Then again, maybe it was the difference between a cad and a responsible, reliable man. This was a frisson of excitement that wasn't meant to last.

She leaned with Owen as they turned into Lakeside Lane, and second nature allowed him to skilfully avoid the pothole. She found herself disappointed that they were home already and wished they had further to go. There was something about being on the back of a bike, on an open road, the wind blasting all your cares away.

When they came to a standstill on the driveway, Owen flipped open the pocket on the sleeve of his jacket and pulled out the remote control to open the garage.

'So was it as bad as you thought it would be?' he asked as the garage door creaked open.

She tried to act as casual as though she did this every day. 'It wasn't bad at all.'

'Sometimes you've got to step outside your comfort zone, Stevens, and take a chance.' They locked eyes. 'You never know what might happen.'

Rosie followed him in through the garage as he parked the bike, and she wondered whether he was right for the second time this evening. Was she so set in her ways, striving for safety and security, that she'd closed herself off to what else life could offer?

Chapter Eight

Rosie went straight up to bed when they got inside the house. Owen sprinkled a few biscuits into a bowl for George and freshened up his water supplies as the cat came running at the sound of the cupboard opening.

When Rosie had climbed onto the back of his bike tonight, he'd expected her to be terrified, but once they were on their way she'd taken the challenge in her stride in the same way as she'd coped with him, her unwanted houseguest. When life threw her something unexpected, it seemed Rosie was a girl who adjusted and made allowances, fitting around other people.

After he'd made a fuss of George and turned out the kitchen light, Owen paused at the foot of the stairs and watched the strip of light beneath Rosie's door go out. She'd been welcoming and friendly once they'd got over their middle-of-the-night meeting and she'd been a distraction, but he still needed answers and hadn't forgotten the real reason for being here in town. He hadn't had much chance to look around the house with her there. Her shifts had fallen on days when he'd either been out of town or busy working and he was getting anxious. He needed to take this opportunity to delve a little deeper, find out what his parents were hiding.

He decided to try his luck in the shed and see if he could find anything amongst the paraphernalia inside.

He rummaged through a carton of tools, packets of seeds stashed in a box, an old tea chest containing nothing more than old books that hadn't made the grade for the inside shelves. He pulled out boxes full of surplus plant pots, he even looked beneath a tool bench that hadn't been used in years, but apart from a cricket bat and deflated soccer ball, nothing.

He perched on the tea chest, arms resting on his legs. Yet another fruitless search. If only his mum hadn't seen the article fall from the bookcase that day. Given the reach of internet searches, it could've given him all the information he needed. Hearing his parents' conversation that night had not only confirmed there was something going on, but it had confirmed the secret was specific to him. There had been no mention of 'the boys' as she often referred to them, only him by name. This wasn't about Tom, or Ben, and that made him feel isolated and determined not to let it go until he found what he was looking for.

With Rosie asleep upstairs, Owen continued his search inside. He checked the bookshelves in the lounge room, climbing up on a set of steps so that he could check the very top but there was nothing. He doubted he'd find anything in the kitchen, but he rooted through each and every cupboard, looked beneath platters, in recipe books in case papers were hidden in those, even lifted up saucepan lids.

He felt as though he was losing his mind.

He tiptoed up the stairs to get the key to the study and then came back down and started on another drawer of folders and papers in the filing cabinet. He was truly amazed at the amount of bumf his parents had hoarded over the years as he waded through everything from old utility bills and insurance details, to information on family healthcare plans.

When he came up with nothing, again, he leant back in the chair. He looked up at the pictures on the walls of him and his dad in their uniforms, father and son team, and another black-and-white photograph of his grandad. He hadn't told Rosie about any of this, shown her any of the pictures that told a lot of his life story. He assumed she hadn't been in the study either if her confusion about his pager was anything to go by, but he'd pushed the boundaries with her tonight and perhaps it was time to stop doing that. Something about Rosie told him she was trusting, and any deception, no matter how playful he intended it to be, wouldn't be something she'd thank him for. And that mattered to him.

After he'd been through one more drawer, tiredness got the better of him. Upstairs in his bedroom he dug out a fresh T-shirt and a pair of jeans, ready for his early morning training session, and climbed into bed. The rain pitter-pattered lightly against the window pane and the smell of the wet outside drifted in through any cracks it could find. Owen stared up at the ceiling, arms folded behind his head. Rosie was the first girl he'd ever wanted to let close to him, but what was he playing at? She was temporary. Plus, she was spoken for, and had the need to settle down … a need he had never shared.

Turning onto his side to get some sleep, Owen also knew he needed to find out more about himself before he could let anyone else in.

*

Owen was up and out before Rosie the next morning. He arrived home filthy dirty from practising lifting techniques in the mud brought on by last night's rain, and there was still no sign of her. He dragged out a lonely slice of quiche from the fridge and a tub of sliced up watermelon. Halfway through a slice of the pink fleshy fruit, he realised why he hadn't seen her. She was in the pool.

He moved to the doors leading out to the deck but kept inside the doorjamb as Rosie swam lap after lap. She was a good swimmer and those petite limbs were stronger than they looked. At the far end she hoisted herself out of the water, her face tilted to the sun as she scraped her long red hair away from it and sent water droplets flying around her body, stunning in an emerald bikini. He couldn't take his eyes away from her.

He pulled back in case she caught him looking, but when he looked out again she was making her way up to the house. Should he pretend he hadn't seen her?

Too late.

'Owen?'

'Hey.' He stepped onto the deck casually as though he'd only just got there.

Rosie grabbed the white towel from the back of an outdoor chair and wrapped it protectively around her torso. 'You're filthy. Where've you been?' Her chest rose and fell slowly as she got her breath back.

'Same place you'll find me every Sunday morning when I'm around in Magnolia Creek.' He was distracted by the glimpse of a tattoo kissing her right shoulder blade and poking out from the top of her towel. Her hair must've masked it when she'd climbed out of the water.

'And where would that be?'

'Training.'

'Are you trying to take the Commando's place on *The Biggest Loser*?' She giggled.

'Something like that.' He turned and went back through the kitchen, calling over his shoulder, 'There's something I want to show you. Come on.'

Rosie looked down at her towel. 'Can I at least get dressed first?'

'Relax, I've seen girls in their swimmers before. I'm not going to jump you.'

Rosie rubbed the towel over her hair to stop it dripping, and he tried not to look at the body she'd had to reveal in order to do so.

He unlocked the study and Rosie followed him inside. She noticed the largest photo on the wall first. 'It's you.'

He stood next to her as they looked at the shot taken of a whole CFA crew standing beside a truck, filthy post-call-out.

'You're a … firefighter?' Her words caught in her throat.

'You're shocked,' said Owen.

She shook her head. 'It's not that.' Her hand rested on her collarbone as though searching for the necklace she must've removed before the swim.

'I'm a volunteer firefighter for the CFA – the Country Fire Authority. It's pretty important around here.'

'I'm sure it is.' The colour still hadn't returned to her cheeks. 'And I know who the CFA are.'

'I'm glad to hear it.'

He watched her, frozen on the spot as she looked at the picture again.

'Training sessions run on Sunday mornings and Wednesday nights, so I go to as many as I can when I'm here. And then there's this thing.' He held up the pager he'd pulled from his pocket, 'This allows Magnolia

Creek CFA to get me whenever they want. I'm on call 24/7.'

Her hand dropped to her side again and her top teeth bit down on her bottom lip.

'What's so funny?' he asked. 'Why are you smiling? Is it the bright yellow uniform, the hat?'

'I thought it was a girl, or girls, summoning you at all hours when your pager went off.'

He'd really kept her on her toes, hadn't he?

Rosie covered her face with her hands. 'It makes perfect sense now.'

'I'm impressed you thought women were so desperate for me that I needed a pager.'

She grinned. 'I wondered why you took so many showers at really odd times of the day.'

It was his turn to smile. 'I clean myself up at the fire station before I come home, unless it's a training session like today, but nothing beats your own shower, especially in the summer and if I've been out on the bike.'

'Oh God, you'll never let me live this down now.' She shook her head. 'Why didn't you tell me in the first place?' she asked.

'Honestly? I enjoyed watching you try to figure it out yourself. You don't like to be surprised, do you Stevens?'

She cast her eyes to the floor and pulled her towel tighter as Owen moved to another photograph of a woman manning a desk, a phone in her hand. 'Do you recognise her?'

She peered closely. 'Bella?'

'She's a volunteer in the non-operational team and organises us all.'

'Wow, it's a real community isn't it?'

He nodded. 'She arranges training schedules, makes sure Facebook and Twitter are updated with any bushfire dangers and organises open days for the Magnolia Creek fire station.

'That's me and Dad.' Owen pointed at a picture where they stood, side by side, helmets tucked under their arms and posing for the camera. 'And this one is a training session. The heat of the day was unbearable, but we trained using hoses, got soaked and it was the best fun we'd had in ages.'

'Who's this?' Rosie pointed to the black-and-white photograph on the opposite wall.

'My grandad. He was the one who started us off in the world of the CFA. He was in a brigade further north, but Dad always wanted to follow in his footsteps, and I guess I wanted the same.' He was close enough to smell the chlorine on her skin and see a lone drip run across her collarbone before it dived into the towel beneath.

'You're all tall,' Rosie observed.

'It's not genetic.'

'What do you mean?'

'Michael is the only dad I've ever known, but he's not my biological father.'

'Oh.'

'Now don't start feeling sorry for me, Stevens.' Her eyes held a watery sheen. Owen hoped it wasn't pity. 'My biological father died when I was really small. I never knew him anyway, so it wasn't a huge loss for me when I found out.'

She seemed shocked and he let her digest what he'd told her.

'It must've been hard on your mum,' she said eventually.

‘It probably was.’ Not that she’d talked about it with him. It seemed another area of her life she’d closed off to him.

‘Thanks for telling me,’ said Rosie.

‘I couldn’t tease you any longer.’

She smiled, her cheeks colouring. ‘I’d better get dressed.’

He pulled the study door shut behind them, and without turning to watch her walk up the stairs, said, ‘Nice tattoo, by the way.’

Chapter Nine

Rosie's skin was dry from the swim that morning. She showered and rubbed a light layer of moisturiser all over her body. She thought about Owen's revelations earlier, embarrassed at the conclusions she'd jumped to about the pager.

In those first few days at the house, she'd thought Owen spoiled, using this place as a base while he made his money in property. But she could no longer think that when he was giving his time and risking his life for his town, voluntarily. His job was so different to Adam's, whose work was safe in both the financial and the physical sense. Those were amongst the reasons she'd been drawn to him.

Downstairs Rosie rinsed out her bikini in the laundry sink. She flushed at the memory of Owen seeing her in so little and spotting her tattoo. Unwittingly, she'd revealed a lot more of herself to him just as he had to her.

She hung the bikini over the drying rack when a tapping sound coming from outside caught her attention. Back in the kitchen she watched as Owen hammered a nail into the fence at the foot of the garden. She'd mentioned that a couple of panels were loose, but she hadn't expected him to get to the task quite so quickly.

'Hey,' he called when he looked up towards the house and noticed her watching. He looked hot from yanking those fence panels back into place and holding them there.

As he made his way up to the house, wiping his brow on his forearm, Rosie opened up her iPad and checked the FireReady app, but Magnolia Creek was still as safe as it had been since she'd arrived.

Owen filled a glass with ice-cold water from the dispenser in the fridge-freezer door.

'What do you do with the CFA when there are no incidents in Magnolia Creek?' she asked watching him gulp the liquid down thirstily.

Refreshed, he answered, 'Magnolia Creek is small, but so is the next town and the one after that. My callouts since I've been back have both been out of town. We're often drafted from here as a strike team.' He refilled his glass.

'A strike team?'

'It's a team made up of the same resources.' He smiled at her interest and leant against the bench, sipping from a second glass of water. 'Members of the CFA are volunteers, so they aren't always available. Many have full-time work or family commitments. Take me as an example. I'm often out of town or out of the state, occasionally out of the country, so I wouldn't be able to take every call and it's the same for lots of members. Sometimes a strike team becomes necessary for the gravity of a situation too.'

'Were you ever tempted to be a full-time firefighter?' Rosie pushed a glass beneath the ice dispenser in the freezer and let the ice cubes crash out. They cracked when the water cascaded over the top of them.

'What's this, twenty questions?'

She smiled sheepishly.

‘Relax, I’m teasing you. I was too into the property business to ever want to give it up, so I never considered anything other than volunteering. It’s hard graft too, I don’t know how people do it full-time.’

‘What made you volunteer? Was it because of your dad?’

‘I used to go down to the fire station with him, and as soon as I was old enough I joined the junior brigade.’

‘How old were you then?’

‘Eleven … I think. It’s a long time ago now.’

‘It must’ve been fun growing up doing things like that.’

‘It was. We learnt about using the radio, the buttons not to click on the truck.’ He chuckled. ‘We had races to connect and disconnect hoses – we got each other soaked in those games. Being part of it kept us all out of trouble anyway.’

‘So how did you get into the property investment business?’

‘When my parents renovated this place, I was always talking to the builders, plumbers, electricians. I was fascinated by how they could take something rundown or very ordinary and turn it into something beautiful. I left school, found work in a real estate agent’s and my interest spiralled from there. I bought my first place in my early twenties, and now I have twenty-three properties in total.’

Her glass of water paused mid-air. ‘That’s pretty impressive.’

‘I learnt a lot with the agency, everything from how to identify the latest hotspots to the rules and regulations of tenants’ right, landlord insurance and basic accountancy. I did a short course to learn more about tax, property law, negotiation skills.’ He hesitated and then added, 'I'm hoping to go over to Europe – the UK perhaps – and invest over there too.'

It was her turn to hesitate as his words reminded her that this arrangement was only temporary. She was letting herself fall into the new world of Magnolia Creek, having someone around her all the time.

'Going to a different country to work would be hard,' she said. 'Especially when the risk is all your own.'

'What's life without a little risk, Stevens?'

Her chest tightened as he looked at her, but then she frowned. 'Hang on a minute. Did you say you have twenty-three properties?'

'Correct.'

'You own twenty-three houses, yet you have nowhere to live?'

'Now you put it like that, it does sound kind of ridiculous.'

She giggled. 'So why buy so many properties? Surely it'd be easier to manage fewer, bigger places.' Rosie tore off a piece of kitchen towel to mop up the water than had pooled beneath her glass as the icy contents warmed.

'Having lots of smaller places makes sense. Then if one, or a couple, aren't rented out for a period of time, I don't lose all my income.'

'Good strategy.'

'I allow pets too.'

'Most landlords wouldn't.'

'And that's exactly why I decided I would. I thought I'd see how it went and if it proved a bad decision then I'd make changes to my future tenancy agreements. There are stipulations – you can't have four German Shepherds in a one-bedroom top-floor apartment for example, and if the pet is causing trouble with regards to neighbours, then it's an issue.'

'You sound like a decent landlord to me.'

When he held her gaze, Rosie got up to move away. 'I'd better water down the garden.'

'Already done,' he said. 'I did it before this morning's training session.'

'Now I feel guilty.'

'No need. I'm earning my keep. And besides, I'm used to living in a bushfire area, so it becomes second nature … a bit like putting sunscreen on that skin of yours to protect it – I bet you rarely forget.'

Before she could get too uncomfortable thinking about him seeing her in her bikini earlier, he said, 'You should come down to the fire station some time and see what goes on.'

Her fingers fell across her necklace. 'Why?'

'It might be fun, you never know. We organise regular open days.'

'I'm keeping up-to-date on the bushfire plan and checking the app every day, but I'm not sure I want to be involved.'

'Oh come on, you can see some of the odd people we get in, the tourists who haven't got a clue. Last summer a lady came in with a cigarette dangling from her gob. She flicked ash too … middle of bushfire season. Bella told her, not too politely, to "put the damn thing out".'

Rosie picked up the shopping list from the kitchen bench. 'I'll see.' She smiled. 'Do you need anything?' She waved the list.

'Why don't you let me go? You went last time.'

'I really don't mind.'

‘Well at least let me come with you and help. We could take my pickup,’ he suggested. He must have seen her face because he added, ‘Okay, too rough and ready for you …’

She grinned. ‘I’ll drive. But you can push the trolley.’

Outside the house, Owen sniggered when Rosie climbed into the driver’s seat.

‘What’s so funny?’

He climbed into the passenger side. ‘Nothing, I’m just thinking the Hubba won’t do much for my street cred.’

She fastened her seat belt. ‘You can drive if it makes you feel any better?’

He held up his hands. ‘Oh no, being a passenger violates my self-respect as it is, but driving this thing?’

Rosie unlooped the hair tie from her wrist and twisted her hair off her neck in the summer heat.

‘I feel as though I’m in one of those revolting Barbie movies where everything is pink,’ he said as she pulled out of the driveway.

‘Oh, shut up and let me drive.’

*

All smiles after they returned from the supermarket, Rosie realised Owen was becoming a friend as well as a housemate. She’d never had a shopping trip like that with Adam, who usually wandered aimlessly, Blackberry in hand. The only time she ever got his attention was when she’d picked up something really naughty like her favourite ice cream, Maggie Beer’s Burnt Fig, Honeycomb & Caramel, or a slab of milk chocolate. Sometimes she deliberately chose something enormously fattening just to get his attention. It was a bit of a game. One day she’d dropped in a few slabs of chocolate, a bumper bag of lollies and a family-size pack of peanut M&M's before he'd pulled her up on it. She didn't even like nuts!

Owen had been a scream to go around the supermarket with. Like a big kid, he'd loaded four tubs of ice cream into the trolley and Rosie had told him to put some back on account of it being greedy and there not being enough room in the freezer, and she'd had to reign him in at the meat section when he tried to buy five different types of marinated red meat to put on the barbecue before total fire bans came into place. He'd argued his case that he was a firefighter in need of sustenance, and for one of the first times she'd found herself thinking of a firefighter's heroic duty without being lost in a world of sadness.

Back at home, George wasn't going to let them cross the threshold without first giving him the required level of fuss. They unloaded the car and he followed them inside, threading himself between Rosie's ankles and then Owen's as they unpacked.

'Ice cream's in the freezer, Stevens.' Owen folded up the chiller bag.

'Hey, it's your ice cream, not mine.'

'And I'll bet you help me eat it.'

They were both grinning at each other when the doorbell chimed.

'I'll get that.' Owen scooted off as Rosie pushed peppers into the chiller in the fridge, milk into the shelf on the door and dishwasher tablets beneath the kitchen sink.

As she balanced the last nectarine on top of the others in the fruit bowl, Owen reappeared minus the smile and the jovial mood. 'You've got a visitor.'

Chapter Ten

The familiar warmth of Adam's body enveloped Rosie.

'This place is quite something,' he said, arm around her shoulders as they stood in the kitchen and Owen unpacked the rest of the shopping. She'd introduced the two men, omitting the tales of trips to the supermarket with her housemate, a visit to the pub, a ride on the back of his motorbike.

'It is,' Rosie agreed.

'I wasn't sure I'd see you,' Adam said to Owen. 'I thought you'd be hot-footing it around the country buying up property.' He hugged Rosie closer.

'Not this week,' Owen replied, halting any further conversation.

She separated the two men by taking Adam outside to see the garden and the pool. With his arm still round her shoulders, he nuzzled her cheek. 'I wanted to surprise you.'

'I'm glad you came.' She wondered if Owen's presence had propelled Adam's little surprise as she listened to him extoll the virtues of the garden, the backdrop, the pool, the cabana.

His blond hair shone beneath the sunlight as they stood beside the pool. 'It's quiet out here.'

'It's lovely,' she answered, almost to herself. Should she mention the derelict cottage in Daisy Lane?

Or should they go for a walk later and stumble upon it accidentally? That way she could judge his enthusiasm and hope it measured up to her own.

'This town is a complete contrast to Singapore.' He stood away from the glass surround of the pool and brushed his shirt sleeve for imaginary dust. 'You wouldn't believe the mayhem at rush hour or even in the middle of the day.'

She'd never shared his thrill of big buildings, a heavy layer of smog, the way people were unable to walk along and appreciate their surroundings. It wasn't looking good for the little cottage on Daisy Lane.

Rosie stayed against the glass fence but reached out for Adam's hand and gave it a squeeze. Adam – reliable, solid, Adam. He bent down to kiss her and she let herself melt into the familiarity of it.

'What's that?' When they pulled apart, Adam caught sight of Bertie as the blue-tongue dragged its body across the top of the rockery and into the bush beyond.

'That's Bertie. He scared the life out of me when I first saw him, but I'm used to him now.'

'But you hate wildlife.'

She shrugged. 'It's not so bad.'

Rosie updated Adam on her part-time job: her duties, the people she'd met, how she was falling little by little for the small town.

'Come on,' she said. 'I'll show you around.'

At the front of the house, Owen was standing beneath the shade of the open garage door, music blaring out. His arm plunged into a bucket of steaming soapy water and then dropped snowy suds across the paintwork of his Ducati. He rubbed vigorously at the headlight and didn't turn round as Rosie and Adam left the house.

Rosie felt sorry for the windshield he moved onto next – she sensed it was about to be scrubbed to within an inch of its life.

When Adam mentioned, again, that they were in the middle of nowhere, she bypassed Daisy Lane and they strolled towards the main street. They went via the lake that sparkled obediently, and even he had to concede that the setting was beautiful.

'You're smitten with this place, aren't you?' he said.

'I suppose I am a bit.'

'Holidays and weekend getaways are one thing …' Here we go, thought Rosie. '… but the commute every day would be hard.'

'I know.'

'And, can you honestly say you'd be happy living in a bushfire area?'

'There hasn't been an incident for years.' A bumble bee wiggled its bum and dived into the centre of a flower as pink as Rosie's Volkswagen.

Adam took Rosie's hands in his. 'I want us to get a place together too, but we may have to be realistic, start with an apartment nearer the city. In years to come we might decide we've had enough of all that, but for now it's not practical to be as far out as this.'

'You said that.' She looked at the dried earth beneath her feet. Adam said plenty of sentences with the word 'we', but Rosie sometimes wondered whether 'I' would be a better fit.

'Rosie, it'll happen one day. It nearly happened before. We'd be in our own place by now if we hadn't been outbid. But perhaps it was meant to be.'

'So you're happy we lost the apartment in St Kilda?' She stood back, arms folded.

'Of course not.' He scooped her hair behind her ears. 'What I'm trying to say is that we lost out on the apartment and soon after I got the overseas posting. But the good thing is that you're not at our place alone, we're both saving money and eventually we'll be able to get a place together.'

He kissed her lightly on the lips. 'Show me some more of the town.'

They made their way to Finnegan's café, where the little bell above the door chimed as they left the warm street for a cooler yet no less welcoming interior. Rosie waved over to Jackie, one of the kitchen staff at Magnolia House, who was sitting with her young daughter busy colouring the disposable tablecloth as her mum sipped on tea.

Bella didn't waste any time coming over to their table to investigate the boyfriend.

'Well, it's a delight to meet you, Adam,' said Bella after Rosie had introduced them to one another. She wiped down their table and swiftly laid out two sets of cutlery and napkins folded into triangles.

Rosie began to realise it mattered to her what Bella thought. Since she'd started going to Finnegan's after work each day, Rosie had told the other woman all about her boyfriend. And now, the more she felt settled and at home as part of the community, the more she wondered how she'd feel in January when her time here would be up.

Adam's crisp, beige chinos left him at odds with the other clientele – a man in the corner wore shorts and sandals, Jackie had on a floaty summer dress and Rosie wore a navy cotton shift dress.

Rosie ordered the scones with jam and cream and a pot of Earl Grey tea for them both to share, and when

Bella went to fill the order, Adam said, 'You didn't even ask what I wanted.'

She looked at him. His top button was undone to show golden-tanned skin beneath, a five o'clock shadow creeping across his chin and up the sides of his face. It was different to his usual corporate image, and ordering for him was certainly something new. But Owen's comment the other day kept cropping up in her mind at the oddest of times. He was right. She needed to step out of her comfort zone, and maybe this was all part of it.

'You'll love the scones,' she said, grinning at Adam, 'and I knew you'd say you wanted something healthier if I let you order.'

'I need to watch what I eat after all these hotels and the flight,' he said, patting his belly and smiling at her.

'Time to take a risk.' Uttering similar words to Owen's made her feel alive, in control.

Adam's hand found Rosie's across the table. 'You look happy. More relaxed than I've seen you in ages.'

She felt her insides flicker. 'I am.'

The food and tea arrived, and Rosie took a huge, delectable bite of the still-warm scone, putting her thumb up in Bella's direction when she looked over.

She caught the crumb at the corner of her mouth. 'How long can you stay?'

Adam dotted a tiny globule of cream onto a piece of scone. 'I'm heading to Sydney tomorrow.'

He'd done it again: thrown her world into disarray and then planned to saunter off. Her face fell and it didn't go unnoticed.

'I'm sorry. I know you think I work too hard and I'm obsessed by my job—'

'Aren't you?'

‘I’m not as obsessed by my job as I am about my girlfriend – the girlfriend I thought would be ecstatic to see me.’

His smile placated her. ‘I’m sorry. I’m disappointed, that’s all.’

‘We’ve still got tonight.’ He poured out two cups of tea and added sugar and milk to his own. ‘I’m assuming I can stay at the house?’

‘Of course, why wouldn’t you?’

‘Owen might not like it.’

‘He’ll be fine. He’s been pretty helpful at the house, actually.’ She didn’t mention that as well as Owen being at the house far more than she’d anticipated, he’d also become a friend. Not wanting to make Adam overly jealous, she added, ‘He’s a volunteer firefighter with the CFA, so he’s hardly ever home.’

‘You sound as though you’re fighting his corner.’

‘Don’t be ridiculous.’ She crammed the remaining piece of scone into her mouth before he could ask her anything else.

They walked back to the house chatting about Adam’s time in Singapore, how he’d got lost on his first day, the heat and the buzz of the city. And when they turned into Lakeside Lane, Rosie couldn’t help but laugh at Adam’s story of hitting the pothole earlier and spilling his bottle of Coke everywhere.

‘You learn to avoid that.’ She grinned. As they passed Daisy Lane, she decided it still wasn’t the time to show him the cottage.

Owen was in the same place, beneath the shade of the garage door, and raised a hand when they approached. The music was quieter now, and instead of vigorously scrubbing and sending suds everywhere, he dabbed a rag in a pot of wax and tenderly polished the paintwork in circular motions as though the bike had gone from being a beast that needed to be tamed to a delicate being in need of tender loving care. A can of WD-40 sat beside the front wheel, and another rag lay across the corner of a gleaming windshield that didn't need the help of the sun for its sparkle.

Rosie nodded hello and left him to it, and a short while later she heard the engine purr into life and drive away from the house. She prepared and cooked dinner with Adam and they ate outside, conversation and wine flowing easily until they giggled their way upstairs for the night.

After they'd had sex, Adam took seconds to fall asleep. But as he lay there snoring softly, Rosie lay awake. She was still wide-eyed when she heard Owen's bike turn in off the main road, make its way down the lane and crunch onto the gravel driveway. She listened to the internal door open and shut downstairs, the sound of boots being taken off and dropped on the floor, his feet as they took the stairs to bed.

Her eyes only shut when she'd seen his shadow block the landing light as he walked past her bedroom door.

Chapter Eleven

'Perhaps Evel Knievel's off fighting fires or saving the world this morning.' Adam tucked into toast topped with mushrooms as he sat having breakfast on the deck with Rosie the next morning.

Rosie speared the last of her mushrooms with a fork. 'Don't call him that.'

'It's a joke. You don't have to be so touchy.'

It was as though Adam had done something in her dreams because she almost resented his presence this morning. Maybe she was tired. Part of getting used to Adam each time he came back was that she had to share a bed. She'd taken a while to fall asleep last night and then when she did, every time he'd moved she'd woken up and found it next to impossible to get back to sleep.

She watched Adam sitting outside, in these beautiful surroundings with the lyrebird trilling its song and nothing much else for company apart from the rushing sound of the wind against the leaves of the gum trees. He was a businessman, and sitting in a Magnolia Creek country house in a suit and tie, he looked as though he was out of a New York film set where he should've been running into the nearest Starbucks shouting for a 'large latte to go' and then dodging between big yellow taxis, his cup held aloft.

‘What time’s your meeting?’ She’d noticed him check his watch.

‘Not till this afternoon, but I fly late morning. I need to run through a presentation on my laptop while I’m at the airport.’ He slurped the remains of his coffee. ‘I’ll be back in a couple of days.’

Rosie hugged him. ‘Looking forward to it already.’

After Adam left for the airport, Rosie relished some alone time in the garden. Her shift at Magnolia House didn’t start until lunchtime, when she would be helping set up for a wedding this afternoon. She picked up the net beside the pool and swished its long pole through the pool water, finding therapy in the motion as she cleared the surface of leaves and a couple of dead cockroaches who’d met their fate.

The water was too tempting to ignore any longer, and after she’d fished out a twig she was afraid could block the filter and tipped the debris into the garden bin, she grabbed her bikini from where she’d left it in the laundry and ran upstairs to get changed. She checked the SunSmart app and slathered on a generous helping of sunscreen, impatiently waiting the requisite ten minutes for it to soak in before she could jump into the water.

Inside the pool’s modern square lines, she glided up and down, notching up thirty-two lengths in all. Satiated, she climbed out of the water and into the teardrop-shaped spa carved out at the far end in front of the gazebo. She pressed the square button to set the spa into motion and positioned herself on the longest seat with jets at the feet, behind the knees and two focused on her shoulder blades. As her breathing steadied into a more sedate rhythm, she rested her head back on the cream leather pillow, tilted her face to the sun and let the massaging waters, penetrating nozzles and millions of bubbles take her away.

Not long later, her eyes flew open when she heard an almighty splash behind her at the other end of the pool. She blinked as the foaming white waters of the spa splashed up at her, and she reached out for the sunglasses she'd left with her towel. When she turned she saw Owen rocketing up and down the length of the pool doing full tumble turns each time he reached the end. Length after length he swam, barely coming up for air, flashing the rose tattoo each time he lifted his arm out of the water and before his hand plunged in to do another stroke.

The buoyancy made her feet float up and flash crimson-painted toes as she moved to the seat facing the pool. Watching Owen, either something was bothering him or he'd chosen to take part in an Olympic swim and had forgotten to train. He finally stopped at the opposite end, and from behind her sunglasses she watched his shoulders move up and down with his breath until he recovered. Only then did he lift his head and see her watching him.

He swam at a more sedate pace towards her, and when he reached the side he rested his arms on the concrete beside the pool, his body still in the water.

'Do you want to talk about it?' she asked.

'Not really.' It wasn't long before he added, 'Your boyfriend can stay here for as long as you like.'

'Thanks. I was going to email your mum and check though.'

'No need, I spoke to her earlier today.'

'Oh.'

'Yeah, I made the mistake of telling her I was here.'

Before she had a chance to reply, he ploughed out another six lengths – Rosie counted – just as fast as the rest. When he reached the edge of the pool again, he adopted the same position: arms plonked on the concrete, chin resting on his forearms, eyes shut as though he needed to take a break from the world.

Rosie saw her opportunity to avoid having fingers that resembled tinned prunes. She flicked the button to turn the bubbles off, stayed beneath the water to check her bikini was properly adjusted and then climbed out. Of course that was the exact moment Owen chose to open his eyes.

They locked gazes for a second before he buried his face and dark hair beneath the water and began shuttling from one end to the other all over again. Rosie climbed out of the spa and grabbed her towel. She was petite, but she still had her gripes: her legs weren't as toned as they could be, and she didn't like the slightly rounded tummy that Adam liked to remind her would only get worse if she kept eating all those freshly baked scones at Bella's café. And Owen had seen enough the other day when he'd come home and shown her the pictures in the study.

'You're pretty fast,' she said when Owen finally came to a stop and she was safely ensconced in the fluffy butterscotch towel beneath the cabana, away from the sun's glare.

'Can I grab one of those?' Owen nodded towards the Diet Coke she'd pulled out of the fridge next to the barbecue.

'I can get you a beer if you like.'

'Can't. I'm on call, and it's way too early.' His mouth curved into a smile.

Rosie pulled another can from the fridge then sat beneath the gazebo at the stone picnic-style bench looking out over the pool and couldn't help but watch Owen as he hoisted himself from the water. His muscles strained to bear his weight and the water cascaded off his body. He shook his head vigorously, sending water droplets flying from side to side, and then rubbed a towel across his face and head, his top half and finally his legs.

'Do you get fed up being on call all the time?' She handed him the can of drink, hoping he hadn't seen her gawping at him.

'I don't mind it. Everyone in the team pulls their weight.' He glanced at the milky white skin of her shoulders. 'You need to be careful, Stevens.'

Rosie noticed a telltale pink tinge that hadn't been there before. She hoped it was just from the heat of the day.

'Have you got sunscreen on?' he asked.

'Of course. The UV index is extreme already.'

The hairs on her arm stood on end when his arm brushed against hers as he lifted his can to take a sip. 'How do you know stuff like that?'

'I've got an app.'

'You're as bad as my mother, checking apps every five minutes.'

They sat for a while, sipping their drinks, letting the tranquillity of the setting fall over them, the glugging of the pool filter making the sounds of summer. Rosie looked sideways at Owen. His eyes were fixed on the water. *Flick, flick*, went the ring pull on the top of his can, as though it could tap into his thoughts.

'Do you know what I wish?' he asked, not looking her way or waiting for an answer. 'I wish my mother knew how to have a row. I'd rather have one of those horrendous slanging matches where I'm called all the names under the sun, but she doesn't seem to know how to let go. The quiet treatment gets me every time. I've no idea what she's thinking.'

Rosie had never had a huge slanging match with her mum either. Her mum had upped and left before she'd ever got the chance.

'Has she always been that way?' She knew this couldn't be the whole story, but she wasn't sure she knew Owen well enough to delve further.

'For as long as I can remember. It's almost as though she detaches herself from half the things I say or do.'

Rosie waited to see if he'd add anything else, but it seemed Jane Harrison wasn't the only one who kept her feelings well hidden.

'I know I'm not the easiest person to live with, Stevens.'

'What makes you say that?'

'I don't think Adam approves.'

Rosie took a deep breath. 'You leave Adam to me.'

'Well if it gets too much, just say the word and I'll move on.'

'Owen, if you were really annoying me, you'd know about it, believe me.'

'Talking of Adam, where is he?'

'He's away for a few days, working.' She looked at him. 'What's that face for?'

'What face?'

'Your judgement face.'

He threw his head back and laughed. 'Oh, I have a "judgement face" now, do I?'

'Yep, you're judging because Adam's working.'

'I'm not judging, and you're paranoid.'

She finished her drink. 'I'd better get ready for work.'

It was his turn to climb into the spa. 'How about a barbecue later?'

'Sounds good to me.' And dizzy with the feeling of belonging, she went inside to get changed.

*

Owen lay back in the spa as he watched Rosie go inside. He did his best to ignore how attracted he was to this girl whom his mum was more worried about than him.

'I don't want to breach the agreement, Owen,' Jane had told him after he'd surprised her with a phone call. He'd had some crazy notion that maybe if she was thousands of miles away she might be more open to discussion, and maybe if he was brave enough he could broach the subject of what she was hiding. God knows he'd found nothing around the house that could enlighten him.

'If Rosie doesn't want me here then she can tell me to go, but she seems to like having someone around,' Owen had insisted. 'I've been clearing gutters, watering the garden, mowing the lawn. I'll make sure she can tell one end of a rose from another too,' he'd laughed.

His comment had met with a deafening silence and Jane Harrison had wrapped up the phone call quickly. He'd gone out on the bike after that, the usual tonic when he was stressed, but when that hadn't worked to clear his head, he'd returned home and jumped into the pool, thrashing out length after length. He'd begged for the coolness of the water and the struggle for breath to squeeze him back into life as he thought over and over about his relationship with his mum.

As a child he'd imagined he had superpowers to make him completely invisible to his mum. He'd pretty much felt as though she couldn't see him a lot of the time anyway when she was physically present yet emotionally not there at all. She'd praised him when he'd done something good, scolded him when he'd been naughty, but growing up Owen had often felt as though whatever he did would never be good enough.

He tilted his head back, letting his face, forehead, nose and cheeks be kissed by the sun. He thought of Rosie lying in this same place, her silky skin and her hourglass figure that set his pulse racing every time he let it. Had he shared too much with her earlier? She was a good listener, not interrupting and not probing too much. He had a sneaky suspicion that she was better at listening to others than she was at confiding her own troubles.

*

Rosie buzzed through the afternoon, loving every minute of setting up for a wedding. She took delivery of exquisite flowers, found platters for the caterers to arrange the most delectable canapés, delivered champagne to the bride and bridesmaids as they got dressed in stunning gowns upstairs. She helped weave fairy lights around the veranda to create a magical atmosphere for guests congregating there for fresh air and chatter.

At home Rosie showered and changed and pulled on a thin cotton dress. Owen hadn't fired up the barbecue yet, so she had a chance to flick on the iPad and check out her handiwork with the Magnolia House website. She'd updated their online profile and added extra photographs, and looking at it on the internet now, she was proud of all she'd achieved in her first public relations position. Once she'd viewed the website, she checked her emails and got rid of all the junk mail before she spotted one lingering in the inbox from Jane Harrison. She clicked on the email and read:

Dear Rosie,

I hope you are well and enjoying your stay in Magnolia Creek. We are managing to sort out my sister's affairs in London, and it's lovely to know our home is being so well looked after in our absence.

I'm writing to you because I understand my son Owen is staying there with you. I know this wasn't in the contract, and I really wanted to make sure everything is okay with that arrangement.

If there's a fire in Magnolia Creek – and I'm hoping there isn't as we haven't had one for years – could you please get in touch with me? Any time, day or night, I'd like you to call on one of the numbers I listed for you. There are some specific items on the property – personal items – that I need you to keep safe for me. I also need your word you won't pass this information on to Owen, not under any circumstances.

Jane Harrison signed off and Rosie was left staring at the screen, re-reading the words. It was a valid request to remove certain items from the property, but to keep them from her own son?

The sound of scraping and scratching outside her window had Rosie's attention, and she looked out to see that Owen had leant the ladder against the house and was clearing twigs and leaves from the gutters again, minimising fuel for any bushfire that threatened to come their way.

In the short time she'd known him, Rosie had begun to feel an overwhelming loyalty towards this man. But she'd also seen him that morning, riled by his mum's behaviour, tearing up and down the pool to vent his anger. Did she really want to mention the email and stir up whatever angst there was between them?

Rosie's own childhood and adolescence hadn't exactly been a breeze, not by a long shot, but as she went downstairs to make a salad and watched Owen take position behind the barbecue, she felt glad there was never any mystery. Her family had been what it was. But for Owen, his family had things lurking in their past they appeared to have let mutilate their relationship with their son. She wouldn't want to be in his position at all.

Chapter Twelve

'I'm sorry about the barbecue last night.' The next morning Rosie squeezed her tea bag before dropping it into the bin and sitting opposite Owen at the kitchen table. 'I think the sun must've got to me.'

Rosie had made the salad and some garlic bread and they'd chatted while they ate rissoles, peppered steak and fresh prawns. But despite the amazing food Owen cooked perfectly on the barbecue, she hadn't been able to get Jane's email out of her head. The words had tapped into her psyche, and whether it was that or the sun, she'd ended up with a headache that sent her to bed before any dessert.

'Did the paracetamol work?' Owen scanned the front page of the newspaper.

'It did, thanks.'

He looked up. 'Are you working this afternoon?'

'Day off.' She sipped her tea.

'I'm going down to one of my properties by the beach. The tenant moved out yesterday and I want to check everything is in order, give the go-ahead for the bond to be released.'

'Doesn't the letting agency do that?'

He rolled his eyes as he stood to take his empty cup to the sink. 'They do, but they aren't quite as pedantic as me.'

'I can imagine.'

Owen nudged her playfully but didn't hang around to see how the feel of his touch had affected her. He pulled a bottle of water from the fridge. 'You could come with me. I'd like the company, and Albert Park is a beautiful spot. The house is one road back from the beach and it's a gorgeous day. You could bring your togs – that is, if you didn't get too much sun yesterday.'

'I'm fine.' She blushed when she thought about him visualising her skin yesterday after the pool.

'We can take your car if you like,' he added. 'I'll need my toolbox in case anything needs fixing, but the pickup is definitely a work truck.'

'Filthy, you mean?'

'Yep.'

The idea was certainly appealing, and with Adam at work she had nothing to do here today. Grinning, she said, 'Give me five minutes to get ready.'

*

'I can't believe I'm gunning towards the city in a *pink* car.' Owen was glad the interior was a tasteful black. 'The local supermarket was one thing, but this?'

'Hey, we could've taken your pickup.'

'Sure, but you'd have made me clean it first.'

She smiled at him because she knew he was right. He caught a waft of Rosie – something citrusy and fresh, shower gel maybe, or it could've been shampoo. When she'd trotted up the stairs that morning to get ready, his eyes had followed her, settling on her behind in a dress that clung in all the right places. He did his best to ignore the same cotton dress now, which sat just above her knees, inching upwards every time her feet operated the pedals.

'Ah well,' he said, 'being a passenger has its benefits. I can sink into my seat when we get near people.'

'I'll make sure I put the roof down later and then you won't be able to hide,' she joked. 'You're too tall anyway. You've got no hope of being inconspicuous.'

He'd had Rosie down as being an overly cautious driver, or at the very least, a sit-in-the-middle-lane-no-matter-what driver. But she was neither. On the freeway she went as fast as he would've done, she did some impressive overtaking, and when they'd stopped near South Melbourne market to grab some food, she did an awesome parallel park outside the supermarket.

They'd walked around the market humming and hawing as to whether to go for stuffed olives or plain, falafels or meatballs, which was the best fizzy drink, and as Owen packed the supplies in the esky he'd lined with ice-packs from home, he couldn't help thinking how well they slotted in with each other. The difference with Rosie was that, unlike other women he'd been involved with, he'd got to know her first, as a friend, without the relationship aspect ever being a part of it. It was a completely new experience for him.

Rosie did as promised and put the roof down before they set off towards the house, and as they overtook the green and yellow tram and trundled across the tracks paving the way towards the beach, Owen realised that travelling like this was liberating in a different way than being on the bike: he could take in his surroundings, stretch out in his seat and shut his eyes if he wanted to. Letting someone else take control for a change was better than he'd expected.

Rosie negotiated the parked cars in the narrower streets of Albert Park with practised ease, and when they pulled up outside his property, he hauled the esky out of the boot while she opened the front gate and let him through.

'Where's the key?' she asked, sunglasses firmly in place with the sun beating down on them outside the cream-fronted weatherboard.

'In my back pocket.' He couldn't help the curl in his lips. He could ask her to get it – he'd enjoy that – but something told him not to push. Instead, he set the esky down on the concrete and pulled out the key, sure he hadn't mistaken a smile creeping its way onto her face too.

'Awesome,' he said, picking up the parking permit from the hallway floor. 'Most tenants conveniently forget to leave these behind. They hold onto their precious beach-side parking for as long as they can.' He scooted back to the car and stuck the permit on the inside of the windshield before he took the esky inside.

Owen unlocked the bi-fold doors in the lounge room and opened them up to a small, square rear courtyard to let the air circulate through the house, which was stifling in the summer heat.

'It's a lovely house.' Rosie peeked into the two rooms off the hallway before she came through to the kitchen and family area.

'Thanks. I had the loft space converted to make another bedroom and bathroom, and I stripped out this kitchen and the downstairs bathroom and then painted everything.'

Rosie pointed to the staircase. 'May I?'

'Sure, go ahead.' Her inquisitiveness sat well with him and he followed her up the stairs. 'This was the first house I bought as opposed to an apartment. I was worried I'd taken on too much, but this place has turned out to be a gold mine. It's my biggest income earner.'

'I can see why.'

'The beach is a huge drawcard, and it's close to the city.'

Rosie gasped. 'Wow, you can see the sea from up here, between those two houses.' She pointed.

At the peaked window he leaned closer to share the view. 'I think I'd be using a fair bit of artistic licence to describe this place as having "sea views".' He tried to ignore the wave of pheromones coming from her hair that smelt so good and caused his voice to falter.

'Nonsense.' She gestured with her hands to the space below the window. 'You could put a window seat in here, about so high.' She showed him with her delicate hands and neatly manicured nails. 'You'd be able to sit here and see the ocean.'

When Rosie put both hands on his shoulders, he froze. She was so close.

'Crouch down so you're a bit lower than my height,' she instructed. 'And now imagine there's a seat right here beneath the window.'

He did as he was told and was impressed at her ability to see what he'd never been able to. Out of the peaked window and between the roofs of two houses were the frilly, white foaming edges of the waves on the ocean as they broke and a strip of sunlight glimmering across the surface of the water. 'Perhaps I should up the rent.'

When she laughed his stomach did a weird lurch, but then she was off again, checking out the en suite, running back downstairs – quicker with her dainty feet than he was with his size elevens – and mumbling something about the ornate fireplaces in the front bedroom.

'So what do you think about having a window seat?' she asked when she'd inspected as much of the house as she wanted to.

'It's a lovely idea, but I'm not sure it'd be worth my while.'

'I disagree.'

He wanted to laugh at her stern face, her stance as she looked at him, hands on her hips just like the first night they'd met.

'I think it's those types of extras that could make all the difference,' she said.

Owen didn't usually listen to anyone else when it came to his property portfolio – with the exception of his sister-in-law, Sadie, who came over and gave places the woman's touch before he advertised for sale or rent, adding a vase of flowers here, a pot plant or painting there. But Rosie did have a point about the little 'extras'.

'I'll bear it in mind,' he said. 'I'll do a quick inspection if it's okay with you, and then we can eat.'

Owen left Rosie smelling the agapanthus and the cherry blossom in the rear courtyard while he walked around checking the wooden floors for extra marks or dents other than what could be put down to wear and tear. He checked the kitchen appliances were all in working order and looked beneath all the sinks for leaks that could've been missed and which could prove costly if he left them while the place was untenanted. He was pedantic, but the only place Owen was willing to cut corners was out on the open road on his motorbike.

'How's it looking?' Sunglasses perched on top of her head, Rosie came indoors as Owen opened kitchen cupboards and stepped back to ensure they were clear and clean and ready for the next tenant.

'I didn't need the tools after all. It's all looking good.'

'You're a perfectionist.'

'So I've been told.' She wasn't wrong. He'd bought property after property and turned monstrous, ugly dwellings into something out of the pages of one of those fancy home magazines, and he got a real buzz in doing it.

Owen held her gaze a moment longer than he'd intended and then patted the top of the esky filled with food. 'Are you ready for a picnic at the beach?'

'I'll get the industrial strength sunscreen and I'm good to go.'

Rosie disappeared into the bathroom to apply her sunscreen, and when she came back to the kitchen he borrowed the tube himself – it was the only way to stop her harping on about the UV index and how everyone had to be careful these days – and they headed down to the beach, away from the Sand Bar to where the crowds thinned out.

He set the esky down and Rosie rolled out a picnic blanket. They unloaded olives stuffed with cheese, breadsticks, kabana sausages, quiche, meatballs and a quinoa salad.

'What can I tempt you with?' Rosie asked, ready to fill a plate with his choices.

What could she tempt him with? There was something, but it wasn't on the list.

'I'll have whatever's within reach,' he said, hoping food would distract him from having thoughts that would get him into trouble.

They watched the ocean as they ate, his mind calming with each wave that broke onto the shore. And when he'd eaten enough he lay back on the blanket, propped up on his elbows, shades pulled down. He watched Rosie carefully put all the lids back onto the containers. 'You're very domesticated.'

'Well one of us has to be. This food will all go yucky if we leave it in the sun for too long, and you might want some more later on.'

If anyone could hear them, they'd think they were an old married couple. That had never happened before with any of the girls he'd dated, and he minded it less than he thought he would. This situation was weird, like a temporary relationship to try out what it would be like before he went back to his lifestyle of living between projects, driving in and out of town whenever he felt like it. Had Rosie not been at the house and had he not wanted time to snoop around, Owen knew he'd have left by now. But without the parent cloud that usually hovered over him, Magnolia Creek really felt like home and he was happier than he'd been in a long time.

Rosie sat on the blanket, but it took her a while to drop back onto her elbows like he had. When she did, her hair blew gently across his shoulder and made him shiver.

He sighed. 'I love the beach.'

'Me too, even if my skin doesn't.' She reached inside her bag and pulled out a wide-brimmed straw hat.

'I thought you got sunburnt at the pool yesterday, but your arms aren't red.'

She fidgeted. 'I think I overheated, but I'll be more careful today.' She looked around them. 'This beach is beautiful.'

'You've never been here?'

‘Not that I can remember. Apollo Bay was the family favourite when I was little. Although Mum would never go in the ocean – lifelong fear of sharks,’ she explained. ‘It terrified her when I’d swim out of my depth, give her a wave.’

He looked out at all the unsuspecting swimmers now. ‘Wasn’t a shark found there recently?’

The bottle of Pellegrino fizzed when she twisted the top off. ‘You’re thinking of Lorne.’ Her smile reached those brown eyes, richer in colour out here in the open air, with the ocean and the golden sand a picture-perfect backdrop.

He scooped sand into his palm and let it fall through his fingers. ‘So are you worried?’

‘About what?’

‘Sharks.’ He pointed to the ocean. ‘Out there, today, right now, swimming amongst us?’

She pulled a face.

‘You are!’ He laughed. ‘You’re a big scaredy cat.’

Rosie stood up, flicked open the buttons down the front of her dress and let it fall to her ankles. She pulled out a brilliant turquoise rash vest from her bag, tugged it over her head and wiggled it down over her breasts, covering the same bikini she’d worn yesterday.

‘You’re the scaredy cat still lying there on the picnic blanket,’ she giggled, and while he was still trying to get over seeing the vision of her stripping down, she was off.

He leapt up. Two could play at that game. He pulled his T-shirt over his head and chased after her down to the water’s edge. He loved the playful Rosie, the Rosie who’d told him her confusion over his pager, the Rosie in front of him now.

‘Last one to go completely under the water has to cook dinner every night for the next week.’ He caught her only ankle deep and waded in past her, up to his shins.

He reached back and grabbed her hand, pulling her in further just as a kid carrying a boogie board came hurtling into the oncoming waves. She shuddered as her body was splashed with cool water. The bumps covered her thighs until the water level met with her bikini bottoms and crossed her tummy, then she stopped, grinned at him, dropped his hand and dived into an oncoming wave like a mermaid. He saw her head surface seconds later, and she was chuckling away as she trod water well out of her depth.

‘Dinner’s on you!’ she yelled back at him.

They swam around for a while, and if it wasn’t for his fitness, she would’ve been one step ahead of him the whole time. When her back was to him, he dived beneath the surface and knew he’d scared her when he purposely grazed past her legs. He emerged and their two heads bobbed in the ocean as they trod water, both lost in the moment.

This was more than harmless flirting, he knew it was. This was flirting with intent. And it wasn’t one-sided. The signals Rosie was sending his way weren’t telling him to back off, not in the slightest.

Once out of the water, they were both ravenous and feasted on the remainder of the picnic. They sat on the golden sands talking about other places they’d been to in Australia, the countries Owen had seen when he’d travelled for six months, the European travel Rosie yearned for.

‘You should go,’ he told her.

She held the stem of a strawberry and bit into the succulent flesh. 'One day I will.'

Owen suspected Rosie had been playing it safe ever since she was old enough to make her own decisions, and it was a hard habit to break. He offered her the last meatball, but she shook her head.

When she took off her rash vest and lay back, hat and sunglasses in place, water droplets formed and tumbled off around her waist, breasts and her thighs. 'Do you need more sunscreen?' He cleared his throat.

She opened one eye suspiciously.

'I'm not suggesting I rub it on for you, I just meant you're wearing next to nothing and it's the hottest part of the day.'

Satisfied with his explanation, she shut her eyes again and wiggled her shoulders to get comfortable. 'I'll only have five minutes lying here. I want my bikini to dry so I can put my dress on again for the trip home.'

Owen lay back too. He figured it was safer than staring at her. His skin tightened as the sun beat down and dried his body and board shorts. When he heard a giggle, he opened one eye. 'What?'

'Either you don't have another tattoo as you implied, or it's on your arse or somewhere equally as inconspicuous.'

He grinned. 'Sorry to disappoint you, but I only have the one.' When she flipped over to expose her back to the sun and let it dry, he asked, 'So are you ever going to tell me?'

'Tell you what?' The soporific effects of the sea and the sun made her sound sleepy.

'About your tattoo.'

‘Oh, that.’ She shifted on the sand, her face resting on her forearms, making it impossible to read her expression. ‘There’s nothing to tell.’

‘You’re lying. The cello clearly has a significant meaning in your life given the necklace *and* the tattoo.’

‘Leave it, Owen.’ The sun’s power got too much for her, or maybe it was his line of questioning, and she sat up and pulled her dress on over her bikini. She plonked her straw hat on her head and from behind her sunglasses she said, ‘My dad taught me to play the cello when I was little, and I love music. What more do you want me to say?’

Her face was fixed towards the vast expanse of the ocean laid out before them.

‘Is your dad a cellist?’

Rosie nodded.

‘Why didn’t you tell me that in the first place? I thought we were friends.’

‘We are.’ She tidied away, packing the rubbish bag into the esky, throwing in her empty bottle of fizzy drink. She gestured for Owen to stand up so she could shake out the picnic blanket.

‘I’ll do that before we get in the car, Stevens. The sand will go over everyone else otherwise.’

‘Fine.’ She picked up the miles-too-heavy esky and set off across the sand.

They walked back to the house in silence, and Owen shook out the picnic blanket at the side of the road before folding it away to stow in the boot along with the esky.

He climbed into the passenger seat. ‘Would you mind if we stopped by the apartment I own in St Kilda before we go home?’ It was the first thing he’d said to her since she’d stormed off. ‘The tenant said he’d leave the newly signed agreement in the letter box. I'll sign it and pop it back in for the agency to collect.'

'Sure, just let me know where to go.' The engine purred into action and Owen forgot all about the fact he was bubbling around in a pink car.

They drove along Beaconsfield Parade and when they arrived at Fitzroy Street, Owen directed Rosie until they pulled up in a narrow side street with a cream-coloured apartment block to one side.

'I won't be a minute.' He grabbed the pen and the letterbox key he'd brought with him and jumped out of the car and over to the mail boxes standing in a row like obedient soldiers. He scribbled his signature on the papers, slotted them into the post box and climbed back into the car next to Rosie.

'Let's keep the roof down all the way home,' he suggested. 'I'm quite enjoying posing in this thing now.' But when he turned, laughing, towards her, she was staring up at the apartment block looking anything but amused.

'When did you buy the apartment?'

He opened his mouth to respond, but she was on a roll.

'Don't tell me,' she said, 'is it number four?'

'How did you—'

'How did I know? Because you're the arsehole who stole it from under our noses, that's how.'

She pulled away from the kerb so violently he was surprised he didn't end up with severe whiplash. Lucky for him he hadn't muttered a glib 'all's fair in love and property dealing' remark because he suspected he would've had a lot more than whiplash to contend with.

They drove in silence all the way back to Magnolia Creek. Every time he tried to open his mouth to talk, to reason with her that she was being bloody ridiculous, she turned the music up, and when he turned it down she used the controls on either side of the steering wheel to override him.

And that was how their fantastic day had ended: silent treatment, then deafening music to drown out his words, followed by one hell of a huff from Rosie as she stomped upstairs and slammed her bedroom door.

Now this really did feel like they were in a relationship.

Chapter Thirteen

That night Rosie dreamt about the cottage in Daisy Lane. When she woke she remembered how she'd left things with Owen yesterday. She'd been childish, she knew, but he'd scuppered her plans to move in with Adam, whether it had been intentional or not. And sometimes it was easier to put the blame onto someone else.

When there was a knock on her bedroom door, she curled into the duvet more and pretended to be asleep. When the knock sounded a second time, she called out, 'I'm asleep … leave me alone.'

The door opened anyway. 'Charming,' said the voice.

'Adam!' She leapt out of bed and flung her arms around his neck, pulling him into the room.

'Evel Knievel let me in.'

Rosie heard the bike roar away from the house. She locked her lips onto Adam's, tugged at his shirt, loosened his belt and welcomed the feeling of closeness, the sanctuary of them as a couple.

Their lovemaking was frantic, urgent, and when they'd finished Adam rolled over and both of them caught their breath.

'I could get used to this kind of welcome.' He propped himself up on an elbow and ran a finger along her jaw. 'What's up? I've known you long enough to know something's on your mind.'

She didn't want to tell him about the apartment in St Kilda. It was in the past and she couldn't rewrite history. Besides, she wanted to enjoy Adam being here until he had to up and go again, and the last thing she needed was to create tension between Adam and Owen.

She turned to face Adam. 'When are we going to be together, Adam? Properly, I mean.' The question had been propelled by dreaming about the cottage in Daisy Lane. She had no time to think about whether she really wanted to know the answer.

'It won't be like this forever,' he promised.

Rosie could tell he was too relaxed for the serious conversation she needed to have and so she settled for a reassuring cuddle. Before long his breathing slowed into the familiar pattern that meant he was on the brink of sleep. Restless, she pulled on some cotton shorts and an old T-shirt and headed downstairs, glad of the headspace. Her limbs ached pleasantly from the ocean swim yesterday, the current more challenging than the crystal calm waters of the pool she looked out at now.

She had some gardening chores to do this morning, but before she headed outside she perused the floor-to-ceiling bookshelves lining one wall of the lounge. She delved into a thick, leather-bound gardening book, flicking through the pictures and imagining what the cottage in Daisy Lane could look like with manicured gardens and roses around the door. She read a section on fungal diseases such as black spot – a pest in late summer and autumn – rust and the importance of removing dead leaves from the ground to minimise the risk. She imagined what it would be like to have her own garden one day and read up on how to best encourage blooms and keep existing plants going long into winter.

Slotting the book back in its place, the travel section fit for any city library was next to catch her eye. She ran her fingers along the spines of travel guides for London, Paris, Rome, Tuscany, Prague. She paused when her finger landed on a guidebook to Florence, Italy. She pulled it out and sat back on the arm of the sofa as her eyes hungrily devoured pages depicting the Ponte Vecchio, the Piazzo del Duomo, the bustling cobbled streets. She could feel the Italian voices falling like soft pillows around her ears, imagine the chatter in the restaurants late into the evening where wine was savoured rather than consumed.

The room darkened as though a blanket had fallen over the entire house, and Rosie looked out to see dense grey clouds hovering in the sky above. Anxious to get at least some of her gardening chores done before the heavens opened, she went to the shed and took out the tools she needed.

Kneeling on the mat, she started with the yellow roses. The majority were still healthy blooms, but a couple were spent, and as per Jane's guidance, she moved the secateurs down to where there was a section of five leaves on the stem, plus a healthy looking bud, and cut off the rest. She hoped she was doing this right. It was a big responsibility for a novice gardener.

As she moved round to the next rose bush and pulled dead twigs from the ground, throwing them into the bucket beside her, a low rumble made her look up. But it hadn't been thunder, it was Owen's motorcycle. She busied herself but knew he had come outside the second he'd seen her tending to the roses.

‘You look like you’re getting the hang of that.’ Owen cast a shadow over her as he walked up behind her.

‘Your mum left clear instructions,’ she answered without looking up.

‘Sometimes I wonder whether she loves those roses more than anything else in the world.’

The undertone of his remark failed to convey the flippancy Rosie suspected he’d intended. She thought about Jane’s email again, how she was keeping something from Owen.

Rosie sat back on her ankles. ‘I’m sorry about yesterday. It was wrong of me to blame you for us losing the apartment. You bought it fair and square.’

They both turned at the familiar sound of the ice maker in the fridge-freezer whirring into action because a glass had been pushed beneath it.

‘Apology accepted, Stevens.’ He looked up at the dark clouds congregating above their heads. ‘I doubt you’ll need to water the grass.’

She smiled at him before he disappeared inside. Adam waved to her from the kitchen, glass of water in hand, before he disappeared back upstairs.

Refocusing on the roses, Rosie picked up dead leaves from the ground around the base of the plants. She dropped them into the bucket beside her and, using a small trowel, dug out a couple of weeds that had poked their way through the soil. When one stubborn weed remained, she dug deeper to prise it out, but it wouldn’t move. She thrust the trowel in again but this time she hit something hard. She jiggled the trowel to work what she assumed must be a rock out of the soil, but it was bigger than she’d anticipated.

She wiped the back of her arm across her brow as the first few spots of rain were unleashed from the clouds above, and this time used her gloved hands to scrape back the earth and see if she could prise out whatever was buried with her hands. But when she peered more closely to see the size of the thing, the deep grey colour definitely wasn't a rock. She hooked her fingers around the outside of what appeared to be a metal box and let a giggle escape as she tried to pull out whatever it was. It was like finding buried treasure, like the magical fairy party when she'd turned six and a fairy lady had visited their garden and hidden treasures all around: silver beads in the heads of plants, glitter sprinkled round the bottom of a gum tree, a silver-coloured pencil found in the cubby house, a beautiful gold trinket box buried beneath a pile of leaves.

But this tarnished grey box didn't look much like treasure. There was no lock on it, and with a bit of wiggling the lid came off easily enough. All that was inside was a see-through bag containing papers of sorts. She opened the bag to find a photograph of a girl Rosie estimated to be in her late teens, possibly early twenties, and another photograph of the same girl in a faded newspaper article with the headline 'Young Woman Killed in Tragic Sailing Accident'. Rosie read the article, taking in phrases such as 'no suspicious circumstances', 'alone', 'survived by her parents and sisters Jane and Sarah'.

Rosie's chest tightened when she realised Jane had lost a sister before now, before the funeral she'd travelled to the UK for. But why hide all this beneath a rose bush in the back garden?

Rosie looked up to check neither Owen nor Adam had come out onto the deck and that she wasn't being watched from Owen's window upstairs. Then she rummaged through the bag again and this time pulled out two magazine articles, one in full colour and the other much older, faded. The coloured article was scrunched as though it had been balled up for rubbish and then flattened out again.

Crouching down, she skimmed over the first article, a story of a school truant and dropout turned businessman, Gregory Falmer, who was the man behind the set-up of a lucrative, thriving holiday home development in Victoria. Rosie's heart sagged when she read about Gregory Falmer's wife, Jane, and son, Owen. The words described a family man as well as a successful businessman, and the photograph told a story of happiness. The story of Owen's life before his dad had died.

When Rosie moved to the second article, the feelings of sadness gave way to curiosity. This article talked about another businessman – this time Declan Roberts, who had two young sons with his partner Claire. But it only took seconds for Rosie to make the connection. The man in the second photograph was older than the man in the first, his hair was silvery grey and thinner and he had a pronounced paunch. But they were the same man, no doubt about it.

She looked at the dates of both of the articles. The first was written many years ago, but the second was dated recently, less than six months ago. Her eyes darted up to the house and the upstairs window as she eagerly digested what was before her now. These had to be the personal items Jane had mentioned, the items she didn't want Owen to see.

Rosie pulled out the remaining contents of the bag. A bundle of papers unrolled to reveal a bank statement with highlighted payments to a C. Gilbertson alongside a description of 'roofing repairs', all twenty thousand dollars each … five of them in total. Her next find was the most disturbing of all: a photograph of the same man – Gregory Falmer, Declan Roberts or whatever he called himself – in his younger years, semi-clothed, in an office, all over a girl who looked young enough to be his daughter.

There was one more thing lurking at the bottom of the plastic bag and, hiding as much as she could to the side of one rose bush, careful not to let the thorns poke her in the eye, she pulled out a letter addressed to Jane. She hesitated. This was more personal than anything else, but she had to read it.

The letter was written by Natasha, the sister who'd died, and the words begged for forgiveness, pleaded with Jane to believe in her.

A voice from the kitchen startled Rosie as the rain started falling more heavily. 'What on earth are you doing?' Adam shouted. 'It's raining, come inside!'

She pushed the items back in the bag and hid them in the box before shoving it back into the hole in the ground. She frantically covered the box with soil and then ran towards the house, her clothes clinging to her as the rain unleashed its full force.

That was the thing about secrets. Those who didn't know wanted to know, and those who knew sometimes wished they didn't.

Chapter Fourteen

'What's for dinner tonight?' Adam pulled Rosie to him as she emerged from the bathroom. Even after a long shower she hadn't been able to wash away the secret she'd found in the dirt outside.

'Earth to Rosie,' he teased when she didn't answer. 'You're working too hard in that garden. If they wanted to have their flowerbeds worshipped, maybe they should've hired a gardener, not a house-sitter.'

'It's all part of the job.'

'No it's not, I saw you out there'—he indicated the garden—'digging away in the pouring rain for fuck's sake.'

'Adam.'

'Come on, why don't you get dressed? I could take you out for dinner?' He moved towards her, toying with the damp strands of her hair.

She snuggled against his chest and stayed there for a while, her mind anywhere but dinner. 'I'm happy to stay in.'

'Come on, Rosie, I'm trying here.' He kissed the top of her head. 'I eat out all the time, but I know you don't.'

'I'm tired. Honestly. Staying in would be perfect.' She kissed him and then tipped her head upside down to dry her hair. As the hairdryer whirred in her ears, she remembered Owen was supposed to be cooking every night following their race into the ocean, but perhaps he'd feel that Adam's presence rendered their deal invalid.

When she was ready Rosie went downstairs and rifled through the fridge for something to cook. Luckily, along with the pantry, it was well-stocked, so there were enough ingredients to pull together a lamb curry. She lost herself in the task of cooking, anxious to avoid thinking about what she'd found and stressing about whether to mention any of it to Owen. She knew more about him and his family now than she suspected he did. He'd grown up believing his biological father was dead, and she now knew he was anything but.

*

Owen appeared as the curry simmered on the stove.

'Whatever you're making, Stevens, it smells great.' Glad Adam didn't seem to be around, he dropped his helmet onto the bench top and peeled off his leather jacket, relieved by the air circulating his torso now he was out of the summer heat. He lifted the lid from the pot, unleashing the smell that had already snaked out of the open windows at the front of the house and pulled him in the second he got home.

'It's lamb rogan josh with vegetable pilau rice.'

'What happened to our deal? I'm supposed to be cooking every night this week. You beat me fair and square.' He looked heavenward when she pulled a spoon from his hand, not wanting him to test the curry before time. 'I'm not one to renege on a deal.'

'I don't mind.'

He liked it when she went all coy. It showed her femininity.

'Can I do anything to help?' he asked.

‘No, it’s all in hand. Just make sure you’re here in an hour and that’s about it.’

He pulled open the fridge and moved a block of cheese, then a basket of strawberries. His last two remaining beers had to be here somewhere.

‘What are you looking for?’ She leaned closer and pulled the white wine from the door of the fridge, and her hair fell against his arm – softly, yet with as much power to make his heart race as fast as a Dodge Tomahawk.

‘I could’ve sworn I had a couple of beers left.’ He rummaged in the crisper at the bottom of the fridge in case she’d shoved them in there.

‘Sorry, mate.’ Adam’s voice sounded from the sofa, where Owen hadn’t looked since his return. He’d been so taken by the smell of food and the sight of Rosie that he hadn’t even wondered why Rosie had the cricket on the television as she cooked when usually she’d be humming away to upbeat music.

‘I had a couple this afternoon watching the cricket,’ said Adam sleepily as he sat up. ‘I’ll go out and replace them. Where’s the nearest bottle shop?’

Taking another bloke’s beer was almost like taking his woman, although when you thought about it like that, Owen knew the time he’d been spending with Rosie – cosy dinners, trips to the shops, picnics and swims – was far less innocent than Adam’s crime. If another man did the same with a girlfriend of his, well, he’d probably have him up against a wall with a serious warning and a smack in the mouth for good measure.

‘There’s a small bottle shop at this end of the shopping strip,’ said Rosie, not turning round from the stovetop. Owen felt the ripple of loyalty and suspected she hadn’t been the one handing out the drinks.

'Don't worry, mate,' said Owen. 'I can pick some up.'

'No, no, I insist.'

Owen felt bad when Adam picked up his wallet. But his guilt was probably more to do with his feelings for Rosie than his forgiveness over the beers.

'How was your day?' Rosie asked after Adam kissed her and headed off to the bottle shop. She stirred the curry, her other arm wrapped around her middle in a comforting gesture.

He leant against the kitchen bench. 'Not bad. I fixed a table in the café for Bella, then helped her with the website for the fire station.'

'That's nice of you.'

'I'm a nice guy.'

His comment hung in the air along with the smell of the rogan josh as Rosie refused to look at him. Yesterday she would've had some rebuke, some comment to make about what he'd said, but today, nothing.

'Are we okay?' he asked.

'What do you mean?'

'Look at me, Stevens.'

'I will if you stop calling me "Stevens",' she teased. She turned to look at him. 'Of course we're okay.'

Owen busied himself washing up the pots in the sink, and when Adam arrived home he decided to make a concerted effort to make the man feel welcome. It was the least he could do when Rosie could've very easily kicked him out of here, and then he'd never be able to have a good search of the house without being interrupted.

Owen got Adam talking about cricket and all things sport, and found himself relaxing in his company. Adam was a reasonable guy once you got to know him, and really, the only thing Owen didn't like about him, he realised, was that he was the one who had Rosie.

'My company paid for some of us to go to the Australian Motorcycle Grand Prix on Phillip Island this year,' Adam told him.

'I'll bet it was amazing.'

'It was awesome. We were on the viewing deck and could see the starting grid, the finish line.'

Owen twisted the top off a beer.

'So, Rosie tells me you're a property investor,' Adam continued.

He gave Adam a brief rundown of the properties he owned already, his intentions to head over to Europe.

When Rosie put the cutlery on the table, Adam pulled her to his side and hugged her close. Owen felt the corner of his mouth twitch.

'Wouldn't it be better to have a bigger house as an investment?' Adam asked, his arm holding Rosie in place. 'It'd be far less hassle, easier to manage.'

This was why people fell at the first hurdle when they thought they could invest in property and get rich quick. Like any career, property investment took work, it took know-how, and if you weren't savvy you risked hefty financial loss.

'Rosie asked me the same question.' He returned her smile, as though they were both in on a secret Adam knew nothing about. 'Having smaller properties spreads the risk.'

Adam nodded. 'Sounds like you know what you're doing.'

Rosie wriggled away from Adam's side and went to check on the rice as Adam responded to Owen's question about what he did for work.

As Owen listened he wondered whether he'd sounded this dull when he spoke about property. The guy didn't do concise, that was for sure, but Owen politely nodded in all the right places. He thought about Rosie as he zoned out, sipping his beer. Usually she'd join him for a drink and a chat, giggling about inconsequential things, but tonight she seemed intent on avoiding sitting with them. A few nights ago they'd drunk beers beside the pool together, laughing at the poor gecko trying desperately to clamber out of the water, slipping on the tiles every time. Owen had eventually fished it out with the pool net and let it scamper off in search of its freedom.

A blunt question from Adam dragged Owen back to the present. 'So, Owen, why didn't you want to be a real firefighter?'

'Adam!' Rosie glared at her boyfriend.

'Sorry, mate. I didn't mean any disrespect. Wrong choice of words.'

You don't say.

Adam sat forwards on the stool, his beer resting on the kitchen bench. 'But volunteer firefighting isn't really the same, is it? I mean, do you train in case there's a fire, spending most of the time rescuing cats stuck up trees for little old ladies?'

Was the guy trying to piss him off? Maybe he'd caught Owen's eyes straying over to Rosie one too many times.

'We did have a call to rescue a cat the other week,' he answered. And when Adam looked smug, he added, 'The lady who answered the phone explained to the caller that we don't do that, and the crew were, at that very moment, out fighting a grassfire forty kilometres away. Had the fire not been stopped it would've spread to nearby towns, maybe even Magnolia Creek.'

'Oh.'

'And the fires on Black Saturday were pretty real too.' Owen was enjoying having the upper hand again. 'One hundred and seventy three people lost their lives, entire towns were wiped out, thousands of homes destroyed.' His gulp of beer didn't slide down as easily as he'd expected as his mind flashed with the memory of a heavy, vicious orange glow that had accompanied those fires back in 2009. It was as sobering as plunging into an ice bath.

'It doesn't get much more real than that, Adam,' he concluded as he helped Rosie bring the dishes over to the table. 'This all looks amazing,' he told her, anxious to change the subject.

'I'm sorry if I spoke out of turn.' Adam had the grace to look sheepish. 'Rosie's da—'

'Adam, enough,' Rosie snapped again, and Adam stopped talking.

Owen wondered what he'd been about to say. It was clearly something Rosie didn't want shared. He thought about probing some more but sensed Rosie wasn't enjoying this situation as much as he was right now, and she didn't deserve a dinner filled with tension and petty point-scoring between two men. Quite frankly, he couldn't really be arsed with it either.

He scooped up a forkful of curry. 'So when do you go back to Singapore, Adam?'

'I've got one more full day here, then I'll be off.' Adam hesitated and then added, 'I'm in line for another promotion.'

Rosie's forkful of curry lowered down to her plate. 'You didn't mention anything.'

'I was going to wait until it was definite.'

Owen concentrated on the hearty meal in front of him, wincing at the conversation going on beside him. So much for a dinner devoid of tension. Rosie's words were congratulatory, but her face said something else entirely and Adam didn't seem to have picked up on it.

He knew he was stirring things up but couldn't resist asking, 'So when do you think you'll be coming back to Australia for good?' It was the question Rosie should demand to know.

'I'm not sure.' Adam shovelled in another mouthful of curry and took his time chewing, presumably so he didn't have to answer the question.

After dinner Rosie and Adam went outside onto the deck and Owen stayed in the safety of the house to clear up. A heady summer evening carried in on the breeze and segments of their conversation drifted in as murmurs, but with the clank of saucepans against the drainer and the swooshing of the dishwasher, Owen couldn't follow it. He kept busy wiping down the inside table, the cooktop and the benches, and when he couldn't pretend to be Mr Domestic any longer, he decided a swim was in order. He needed something to awaken his senses, something to get him away from Adam and Rosie, who didn't look to have resolved anything.

'I think I'd sink after all the food and beer,' laughed Adam as Owen headed outside in his board shorts.

It looked as though Rosie and Adam were past the stage of talking and had moved on to giving one another the silent treatment.

When Owen headed down the steps and across the garden, he didn't expect Rosie's voice to follow him.

'It's a nice night for it,' she said. 'I'll get changed.'

Despite the generous dinner tonight, Owen still swam ten lengths of the pool before Rosie appeared. The moon glowed up above, the blue pool lights illuminated the water below him, and he tried not to stare as she made her way gingerly down the steps from the deck. She was wearing what girls called a 'tankini' – bikini bottoms, but a top part covering her midriff. Shame. He clocked her tattoo as she draped her towel over the glass fence and pulled the latch for the gate.

Adam came down to the glass fence, beer in hand, to watch them. 'I told her not to get any more,' he said.

'Any more what?' Owen asked as Rosie dived in at the deep end.

'Tattoos. I saw you looking.'

Yikes, he'd better be careful. He'd thought he was being discrete.

'It's a great tattoo.' Owen cleared his throat as Rosie did a tumble turn close to them and headed back to the other end of the pool. 'I've got one myself so I'm always admiring others.' Was that a plausible excuse for ogling another man's girlfriend?

Adam nodded at the rose on Owen's upper arm. 'What's the story behind it?'

He shrugged. 'I'd always wanted a tattoo.'

'It never appealed to me.'

Now why didn't that surprise him?

'I got this one when I was seventeen,' said Owen, 'but don't ask me why it's a rose – it's nothing to do with the heavy metal band Guns N' Roses, by the way. I guess I just liked it.'

When Adam disappeared inside to watch the cricket, Rosie finally came to a stop beside Owen to catch her breath.

'Is everything okay, Stevens?'

‘Of course.’ She smiled unconvincingly before ploughing back the other way, her head turning every third stroke to take a breath.

Adam had no idea how lucky he was to have Rosie, and Owen was left wondering whether she would ever put herself first in their relationship. God knows she deserved to.

Chapter Fifteen

Miss Marple's Tearoom in Sassafras resembled an English Tudor style cottage, quaint windows rounding out from the second-storey of the building, window boxes full of blooms beneath. Rosie had brought Adam out for lunch today because she needed to talk to him, away from the house, about the promotion bombshell he'd dropped at dinner.

They were shown to a table, and Rosie eyed an enormous dessert big enough to feed a family of four as a waitress delivered it to a couple sitting beside the window.

'I swam all those lengths last night, I feel like I deserve something naughty,' she told Adam. A bit of sustenance before she asked him to be straight with her wouldn't go astray either.

She watched Adam dither over the menu, trying to find something healthy. This man had made her feel safe and secure for a long time. He was perfect for her. His sandy blond hair was cut straight at the back, neat at the sides, as sharp-edged as the business suits he wore, and a Tin-tin-like quiff at the front hinted at a softer side to him.

He looked up from his menu. 'How about after this house-sit, you come over to Singapore for a while?'

His suggestion met with a smile. 'I'd love to, but there's my job at Magnolia House to consider.'

'It's only part-time, they won't mind giving you a bit of time off.'

'I can't, Adam. It wouldn't be right. And I need to be here in the New Year to look for another house-sit or somewhere to rent fairly nearby.'

She'd prefer to be buying somewhere with him but there were only so many hints you could drop. 'It's not that I don't want to come,' she said. 'It's just—'

He sighed. 'I know. You have your work. And it's the same with me.'

Either he was very understanding or he'd set her up to make the point that work was important to both of them.

The waitress, dressed in black with a white pinny, brought over a jug of water and poured it into two glasses before setting the jug down in the middle of the table.

'Tell me a bit more about this promotion,' Rosie said when the waitress left. She'd been so defensive last night that she'd barely taken anything in as he'd told her about this new position he was in line for.

His blue eyes rounded and his naturally curved-up lips broke into a bigger smile as he told her all about it: more responsibility, a salary increase and better long-term prospects.

'It could be what we're both looking for, Rosie. I didn't want to say anything to you before, but you'd love it in Singapore. Some of the apartments are amazing and there's a huge expat community. A lot of people have a maid, so you wouldn't even have to clean.'

'Hold on a minute. Another country has never been on the agenda for us.'

'We wouldn't need to stay forever. I'm doing this for us, to build us a fantastic life.'

In this entire conversation, he was telling her what was happening when really he should've been asking her what she wanted for their future. Her mind flashed momentarily to the cottage in Daisy Lane.

A plate of champagne ham, English cheddar and chutney fingers appeared in front of Rosie, but her appetite had disappeared. She felt nauseous. All the while they'd been separated, she had thought she knew what direction they were heading in, and now she had no idea.

A fruit salad was set down in front of Adam. 'Rosie, I want us to be together as much as you do—'

'Do you?'

'I may not even get the promotion.'

Rosie knew him well enough to know he wouldn't have mentioned it if it wasn't almost a done deal. 'What happens if you get this promotion and I don't want to go to Singapore?'

Adam's fork speared a chunk of melon. 'Why don't we wait and see?'

Rosie managed to eat half of her lunch and try to make the most of some togetherness before Adam jetted off again. But the atmosphere between them in the car on the way back to the house was strained. Adam tried to rest a hand on her thigh, but it felt more obligatory than loving, as though if he didn't do it, the boat would rock even more.

When they pulled up at the house mid-afternoon, Owen's bike was in the driveway. It was funny how Owen's presence here felt natural, whereas Adam's presence was beginning to feel increasingly out of place.

Rosie grabbed an ice-cold can of Diet Coke from the fridge, and Adam picked up the local newspaper from the kitchen bench without a care in the world and went outside to the deck.

'Well, well, well,' he said when Rosie joined him. 'Evel Knievel has a girlfriend.'

She waved back when Owen spotted them looking over and did her best to appear indifferent, grateful to hide behind her sunglasses and a newspaper supplement.

She'd known Owen wouldn't be short of women to choose from, but so far he'd kept that part of his life private. The girl with him was clinging to him like an overzealous koala, and Owen threw her back into the water. She squealed in the annoying-girlie-protest way, translating, literally, to keep-doing-it-I-love-it.

Owen eventually hoisted himself out of the pool and came up to the house, the girly-giggler following closely behind.

'Hey guys. This is Carrie, Carrie this is Rosie, my housemate, and Adam, her boyfriend.'

Carrie flashed them a perfectly white, straight-toothed smile. 'It's lovely to meet you.' All tanned, Rosie wondered if the girl had ever had to put an ounce of sunscreen on in her entire life.

Rosie forced a polite greeting. 'It's nice to meet you too.'

'Owen tells me you work at Magnolia House,' Carrie said. 'My sister's getting married there in December. It's a beautiful place.'

Rosie thawed. 'It is. She'll have a beautiful day.'

'I'm sure she will.' Carrie giggled as Owen dragged her inside and up the stairs, laughing all the way.

They were dripping water all over the carpet, Rosie noticed.

‘So Evel Knievel does have a life apart from you.’ Adam made his remark without looking up from his newspaper.

‘We’re sharing a roof, nothing else.’

‘No need to get defensive, I was kidding. Carrie seems nice anyway.’

Rosie tried to relax, aware of the murmurs and laughter drifting from the open window of Owen’s room looking out over the back garden.

When Owen and Carrie appeared in the kitchen almost an hour later, Carrie was still all smiles.

‘How are you enjoying Magnolia Creek?’ she asked Rosie as her perfectly shaped nails settled around a bottle of water Owen had passed her from the fridge.

‘It’s beautiful, very friendly,’ Rosie replied. ‘Are you from around here?’

Carrie’s blond hair had dried wavy, and as she stood at the bench, she wound it up in a hair tie and Owen kissed the back of her neck.

‘I’m a Gold Coast girl,’ she told Rosie when Owen left her alone.

That explained the tan, then. She could imagine Carrie at the beach every single day, bronzing her perfect body.

‘My sister relocated to Melbourne a couple of years ago and I followed her in June last year,’ Carrie went on. ‘I met Owen a couple of weeks ago at the petrol station. I couldn’t open the petrol cap, so he came to the rescue. I know it sounds ridiculously girly, but it was stuck fast.’ She grinned. ‘I’m not a total airhead though.’

‘Carrie is a paediatrician.’ Owen hooked an arm around her shoulders. ‘She works in the emergency department.’

Well that made Rosie feel *so* much better about the epitome of physical perfection standing in front of her. It would've been some consolation to know Carrie didn't have much in the brain department. But not only was she beautiful, but the girl saved children's lives too. It seemed she had the whole package.

The image of perfection had pulled Adam inside, and Rosie leaned against him when he hugged her.

'It was lovely to meet you both,' said Carrie. 'But I'm on an early shift tomorrow, so I'd better have Owen give me a lift home now.' She turned to Owen. 'You could always stay over at my apartment tonight.'

Well this would be interesting since Owen had confessed he didn't like to spend the night with a girl and give her the wrong impression.

'I'd better not.' Owen kissed Carrie and squeezed her shoulders. 'The weather's hotting up, so I need to be around in case the team are called out.'

He'd sidestepped her request well.

Adam nuzzled at Rosie's neck after the others left. 'I was beginning to wonder if Owen had his eye on you, but now I know he has a girlfriend I can rest a bit easier.' He trailed kisses up her neck until he reached her ear lobe and then he took her hand and led her upstairs. 'Let's enjoy having the place to ourselves before he gets back.'

Rosie trailed behind him with a hollow feeling in the pit of her stomach.

Chapter Sixteen

Rosie was up early the next morning despite tossing and turning most of the night. She shared breakfast with Adam and waved him off – again – but this time it was more of a relief than anything else. As her shift didn't start until ten o'clock, she took a walk to clear her head. It was swimming with thoughts of a potential move abroad, thoughts of the secrets she'd found beneath the rose bush.

She wandered past the cottage on Daisy Lane again, glad she hadn't shown Adam. With a promotion on the horizon, there was no way he would've ever matched her enthusiasm. At least this way he couldn't completely take the dream away from her. She did the sums in her head yet again, but even if she worked full-time, there was no way she could make buying this place work, not on one salary with all the renovations the cottage would need.

To satisfy her coffee craving, Rosie stopped at Finnegan's on her way to work and ended up telling Bella all her woes about her love life. Well, most of them anyway.

'I suppose the big question,' said Bella after she'd handed Rosie her drink, 'is whether you still love him?' She finished lining the cinnamon scrolls up on display and then she and Rosie moved to the side of the café as Rodney served the next customer.

'Maybe we've both changed,' said Rosie. 'It isn't fun like it once was. It's different now.'

'Oh, Rosie.' Bella wiped her hands on her apron. 'I think that's life. Rodney and I are different people to who we were in the beginning. Back then it was all excitement and we couldn't keep our hands off one another.'

Rosie smiled. 'I don't mean different in that way.'

'Then how?'

'In the beginning, I admired Adam for his ambition, the way he knew exactly what he wanted in life and went for it at every opportunity. But I'm starting to realise his dreams are bigger than mine.'

'Go on …'

'I want the simple life, Bella.' It was what her mum had wanted too, and probably the reason behind her parents' marriage breakdown. Her dad was a simple man, but he'd taken risks and it had been a deal-breaker in the end.

'I'm not sure it'll ever be enough for him,' said Rosie.

'Well then, perhaps it's time you sat down and talked about what each of you really wants. And if it isn't the same thing, then there's your answer.'

'You talk a lot of sense.' Rosie smiled.

'I've been around for a bit longer than you, that's all. So will you talk to him?'

'I will, but he's in Singapore, and it's not the sort of discussion I really want to have over the telephone.' Then again, in person she found it hard to get her feelings across. She'd always been independent, but for some reason she always let Adam take control. Perhaps sometimes she just had enough of being the leader, the person who always made things happen.

'You'll work things out,' Bella assured her. 'Anyway, how's Owen treating you?'

'We're getting along fine.' Rosie sipped her coffee.

'Can I ask whether he has anything to do with the doubts surfacing about Adam?'

Rosie's coffee went down the wrong way and she coughed. 'You're certainly blunt.'

'And you're avoiding the question.' Bella kept her voice down and moved out of the way of the latest customer perusing the jars of homemade jam lined up along the shelf next to where they were standing.

Rosie couldn't deny she was attracted to Owen, but more than that, she felt an emotional connection to him since she'd found out more about his family. But she did owe it to Adam, and to herself, to put her relationship first before any fleeting crush with a man who was very different to what she needed.

As Bella took her position behind the counter and took payment from a customer for the homemade raspberry jam, Rosie desperately wanted to mention the box beneath the rose bushes. She was tired of carrying this secret alone, but with more customers flocking into the café and Bella whipping up skim lattes, hot chocolates and so many combinations of eggs, toast and side orders that even Rosie was confused, she said goodbye and went to work.

*

At the fire station that afternoon it was all systems go with a call to a structure fire. The crew had their routine down pat and Owen pulled on the bright yellow trousers, looped the braces over his navy T-shirt and pushed his feet into the steel-capped boots. The only thing different this time was that he was on his way to a venue close to home, a venue where he knew Rosie was working a shift.

Sirens blaring, the truck swung out of the fire station on the short journey to Magnolia House. They'd been called out last week and the week before to the same place – Rosie had been safely at home both times – and it had turned out to be a false alarm on both occasions.

He had hoped that was the case today, but when the fire truck screamed to a halt sending dust on the driveway up into air already tarnished with smoke, he knew this was the real thing. Smoke billowed from a side window as the crew leapt from the truck. Their first in command yelled to confirm, 'Gas supply and electricity supply switched off.'

Owen was trained to use breathing apparatus gear, but even now, when it was time to be kitted up, he knew he'd have to take a deep breath before he pulled on the face mask and had the BA cylinder fixed to his back. The first time he'd ever donned all the gear he'd felt claustrophobic and panicked, and he'd been pissed at himself for freaking out. He'd been told it was understandable if he wanted to pull out of the training, but the challenge had become like any other in his life and he'd met it head on.

Hurrying, he fitted the mask over his face and tightened the rubber straps, finishing with the one that ran from the middle of his eyebrows right down the middle of the back of his head. He pulled the flash hood over the top to protect his ears and neck and then pushed his helmet on, securing it in place by tightening the chin strap. He assisted his colleague Gus putting on a BA cylinder, and Gus returned the favour for Owen.

When someone yelled out that there was a body inside, Owen's head snapped round, his legs juddered, and the weight of the potential tragedy faced him head on. His heart hammered away, beating out Ro-sie, Ro-sie, Ro-sie. Suddenly, the prep before entering a structure that took seconds because they were all so familiar with the routine felt as though it was taking forever. He pictured Rosie's face, heard her voice and her laugh, imagined her hair tumbling around her shoulders.

He took a deep breath and turned on the BA cylinder strapped to his back. Something Owen had learnt from the start, back in the days of junior brigade, was that whether you were a voluntary or career firefighter, brigades were like a second family and someone always had your back. So, when Owen entered the structure fire first, Gus followed.

Owen pointed the Thermal Imaging Camera straight ahead. The thick smoke made it impossible to see anything without the device that read heat signatures and indicated vital information, including the source of the fire and anybody who may be trapped inside. He moved cautiously through the corridor, turning the TIC left and right, searching quickly but thoroughly, glad he knew the layout of the place already thanks to the previous two false alarms.

The fire was confined, for the moment, to the side of the venue where a second kitchen was located. He moved left from the corridor and as he turned, patches of red showed on the TIC and led him to a person trapped inside. The body was curled up on the floor at the side of the room, but the camera showed movement. Thoughts of Rosie ricocheted through his mind as he panned the camera to rule out danger from the heat sources shown beyond the victim's position. The flash hoods they were required to wear made what was almost audible damn near impossible to hear, and he used hand gestures and yelling to tell Gus to take over the TIC so he could step forwards and rescue whoever it was lying there.

Owen took only seconds to reach the victim and haul them to standing. With every step he took he cradled the person's weight, every step towards their escape pounding in his ears that this could be Rosie. He exhaled hard into his BA, determined not to let panic get the better of him.

The second he stepped outside, paramedics took the victim from his arms and sounds of his own breathing filled his ears. Owen's job was to get back and help Gus now, watch his back. But he had to know. He had to know if it was Rosie. His breathing came in rasps despite the BA and sounded eerily Darth-Vader like.

He rushed to the ambulance. He saw the victim's face. It wasn't her.

And now he still had a job to do.

Back inside, the TIC in Gus's hands showed deep patches of red, which guided them towards the source of the fire. They fought it, watching one another's' backs the whole time, annihilating the angry orange flames and debris. Flames licked the walls and threatened to go higher, but it seemed they'd got here early enough to avoid the structure being brought helplessly to the ground.

The heat inside the head gear and clothing made Owen feel as though his entire body had been dropped into an incinerator as they worked tirelessly until it was confirmed the fire had lost this particular battle. Owen and Gus made their way outside. It was a walk of mere metres but felt so much longer. When he reached fresh air, Owen ripped off all his gear, throwing away the helmet that felt so heavy, the flash hood that made the blood inside his head boil, the rubber straps that held his entire head in a tight grip and triggered the hyperventilating.

'Whoa. Easy there, mate.' It was Gus, armed with bottled water. 'Breathe.'

Owen shut his eyes and felt the breath struggling to get in and out of his body until he took control, refusing to let panic get the better of him. Gus coped with BA a lot better than he did, but Owen knew his own reaction today wasn't only because of the restrictive gear. It was because of his personal involvement. He looked anxiously towards the front entrance of Magnolia House where a paramedic was shutting the double doors at the back of the ambulance. The victim could so easily have been Rosie. The victim could so easily have been a lot worse had they not found her quickly.

His breathing threatened round two of hyperventilation.

'You okay, mate?' Gus rested a hand on his shoulder.

Owen steadied his breathing again. 'Who was it? Who was in there?'

'It was Tilly, the new head chef.'

The ambulance sirens whirred into action and the ambulance crunched its way over the gravel.

Owen bent over, his hands on his knees.

'She's going to be fine,' Gus assured him. 'We saved her and Magnolia House. All in a day's work, eh? Now take this.' He handed Owen a bottle of water. 'Drink it, mate, keep your fluids up.'

Owen slumped down on the gravel, his legs unable to take the weight of the day, the smell of smoke lining his nostrils and blackened soot clinging to every part of him. Even with all the headgear, the smoke had still got into his eyes, and he shut them and squeezed the bridge of his nose as he tried to let go of the fear he'd had inside him the whole time he was fighting the structure fire. He was proud of his position with the CFA, but it was moments like this that threatened to undo him. The adrenalin surge, the sheer terror, the physical demands of the job and the unpredictability were the reasons why he thrived on being a firefighter, but some days it was harder than others.

Owen took the water from Gus and filled his mouth with the liquid, holding it in his cheeks before he swallowed. He tipped the second half of it over his head, blinking as dirt ran from his hair to his temple and into his eyes.

'Tilly told the ambos there was a bain-marie on the stove,' Gus explained, giving him a second bottle of water. 'It was forgotten about and covered with a tea towel, of all the stupid things. It must've caught on the flame beneath.' Gus looked up at Magnolia House. 'It'd break my heart if that place got destroyed. I got hitched there.'

Owen smiled. 'I hadn't forgotten.'

'I'll bet you haven't. I seem to remember you got pretty friendly with Sharni, the maid of honour.' Gus chuckled, light relief from the day. 'I heard on the grapevine you told her from the start that it was no strings attached.'

Owen, glad of the reprieve from thinking emergency-fire-rescue, said, 'I lay my cards on the table. I don't lead women on.'

'Fair point,' said Gus. 'Speaking of women, I met your Rosie the other day.'

Owen ran a hand through wet and grimy hair, willing his voice to stay steady. 'She's not "my" Rosie. She's house-sitting, that's all, and was nice enough not to turf me out.'

'Well, whatever she is to you, mate, she's a lovely girl. She's not bad to look at either.' He winked. 'See you at the pub tonight?'

'You're on.'

Owen climbed into the truck, and as the others dissected the fire call, he zoned out, well aware that where Rosie was concerned he was in deeper than he was prepared to admit.

*

When Owen walked through the doors of the pub in the early evening, Rosie smiled. She took in his freshly-shaven jaw, the plain white T-shirt and jeans, the waft of a linen-fresh shower gel.

'Well done this afternoon,' she said. 'I heard all about it.'

'Good news travels fast.' He grinned across the room at Gus, who had been recounting the drama to as many people as he could find and looked as though he was still doing so judging by his hand gestures to bring his audience into the moment.

The smell of smoke had pulled Rosie out to the front of the house earlier and she'd been greeted with grey clouds pluming in the distance. She'd leaned against the wall to steady herself, her legs weak at the threat of what could happen.

She cleared her throat now, talking to Owen. 'I heard Tilly was in the building.'

'She's going to be fine, she was lucky.'

They watched one another for a moment, until, noticing the absence of a jacket and helmet, Rosie asked, 'Where's the bike?'

Before he could answer, Bella spotted him through the throng and she wrapped him in an enormous hug. She requested a Guinness for one of Magnolia Creek's heroes. 'Drinks are on me tonight, love.'

'Thanks, sweetheart.'

Bella ruffled his hair in a mumsy way.

'Sweetheart?' Rosie asked, the pieces falling into place.

'To outsiders I guess it sounds weird,' he said. 'But when I was a little boy she'd always ask "What are you, Owen?" and I'd answer "Bella's little sweetheart". Sounds daft, I know. When I grew up I was way too manly to be called such a name so I turned it around and started using the same name for Bella. I guess it kind of stuck.'

Rosie realised now that the night she'd thought he was answering a page from a woman when he'd shaken his head and muttered 'Not tonight, sweetheart', he'd actually been responding to a request from Bella. The skin on her neck tingled.

Owen thanked Bella for the Guinness and sipped the cream top. 'I didn't bring the bike tonight. I wanted to clear my head after today. And God knows I could use a drink.'

Owen's tongue darted out to lick his lip free of the creamy froth, and Rosie tried not to stare. She hid behind a gulp of her own Merlot.

'How long do you think it'll be before Magnolia House reopens?' she asked.

'I don't know. They'll have to clear up and then the building will need to be certified as safe.' He took a sip of Guinness as Rosie's phone bleeped with an incoming text. 'Is it Adam?'

'He just landed.' But instead of his absence making Rosie's heart grow fonder, it seemed her heart wanted nothing more than to wander off elsewhere, particularly with this man who spelt danger compared to the safe life she'd mapped out for herself.

Her life had reached a whole new level of complicated lately.

Bella swept in again and put an arm across Rosie's shoulders. Then to Owen she said, 'So who's the mystery blond I saw you with yesterday?'

'No mystery,' he said. 'That was Carrie.'

'She's nice,' said Rosie who got the eye raise she'd predicted from Bella when she realised Owen had introduced this woman already.

'I've met her,' Rosie continued, stirring up trouble. 'She lives in the city and wanted Owen to go back with her.' She took a generous swig of Merlot. 'But Owen doesn't spend the night with women, do you?' Oh dear, maybe she should've eaten more before she came out rather than the paltry slice of toast with butter. The alcohol was going to her head.

Bella hovered. 'Go on, sounds an interesting story.'

Egged on by her audience, Rosie said, 'Owen thinks spending the night with a woman would be leading her on and invite questions like "Where is this going?"'

'What a load of old nonsense.' Bella giggled. 'That's the poorest excuse I've heard in a long time for playing the field.' She looked past Owen. 'Excuse me. Rodney's come in the door over the other side of the bar. I'll go and grab him.'

When she went to look for her husband, Owen turned to Rosie. 'It'd be great if you didn't share quite so much of my personal life with the entire town.'

'Bella's a friend,' she protested. 'She's *your* friend.'

'True. But in many ways she's more like a mother to me. She probably changed my nappies once upon a time.'

Rosie spluttered on her wine.

'All I'm saying is that it's like talking to my mum about my sex life.' He fought a grin. 'Would you want to talk to your mum about your habits with men, your behaviours?'

Rosie's glass stopped on the way to her lips. 'No, I wouldn't. I'm sorry.'

'Apology accepted.' His eyes held hers, although they dropped to her lips a couple of times before Bella and Rodney came to join them.

Rodney and Owen went to play a round of darts and left Rosie alone with Bella.

'So,' Bella began, 'what's this Carrie really like? Is she good enough for Owen?'

She couldn't lie. 'She seemed lovely, but I didn't talk to her much. Owen doesn't share much about his personal life.'

'You know, I don't think Jane and Michael ever met any of his girlfriends.'

Somehow it didn't surprise Rosie.

They changed the subject – Rosie's doing – and chatted about Magnolia Creek. Bella told Rosie all about the snowfields come winter, the walking trails and the must-visit wineries of the Yarra Valley.

'If you ever get a chance, take a flight in a hot air balloon,' said Bella. 'Rodney surprised me on our twenty-fifth wedding anniversary, and it was such a thrill being so high up, soaring over the ranges.'

Rodney waved to Bella and Bella finished her drink. 'I'd better go. It's another early start in the morning for us. Don't ever start your own business if you value your lie-ins.' She hugged Rosie.

'I bet you wouldn't have it any other way.' Rosie waved goodbye to them before nipping to the ladies, glowing at being a part of such a great community. It was like a family with no blood-ties, people who were close because they wanted to be. Her spirits only waned when she thought of the Harrisons' return from overseas. She wasn't sure whether she'd be able to find a rental property so nearby that she still felt a part of all this.

When Rosie emerged from the bathrooms, Owen was still playing darts, this time with Gus. She weaved through the crowd at the bar, but as she was about to sit at the table with the best view of the dartboard, she saw Carrie, her arm possessively tugging at Owen's waist, the familiar laughter ringing out. And when Carrie planted a kiss on Owen's lips, Rosie's heart sank.

Oh well, time to leave.

She stepped outside into a warm evening with a light breeze on the air. It gently lifted her hair as she walked away from the pub beneath a sky that had carefully fallen across the trees but still allowed the moon to emerge from its hiding place. Doubts about Adam had surfaced over the last couple of days, but perhaps it would be best to get everything out in the open. She'd go home and FaceTime him, maybe even tell him all about the dream house on Daisy Lane. She needed to tell him she didn't want to leave Australia. She needed to make him hear what she was saying.

Streetlamps lit the way along the high street for the first part of the walk, but when Rosie left the stretch of shops the lamps were scant. The moon seemed to shrink behind the trees, unable to peep over, and when she heard a rustling in the bushes lining either side of the road she quickened her pace.

She was being paranoid, she was sure of it. She hesitated, wondering whether to turn back. She was less than a few hundred metres away from the pub. But the thought of playing the damsel-in-distress card with Carrie looking on was enough to persuade her to put one foot in front of the other and keep heading for home.

But then she heard another noise. And this time it was footsteps behind her.

Everything happened so quickly. One minute she was spinning round to see who it was, the next she was pushed to the ground. Her head cracked against the pavement and her purse was whipped from her hand.

She shielded her face with her arms. She felt a tightening around her neck, something digging into her skin, and she wondered if she'd ever be able to breathe again.

Chapter Seventeen

'Have you seen Rosie?' Owen asked Gus and then several others in the pub. He'd seen Bella and Rodney leave and then Carrie had appeared out of nowhere. When he'd finished the game of darts, he'd expected to see Rosie watching on, but she wasn't anywhere to be seen.

'She must've left,' said Carrie. 'Let me drop you home, you look beat.' Her hand sneaked around his waist and her fingers tucked into the rear pocket of his jeans. He knew she'd been shaken up by meeting Rosie the other day, and why wouldn't she be? Rosie was an attractive girl, and the fact she clearly had no idea this was the case made her even more appealing.

'I'd like the walk.' He planted a kiss on her cheek, saw her to her car, and then set off on the short walk home, past Finnegan's, past the gift shop.

He hoped Rosie wasn't in bed yet. He'd assumed they'd carry on chatting after he'd played darts. He'd envisaged having one of those evenings where they lost track of time and talked into the early hours of the morning until it was impossible to keep their eyes open any longer. He was beginning to realise that his reasons for being at the house had changed somewhat. Over the last couple of weeks he'd continued his search, snatching moments here and there to go into the roof space, rummage through laundry cupboards, go through the shed in case he'd missed something. But whatever evidence there may have once been, it had clearly been destroyed so that he could never find out what was being kept from him.

And now, he had no reason to be in Magnolia Creek or at the house any more. No reason, that was, apart from Rosie.

He turned the corner, and as he passed beneath the second streetlamp, he stopped at the sound of muffled crying.

It took seconds for his vision to adjust to the dark, and that was when he saw her.

Slumped on the ground, Rosie had blood running from her knee and she tugged at her dress to cover herself.

'My God, what happened?' He hoisted her up to standing. Blood ran down one side of her face from a cut to her head, and she was clasping her neck.

'He took it,' she sobbed.

'Slow down, breathe.' He held her close and she leant against him as his arms enveloped her.

'He took my necklace.'

'You're okay, that's the main thing. Anything taken can be replaced.'

Rosie pulled back, brown eyes wide. But before she could speak, her legs buckled beneath her and he caught her in his arms.

'I need to get you home,' he said, helping her to stand upright again. Thank God he'd walked tonight. If he'd been on the bike, he wouldn't have heard the crying and he probably wouldn't have seen her either. Who knew what else could've happened to her.

She put her arm round Owen's waist and tugged at his T-shirt, trying to grab a hold of him. He wrapped one arm across her shoulders and the other around her front, gripping her forearm, leaving her in no danger of falling as they staggered the rest of the way home.

Back at the house he settled her onto the sofa. 'I think I've twisted my knee,' she said.

'I'll call the police and then I'll get you an ice pack.' He touched her hair lightly and winked at her, and once he'd made the call he wrapped an ice pack in a tea towel and crouched down to place it to her knee. She winced. 'Sorry.'

'It's okay.' She relaxed back against the sofa as the ice began to soothe, but when her hair fell away from her neck, he dropped the ice pack.

'Bloody hell, Rosie.' He reached up and pulled the rest of her hair out of the way to reveal the red, raw marks where her necklace had once been. 'If I ever find out who did this, I'll—'

Her hand settled on his. 'Can I have the ice pack back now?'

He crouched down beside her again and gently held the pack against her knee. 'Does it hurt?' He couldn't stop looking at her neck, at the space where her necklace had once been.

She gave him a look.

'Sorry, dumb question.'

The police arrived less than fifteen minutes later, and a female officer spoke with Rosie while another officer made notes. Owen offered tea all round and tried to give Rosie the space she might need and privacy if she wanted it. He was making tea when the officer asked whether the man had sexually assaulted her. The boiling water splashed all over one hand and he wasn't sure how he managed to quash the 'fuck!' under his breath.

He ran his hand under cold water and felt immediate relief not only from the burn but also from Rosie's confirmation that, no, all the attacker had been interested in was her purse and necklace.

The officers left half an hour later, sounding doubtful about catching the mugger given the lack of physical description Rosie had of the man. Owen sat on the armchair next to the sofa where Rosie was sitting, cup of tea clasped between her palms, left leg outstretched across the ottoman with the ice pack doing its job.

'How's it feeling?' He nodded towards the knee.

'A bit better.'

'Can I get you something to eat?'

'I'm not hungry.' Her fingers moved towards her neck but fell away again. 'Do you think they'll be able to get my necklace back?'

Owen shook his head and Rosie's shoulders slumped. He wondered whether shock did that to you, whether it made you forget your own safety and how lucky you were to come away with only the loss of possessions, your life still intact. He'd seen it before – house owners risking life and limb to grab valuables from their homes and not lose everything, when all that mattered in the end was keeping themselves and their loved ones alive.

'You can get another necklace, Stevens.'

She leapt up and the ice pack dropped to the floor with a thump. 'Don't patronise me.'

'I'm sorry. It wasn't my intention.'

'Yeah, well, we're not all robotic, switching our feelings on and off whenever we feel like it.'

‘And what’s that supposed to mean?’ He kept his voice calm, watched her, hands on her hips, face heated with anger.

‘I’m talking about the way you treat people, involved with them one minute and keeping them at arm’s length the next.’

‘I’m not sure I follow.’ His mouth set in a firm line, unsure of where this was going.

‘All this crap you spout about not spending the night with a girl, not leading her on. Well that’s the biggest load of bull I’ve ever heard!’

He was on his feet now, towering above her. ‘What’s brought this on? I’ve gone out of my way to help you tonight, so why the personal attack?’

‘Because that necklace meant something to me, it was more than just a piece of jewellery. But then I don’t suppose you’d understand. You move around, flit from place to place, not getting close to anyone so how could you possibly get it?’

‘Now steady on. I know you’ve had a shock and everything, Stevens—’

‘Don’t call me that!’

He balled his fists up tightly to eradicate the desire to yell at her. It wouldn’t be fair, not after tonight. ‘I’m not listening to this any more. I’ll lock up and say goodnight. Let me know if you need anything, you know where I am.’

He didn’t hear what else she hollered at him because he slammed the door on his way out of the room.

*

It was almost three in the morning and Owen lay on his bed, staring up at the ceiling, knowing he’d never sleep unless he got some air into the house. The upstairs held onto the heat of the day for much longer than downstairs, and he staggered over to the window to open it. He went out onto the landing to open the window at the far end, past Rosie's bedroom. With any luck come morning, the house would be a bearable temperature. He hoped the atmosphere with Rosie would be a bit less scorching by then too.

A welcome rush of cool air filtered in, and Owen was unsurprised to see that George wasn't in his usual spot on the landing. The cat had probably curled up in the kitchen where it was cooler.

Owen turned to creep past Rosie's bedroom, the only sound in the house coming from whispering leaves outside the window or perhaps from the creak of a tree, but he soon realised it was neither. He stopped outside her bedroom door, listening to the gentle sniffing, a sound that requested privacy. But when the sniffing changed to full-on sobbing, he quit hesitating. He didn't even knock. He pushed open the door, went straight over to the bed where she was curled up in a ball. Her bedside lamp was on as though she was terrified the darkness would make her relive last night's nightmare. He took her in his arms and she didn't resist. She leant into his bare chest, her T-shirt barely covering her undies as it rode up her legs. He pulled the sheet over her to give her some dignity. She was so upset she wasn't even thinking, not conscious that she was half naked and so was he in only a pair of boxer shorts.

'You're safe now.' He held her, rocked her until she calmed and her breathing evened out.

He pulled a tissue from the box on her bedside table and handed it to her. She wiped her eyes and blew her nose.

‘How’s the neck?’ He wanted to reach out and magically heal those nasty red marks.

‘I’m sorry about last night.’ She completely bypassed his question.

‘We don’t need to talk about it now.’ His pager went off in his bedroom, the buzzing loud enough in the still of the night to hear from this part of the house. ‘Excuse me. I’ll be one minute.’

He ran to his bedroom and was back at Rosie’s side moments later.

‘Do you have to go?’ Her brown eyes pleaded with him to stay.

‘I’m not leaving you here on your own.’

‘I’ll be fine, go on.’

He looked at her. ‘We’re a close-knit team in the CFA, but we all understand that what we do is voluntary, and sometimes you can’t make it.’ He made a grave face. ‘Mind you, given my robotic tendencies I guess I could head down to the fire station and forget all about someone who might need me more tonight.’

He’d done it. He’d coaxed a smile out of her, no matter how small. ‘That’s better.’ He smiled back at her.

‘I didn’t mean what I said, Owen.’ Her hand reached for the necklace that was no longer there. ‘Force of habit,’ she said when she saw him looking.

‘Did Adam give you the necklace?’

‘No.’ Her face crumpled again. ‘I’m sorry, this is so ridiculous. I should be glad the man didn’t do anything else to me. It could’ve been a lot worse.’

‘True. But you’re not being ridiculous.’

She lay down again and curled into a ball on her side. When Owen saw a tear escape as she closed her eyes, perhaps so he wouldn’t see, he lay down next to her. When her breath caught, he knew she was crying again and he curled his body around hers and held her tightly.

Her hair tickled his face as their heads lay together on the pillow. He couldn't deny how attracted he was to her – he'd felt that way from the moment she'd confronted him in the hallway that first night – but tonight there was no hidden agenda, no ulterior motive. She'd become special to him, and even though she was off limits, he wasn't about to abandon her, not tonight.

'Do you want me to call Adam for you?'

She didn't answer right away. 'No, he'd only worry.'

Owen began to feel the exhaustion creep up on him from the adrenalin of the fire yesterday, finding Rosie and then dealing with the police. He ran a hand across his eyes, still heavy from the effects of the smoke the day before. But Rosie's voice stopped him surrendering to sleep.

'My dad bought me the necklace. For my twenty-first birthday. That's why it means so much to me.'

He waited for her to talk again. This was her time and he let her voice echo into the stillness of the night, falling over him like the air from her open window.

'I'd always been close to Dad and became even more so when Mum left us when I was in my early teens. He was a brilliant cellist. And … he was a firefighter.'

More alert now, Owen propped himself up on his elbow.

'He was killed in the line of duty.'

'God, Stevens. I'm so sorry. When?'

'Eighteen months ago now.' Her voice wobbled. 'The day he died, he'd been part of the team who rescued a family of five from a house fire. The roof caved in on them, killing my dad and his best friend.'

'I don't know what to say.' He knew any words would be of little comfort.

'Mum always struggled with having a husband who did a dangerous job. She had depression on and off too, which didn't help. I think it all got too much for her in the end – the worry he wouldn't come home one day, the newsagency she was running on her own. When I was fourteen I came downstairs into the shop and it was quiet, eerily quiet. There were no customers and Mum and Dad stood there, looking at each other. When my eyes fell on the suitcase at my mum's feet, I knew what was going on.'

'But she didn't just leave a marriage, she left you too.' Rosie was a good person and he hated how people seemed to treat her with no regard to her feelings.

'I know she did, but I also know she was depressed. Depression does funny things to people, things we can't even begin to understand. My Auntie came down from Brisbane and settled Mum into her new home down in Geelong. Slowly I began to see that the reasons she left weren't because we did anything bad or that she no longer loved us. She just couldn't see any other way.'

He waited for her to continue.

'Over the years since Mum left, I've done whatever I could do to keep my life stable, without surprises, and since Dad died I craved safety and security all the more. I guess it was my way of coping without my parents around. It's the sort of hurt I wouldn't wish on anyone.'

He gulped as she told him more about her relationship with her mum and the closeness she had with her dad before he died.

'Are you angry with your mum for leaving you?'

Rosie shook her head. 'What's the point? I'd have been angrier if I hadn't been happy with Dad, but we were so close that he took away the pain of living without Mum. I saw her regularly, and in a way I realised she was becoming a better person out of the marriage.'

He had to hand it to Rosie, understanding like that. He doubted he would've done in her position.

A small smile crept across Rosie's face. 'The family Dad helped to rescue wrote to the fire station to say thank you and to pay their respects. It helps lessen the pain to know my dad wasn't only my hero but other people's too.'

'Why didn't you explain all of this when I told you about my biological father?'

'Talking about it is still painful, Owen. It's only been eighteen months.'

She turned to face him and he held his breath at how close they were, bodies almost pressed against one another. He was acutely aware of the heat from her thigh against his own, her breasts beneath her T-shirt almost in contact with his chest.

'Now do you see why I was so upset about the necklace?' she asked, relaxing her head against the pillow.

'Of course I do.'

Her hand rested on her neck. 'I remember what it felt like when his strong hands fastened the chain around my neck.' She laughed. 'You wouldn't think a firefighter could be so strong yet have hands that put on delicate jewellery and played beautiful music, would you?'

'I guess not,' Owen whispered in the still of the night.

Lost in thoughts of her past, she told him, 'He could make the cello sound weighty and powerful, like he was, yet pure and sensuous too.'

Smiling now, she said, 'You know, you remind me of him. You're a similar build, tall, broad shoulders. Brave.'

'A wicked sense of humour …'

'I'm not sure about that.' She giggled, but the smile soon faded. 'I remember the knock at the door – the knock every relative of anyone in the fire service, police service or armed forces dreads, the knock at the door that changes your life forever. From that day I never wanted to put myself in the same situation, never knowing what was around the corner.'

Owen lay there, disorientated by the emotional intimacy.

'Now I understand the reluctance to talk about your music degree.'

Her eyes sparkled in excitement, enhanced with the sheen of tears. 'Dad and I would play our cellos for hours. We were pretty good.'

'Modest,' he teased, pushing her on the arm.

'I wanted to play for him one last time, at his funeral, on his cello.'

'Bloody hell. You've been through the wringer.' He shook his head. 'What piece did you play?'

'Bach's Cello Suite Number One, Prelude in G Major.'

'I'm sure it was beautiful. I, of course, have absolutely no appreciation for classical music and have no idea at all what that piece sounds like.'

They both laughed, and when she stopped she turned onto her back and looked at the ceiling. 'You were playing it in the kitchen the night you cooked me lasagne.'

Finally, an explanation for her mood change that night when he'd given her a glass of red wine thinking she was just uptight and needed to well and truly relax.

'I spent hours practising the piece,' she said. 'I was frustrated because no matter how much I tried, it never sounded as perfect as it did when he played. My efforts felt clunky, a long way from the beauty he was able to coax out of the instrument.'

'I'm sure a lot of that was in your imagination.'

'It probably was.' She shrugged.

'So you haven't played since?'

She shook her head.

His voice soft, Owen said, 'What happened to the cello?'

'It's in Mum's attic. I sold mine, but I kept his.'

'You've never been tempted to play it again?'

Rosie exhaled. 'I can't even listen to cello music, remember.'

He waited a moment, and then, 'When did you get the tattoo?'

'Not straight away.' She smiled. 'I'm not the best with needles.'

He was pleased to detect the note of humour in her voice.

'I went on holiday with a friend the month after the funeral and got the tattoo on a whim. But I've never regretted it. Adam wasn't too pleased when I told him, but I think he felt he couldn't say anything, not when my dad had just died.'

They lay there without talking, the sounds of their breathing and their thoughts keeping them company.

'It'll soon be Christmas,' said Rosie after a while. 'My dad was always big into Christmas.'

'You never spent Christmas with your mum?'

'A few times, when Dad was working, but she never got as excited by it as he did.'

Owen clasped his hands behind his head, looking up at the ceiling as they lay side by side.

She watched the ceiling too. 'The Christmas before he died, Dad and I got really silly and wore winter cardigans, woollen scarves and gloves despite the summer weather. He made mulled wine and we had tacky Christmas crackers with appalling jokes in the middle.' She giggled. 'We played Christmas carols on the cello too. When I get my own place, I'll have the real tree, the big Christmas dinner and the mulled wine. Even if it's forty degrees outside.'

'You'll need air conditioning, then.' He grinned. 'So where will this dream house be?' He turned on his side to face her again and didn't miss the twitch of her mouth as she stopped herself from saying something. 'Come on, out with it. Have you seen somewhere?'

'I couldn't possibly say.'

'Oh come on, Stevens. You can't leave it at that.'

'Okay, okay. I've seen somewhere.'

'And …'

'Well, it's a house I'd love, but it won't ever happen.'

'Why not?'

'I can't afford it and besides, Adam will never go for it. I don't think he's ready for life in a small town.'

The mention of the boyfriend halted the conversation for a moment, but not for long.

'It's in Daisy Lane,' she said.

'Around the corner from here?'

'Yes.'

'I never realised there was much down there any more. I don't think I've been down there since I was a kid. I pretty much leave the house and, at the end of the road, turn right for the city or left for the main street in Magnolia Creek.'

'I discovered it when I was out exploring one day. It's so quiet down there, and the house could look amazing.'

'Have you mentioned it to Adam?'

'No.'

'Why?'

'I guess I didn't want him to shatter the illusion.' She paused. 'This is embarrassing to admit, but in my dreams I've renovated the lounge, I've put in a character fireplace with a beautiful surround, and a claw foot bath in the brand new bathroom. I've even decorated a Christmas tree to stand in the window.'

'You live in your own little world, don't you, Stevens?'

She frowned. 'I've done the finances in my head and it really is a dream. Sometimes we need those though.' She turned to face him. 'So enough about me. Tell me a bit about the *real* Owen Harrison.'

If she'd been a girlfriend, lying next to him in the middle of the night, Owen would've taken this as his cue to run a mile. But this was Rosie and she was different.

'It's late. Another time.'

'I'll hold you to that.' She lay back, eyes on the brink of giving up their quest to stay open.

He watched her for a while, with every intention of going back to his own room, but sleep grabbed him too and didn't let go until the morning.

Chapter Eighteen

Rosie stretched out her legs and met someone else's. Eyes heavy and swollen from the tears last night, she turned to face Owen. Tiny creases fanned out from the sides of his shut eyes. She'd never noticed them before. Her fingers wanted to trace the lines, reach out and feel the muscular arm thrown across the pillow behind his head. The sheet covered his bottom half, and she watched his chest rise and fall with his breath. Her eyes moved down to his stomach and the smattering of dark hair diving down his abdomen and into the sheet below.

When Rosie looked at his face again he'd opened his eyes. She jumped.

'Were you checking me out me, Stevens?' he asked sleepily, awake enough to grin though.

'I was—' Her iPad chimed and she leapt out of bed, the pain in her knee almost gone after keeping her weight off of it during the night.

Owen sat up, fully alert, the sheet falling that little bit further. 'Is it likely to be Adam?'

She nodded. She saw on the iPad that she'd just missed a FaceTime call from him. Suddenly she was aware of her barely-there T-shirt and the man in her bed who wasn't her boyfriend.

'Rosie, nothing happened.'

She raised an eyebrow. 'Would you see it that way if you were Adam?'

'You've got a point.' He grinned, his stubble darkened from the overnight growth. He rubbed his eyes with the heels of his hands and shuffled towards the doorway, calling over his shoulder, 'Call him back, Stevens. We'll pretend this never happened.'

Rosie looked at the closed bedroom door, FaceTime chiming again but unable to bring her out of her trance as she thought about how she'd fallen asleep with another man. When the iPad quietened she looked in the mirror. She touched a hand to the red marks on her neck that didn't look anywhere near as angry as they had last night.

When the iPad chimed again, she answered the call, angling the device so her neck wasn't in the picture. She couldn't face telling Adam about what had happened, not yet. She'd cried all her tears last night and right now she didn't want to relive her ordeal.

Instead, she smiled at Adam and listened about a presentation he was preparing, the dire food at a client dinner the previous night, and for once she couldn't even summon the energy to worry about what his work life meant for her personal life. The only thought on her mind now was that last night she and Owen had crossed both a physical boundary and an emotional one too. When she first met him, she'd thought him arrogant, over-confident and selfish. She'd thought he looked after number one, never mind anybody else. But she didn't think that any more. Not since she'd spent the night alongside him, sharing her innermost thoughts. She'd seen a softer side to him and so, after she'd finished talking to Adam and heard Owen ride away on his

Ducati, she decided she needed to know more about the secret being kept from him.

Last night had been about her. Today, it was about him.

She thought about digging the box up and showing Owen what she'd found, but she didn't want to hurt him, so she left the house in search of finding answers some other way.

As she walked along the lane and turned left towards the main street, the floral salute of sweet-smelling purple-blue blooms from the jacaranda trees and a sense of determination was enough to carry her past the spot where she'd been attacked last night and all the way to Finnegan's café.

Bella was wiping down a table in the front window, an empty cup and saucer in her opposite hand, until she saw Rosie. 'What on earth happened to you?' She gestured towards the red mark on Rosie's neck, and when Rosie stepped into the café, past the tables, Bella saw the plaster on her knee – Owen had cut a pretty generous square from the roll of Band-Aid.

'I was mugged last night.'

'Oh my God!' Bella dumped the crockery down on the nearest table and pulled Rosie into a hug as she told her the whole sorry story of her journey home from the pub.

'We should've walked you home, we shouldn't have left.'

'Stop it, Bella. I've walked that way plenty of times and I've always been fine.'

'Why didn't Owen walk you home?'

'Carrie turned up and I didn't want to intrude.'

'When I see that boy, I'll—'

‘No, Bella. He didn’t do anything wrong, I sneaked out without him seeing me. It was Owen who found me when he walked home himself. He called the police, stayed with me while I made a statement.’ She didn’t add that he’d stayed all night with her too.

‘I’ll whip up some fresh scones, jam and cream. On the house, I insist.’

‘No, it’s fine, really. I’m over the shock now.’

‘I’m not!’

Rosie grabbed Bella’s arm before she could escape to the kitchen. ‘The scones can wait. I need to talk to you about something.’

‘Oh no, the mugger didn’t try anything else did he?’

‘No.’ She smiled gently. ‘Apart from a grazed knee and marked neck, no necklace and a few dollars lighter with the loss of my purse, I’m fine. Thankfully I’d left my credit card and other paraphernalia at home.’

‘Well then, what’s so important you can’t take pause for my scones and homemade jam?’ Bella joked.

‘I don’t know where to start.’

‘Why don’t you try?’

‘I had an email from Jane.’

‘Okay.’

‘And I found something.’

‘Found something where?’

Rosie took a deep breath. ‘I found a box, buried in the garden at the house.’

When Bella’s face fell, Rosie knew that in her search for answers, she’d come to exactly the right place.

Chapter Nineteen

Rosie wrapped her hands around her mug of tea. Goose pimples peppered her arms in her short-sleeved dress, but she didn't know whether it was from the air conditioning or from the shock that Bella not only knew about every item in the box, she knew a whole lot more.

'Have you mentioned the box to Owen?' Bella hooked her fingers through the handle of her mug.

'I haven't said anything.'

'Good.'

'I didn't ask to be a part of this secret. I shouldn't have been put in this position.' Rosie's defensiveness unleashed.

'Calm down, Rosie.'

'No, I won't calm down. If Owen hadn't turned up in Magnolia Creek, if we hadn't become … friends, then I'd be able to stay out of it. But the fact is, he did, and we are, and he doesn't deserve this.'

'He does that to people.' Bella smiled.

'Does what?'

'Owen comes across as being very different from the man he is inside, and when you get to know him, he's someone you value as a friend. He's a keeper.'

Ignoring Bella's character analysis, Rosie told her, 'It's not my place to show Owen what I found, or to tell him what you've told me. But I'm fighting with myself that that's exactly what I *should* do.'

Bella looked across the room, past Rosie, way out the window to the bush the other side of the road. 'I wrestle with my conscience every time that boy looks at me, each time he winks at me when he leaves the café and when he smiles and calls me sweetheart. When he looks out of sorts, I want to hug him and tell him why his mum is the way she is.'

Rosie looked down into the depths of the brown liquid in her cup. This house-sit had pulled her into a family who had woven a web of lies yet still held strong. 'It was all well and good when Owen was doing his thing and I was doing mine, but—' She glanced up to find Bella looking at her, eyes begging the question. 'We're just good friends.'

'We'll see.'

No matter what Owen had become, or became, when Rosie left the café her only dilemma now was how she was going to face him knowing what she knew.

*

Owen pulled off his helmet and rested back on the Ducati's seat as Rosie walked up the driveway. 'Hey, I wondered where you'd got to.'

'I walked to the shops.' His face must've registered surprise because she added, 'It was fine. It's daylight.'

'I know, but after last night—'

'I'm a big girl, Harrison.'

'Nah, it doesn't sound as good as "Stevens", Stevens.' Smiling, he rested his helmet on the Ducati and unzipped his jacket, shrugging off the heat of the day that was trying to cook him. 'How's the knee?'

'It doesn't hurt this morning, and the mark on my neck is already fading.'

‘I can see.’ He had to stop himself from reaching out his fingers and gently tracing the outline of the mark.

She scurried off inside the house before he could say anything else. The space between them today was like the Grand Canyon compared to the closeness they’d shared last night. But after what had happened, he couldn’t blame her. If he ever got his hands on the fucking lowlife, he’d string him up by his balls for what he did to Rosie.

*

‘It’s great to hear your voice,’ Rosie spoke into the iPad for FaceTime with Adam. She desperately needed some semblance of normality right now rather than thinking about the mugging and the secret she’d found and wished she knew nothing about.

‘I hope you’ve got some champagne handy.’ Adam grinned into the camera.

‘Why?’

‘I didn’t get the promotion that keeps me in Singapore, but I did get headhunted for a nine month contract in the U.S. It’s much more money, more responsibility.’

‘It’s great news,’ she said flatly. It looked as though bad things really did come in threes.

‘Come on, Rosie, once I’ve got this experience I’ll be heading home to Australia with much more to offer. I’ll buy us the dream home you deserve.’ He breathed deeply. ‘I know you like life to be laid out in front of you and you don’t like too many surprises, but this is an amazing opportunity to set us up for a great future.’

She grunted.

‘Rosie, come on. We can’t live our lives adhering to some master plan.’

Fuelled by the pressure of secrets she didn't even want to know, she yelled, 'I don't have a master plan, you arsehole!'

'Rosie!'

'I'm sick of it, Adam. You make out that it's me wanting this, wanting to buy a place together, settle down and have a family, when all along you've wanted the same. Or at least I thought you did.'

They let the air settle between them, and when Adam spoke again Rosie softened.

'I'm sorry about my *master plan* jibe,' he said.

'It's okay.'

'Do you really think I'm an arsehole?'

'A big arsehole,' she laughed. 'A big arsehole with a big promotion.' She couldn't help but beam a smile back at him, and she forgot all about positioning the iPad to hide her neck.

His face got larger as he peered into his own device. 'What happened to your neck?'

Rosie opened her mouth and surprised herself at the words that came out. 'I caught my necklace on a door, ripped it right off.'

'Bloody hell, were you running? It looks a nasty mark.'

'It's fine.'

'Are you really upset?'

Tears sprung into her eyes at his sympathy. 'I'll find another one.'

'That's the spirit.' He ran a hand through his fringe and it flopped right back where it had been in the first place.

'Do you think you'll be able to come home for Christmas?' Rosie asked.

‘I can’t, I need to wrap things up here, get myself organised for the new job. I’ll be back in the New Year, and by the end of next year we should be sharing a place. We’ll be together next Christmas and every single one after.’

‘Sounds perfect.’ The thought of every Christmas in the future was enough to placate her.

‘Is Owen going to be around for Christmas?’ Adam asked. ‘If he is, then you could always come here.’

‘Adam, we’ve been through this. When Magnolia House is up and running again it’ll be all hands on deck.’

‘Did I ever mention how proud I am of you, Rosie?’

‘No, tell me again.’

‘I’m very proud of you, and I love you.’

‘I love you too.’

When they hung up Rosie lay on the bed and traced the pillow where Owen’s head had rested last night. She’d felt guilty the second she saw Adam’s face today and heard his voice. She’d never, not for even a minute, thought that she’d share a bed with another man as she told him her life history. Life had caught her out good and proper this time, but lately it felt as though Owen lightened the load of life on her shoulders, whereas Adam continuously added to it.

Chapter Twenty

Tom Harrison laid something called a BabyBjörn on the sofa and untangled its straps as Owen watched on, fascinated. 'It's like watching *The Krypton Factor*.'

'What's that?' Tom successfully attached the baby carrier to his body and scooped ten-month-old Ryan up from where he lay on the kiddie gym on the lounge room floor. He expertly slotted his son into the carrier and pulled the straps at either side to hold him in place.

'It was a British game show,' said Owen. 'Mum visited Auntie Sarah once and was hooked on it. I watched it with her a few times on Foxtel. I'm pretty sure the contestants would've had a big challenge in the intelligence test if they were given that baby carrier thingamajig.'

Owen tickled Ryan's cheek and coaxed a giggle from his nephew, who was well-practised at the art of blowing bubbles at the side of his mouth. Like Owen and Tom, Ryan had dark hair curling in wisps over his ears when it was allowed to get too long. All three of them had Jane Harrison's deep-set green eyes too.

'Right, let's go.' Tom grabbed the navy-blue sunhat from the side table in the hall, put it on Ryan's head and scooped up a big black bag.

Owen gallantly took the bag from his brother, surprised by its size. 'What's in this?'

'Nappies, wipes, nappy sacks, hand sanitiser … the regular stuff you need for a trip out the door with a baby.'

'Whatever happened to grabbing your wallet and keys?'

'Those days are long gone, bro. And lucky for you, Sadie chose the masculine-coloured change bag rather than a bright pink, orange, or worse, something covered in flowers.'

'Lucky for you, you mean,' Owen retorted, 'otherwise I would've made you carry it yourself.'

They left Tom's house in Port Melbourne and Owen acted as Ryan's assistant, picking up the hat every time the kid threw it on the ground. He soon realised he was merely a pawn in his nephew's game.

'So how's the property business treating you?' Tom tilted his head to indicate the park across the road.

'Not bad.'

'Still hoping to make it big in Europe?'

'I'm hoping to expand, yes, maybe nab a bargain while the UK property market is still moving slowly. It's a big commitment though.'

Tom lifted the latch on the gate and let them into the park. 'I guess it'd be difficult, too, if you weren't there to oversee the rentals or renovations.'

'If I ended up going for it, then I'd have to spend a bit of time over there, probably six months or so. I think I could get a visa easily enough.'

Owen noticed heads turning as they walked past the swings and over to the grass area. 'So having a baby strapped to your chest appears to be a real babe magnet,' he whispered to his brother.

'They probably think we're gay dads,' said Tom.

Owen almost turned around to say that he was as heterosexual as they come, but actually it was quite amusing. Let the three women sitting on the bench, hiding behind their sunglasses, think what they like.

'Have you heard from Mum and Dad?' asked Tom.

'Not since I told them I was in town.'

'I wouldn't read too much into it. Mum's probably preoccupied with the funeral and sorting through Auntie Sarah's things.'

As the boys journeyed into adulthood and Tom had moved out, Owen had confided in him about his feelings towards his mum and how he'd never felt good enough in her eyes. But he still hadn't shared what he'd overheard his parents talking about that night, or about the article, because in a way he wanted to protect his brothers. He was terrified, too, that the truth could be something devastating, or worse still, something that could come between the siblings.

Owen played tug of war with Ryan using the navy-blue cap. When Owen fell backwards, feigning weakness, Ryan thought it hysterical. 'Have *you* heard from Mum and Dad?' He returned Tom's question even though he already knew the answer.

'We've had iPad FaceTime calls for Ryan. Mum likes to read a bedtime story.'

'She was always good at those.' Owen smiled at the memory of cuddling up to her on the sofa in his pyjamas – usually of the superhero variety – and Chanel N°5 the cloak of familiarity around him. In those moments she'd never been a better mum. As he got older she'd been there too, at least physically, watching sporting events, applauding when he'd won the school chess tournament one year.

‘She’s always been proud of you, you know.’ Tom took over the tug of war game Owen suspected Ryan could carry on all day. ‘She told me so.’

‘I’m sure she has.’

Tom rolled his eyes. ‘She did. Why would I lie? She’s always running on about her independent son with the successful property business, his voluntary work with the CFA, how great he is. Actually, it gets on my bloody nerves. It makes me feel pretty inadequate.’

The congratulatory remarks over the years had always felt weak. The words had always been there, the smile too, but something had been missing, and it was as though in some way Jane Harrison had always held herself back when it came to her eldest son.

Owen lifted Ryan onto his lap when he started fussing, and Tom passed his son a teething rusk to chew on. The rusk felt as hard as a rock, but Ryan slobbered over it quite happily.

‘I don’t get why Mum’s making such a fuss about me being at the house when Rosie’s okay with it.’ Owen pulled a face when the brown, now soggy, rusk landed on his hand.

Tom sniggered and handed him a wipe. ‘You know what Mum’s like. She likes to know what’s happening and she wants everything aboveboard. If she had a formal agreement with a house-sitter, she’d want to honour that.’

‘Yeah, I suppose.’

‘Talking of *two* people in the house …’

‘Rosie’s the house-sitter. Nothing more, nothing less.’ It had been a week since they’d spent a night in the same bed. A week of doing his level best to see her as nothing more than a friend.

'So why did she let you stay? Why didn't she find somewhere else?'

'She has a job in Magnolia Creek, and there's nothing much available to rent within a distance that doesn't involve a ridiculous commute. I think she also realises that she needs a man around the place.'

'You'll be a real catch one day, you sexist pig.' Tom threw the rusk at Owen's head, which caused much amusement to Ryan, who reached down and picked it up and threw it too, clapping his hands together when it flew through the air.

'I think Rosie's lonely,' said Owen.

Surprised, Tom said, 'Wow, my brother: "Mr Sensitive".'

'Seriously. All joking aside, I really think she is. This boyfriend of hers works away and, well …' He didn't want to tell all of Rosie's secrets now she'd confided in him. 'I help out around the house, cleaning gutters and keeping it bushfire ready, and I think she sees the value in having someone else there.'

Tom nodded. 'I guess Mum's master bushfire plan and instructions could freak anyone out if they weren't used to it.'

Not to mention the fact she'd lost her father in a fire, Owen thought. But he kept that to himself.

When Owen caught a waft of something distinctly non-edible, he promptly handed Ryan back to his dad.

Tom rolled his eyes. 'Are you sure you don't want to change his nappy? It's all good practice.'

'I'll leave it to the professional.'

'So what's she like?'

'Rosie?'

'Yes, Rosie.' Tom pulled out a change mat from the magic bag that contained just about everything and set about changing Ryan's nappy as though it were a military operation. 'It sounds as though you two have become friends.'

'She's a nice girl and yes, we're friends.' When Tom glanced at him, Owen added, 'I'd probably make a move if she wasn't attached. But she is. End of story.'

Tom's look told Owen he didn't believe a word of it, but he went along with his brother's claim. 'Are you still seeing that other girl?'

'Carrie? On and off, it's not serious.'

'It never is with you.'

Owen had wondered whether part of his attraction to Rosie was her unavailability, but after the night they'd laid next to each other, bodies touching, he knew it was more than that.

'I can't take a man seriously when he's using hand sanitiser,' he said, watching Tom. 'You'll be whipping out the hand cream next.'

'Oh, get stuffed. And I'd be using a far more severe phrase if little ears weren't listening. So, is Rosie's boyfriend coming over for Christmas, or is she going away?'

'We haven't really talked about it.'

'Well, we always have Christmas in Magnolia Creek. I know Mum and Dad won't be there this year, but are we still going to get together and honour tradition?'

Owen knew of friends' parents who told them to please themselves during the festive season, or there were those who went away without their tribe to Europe for the classic white Christmas, or to Fiji to get away from it all. But this was the first year Jane Harrison hadn't pulled the whole family together for that one day.

She usually insisted on it and truth be told, Owen loved the concentrated time with his siblings.

'Ben will still be away too,' said Owen, 'so I guess we could skip the traditions for one year. What's that face for?'

'I was looking forward to being with family this year.' Tom stroked Ryan's downy dark hair. 'It'll be Ryan's first Christmas.'

'True. But what about Sadie's parents? Won't they want their grandson with them this year? If you go there, you won't have to do the Christmas battle this year or next because it'll be Mum's turn next year.'

'You've got a point, but Malcolm and Nadine are in Canberra this year with Sadie's gran.'

'So you're going to force me to put on an apron and rustle up a Christmas lunch for you?'

'Oh come on, it'll be fun with the four of us.'

Owen laughed, his face tipped upwards towards the sun. 'Well, well, well … look how that worked out. You're not trying to do a spot of matchmaking are you by any chance?'

Tom smirked. 'I actually meant Carrie.'

'You're pissing me off now, Tom.'

Tom covered Ryan's ears.

'Oops, forgot his lordship here.' Owen pulled a face. 'Carrie will be skiing in Aspen this year with a friend.'

Tom whistled. 'Well, why don't you ask Rosie first? If she's going to be there and doesn't want us descending then we won't do it.'

'I guess it wouldn't hurt to ask.'

'Did you hear that, Ryan?' Tom tickled his son's tummy. 'Uncle Owen is cooking Christmas dinner this year: the full works with turkey, stuffing, cranberry sauce and a nice big Christmas pudding.'

'We'll see.' Owen laughed as Tom fixed the BabyBjörn back in place and slotted Ryan into it.

So far Rosie had done a grand job putting up with him, and he made up his mind there and then that if she agreed, and if she wasn't flying out to see Adam, then he'd make this Christmas at home the best one ever.

Chapter Twenty-One

'I'd love to.' Rosie couldn't answer quickly enough when Owen suggested Christmas at the house in Magnolia Creek.

'Be warned. It'll be four Harrisons versus one Stevens.'

'I think I'll cope.' She sat on a stool at the kitchen bench, swinging her legs.

Owen spooned coffee granules into two mugs and handed one to Rosie.

'I can't wait to start making plans,' said Rosie, giggling at Owen's freaked-out expression, and a seasonal warmth enveloped her as she realised that, without even looking for it, she'd found a family Christmas this year. The thought kept a smile on her face even when she wondered what Adam would say to this cosy Christmas plan for four plus a baby.

'You'll burn your mouth if you drink too fast,' she told Owen, who was gulping down his coffee at a ridiculous speed.

'I can't stick around. I've got a meeting with my accountant and straight afterwards I'm heading out to the property I bought recently.'

'I didn't know you'd bought another. Where is it?'

Owen tipped his head back to get the last of the liquid. 'Now that would be telling.'

‘I could come with you … give the place the once over from a female perspective.’

‘Another day, Stevens.’ He plucked his keys from the kitchen bench.

After she’d given him her opinions on the house in Albert Park, Rosie thought he might appreciate a woman’s point of view. But perhaps he needed headspace today. She tried not to read too much into it.

*

A few days later the bell tinged above Rosie as she stepped into Magnolia Gifts, a small-fronted-shop on the main street in town. She’d seen the Christmas village scene in the window a month ago, vowing to buy it ‘one day’ when she had a place of her own. And although that still hadn’t happened, having Christmas in a home with a family was all the excuse she needed now.

The set, full of meticulously hand-painted pieces, featured a cottage covered in snow, with orange windows showing lights glowing from within; a figurine of a boy holding a broom to sweep the snow from the path outside; a girl wrapping a scarf round the neck of a snowman. There was a ski lodge as well as olde-worlde streetlamps with red ribbons tied around the top, a guest house and a train station all covered in snow.

Adam was part of a large family, but none of them had ever seemed that enthralled by the Christmas season. She wondered whether her memories of her childhood had got bigger, more vivid, with the absence of anything similar since.

She stood at the counter in the shop with her fingers crossed on both hands that the owner, Mal, would find a complete set out the back, and he didn’t disappoint.

‘Are you sure you don’t need a hand?’ Mal held the door to the shop open for her.

'I'll be fine, thanks.' With boxes piled up in her arms, Rosie left with a smile on her face.

She made it to her car, but as she was negotiating how to balance the boxes and retrieve the key from her bag, a voice came from behind her.

'Let me help you.' It was Bella. Rosie hadn't seen her since their conversation more than a week ago. She let Bella hold the boxes while she pulled out the key and opened the boot.

'You've been keeping a low profile,' said Bella.

Rosie couldn't help but smile. 'Okay, I'll admit I have been avoiding you a bit. But it's really tough keeping the secret from Owen. I really think Jane needs to tell him.'

Her red lips relaxed. 'I couldn't agree more. I've been lying awake at night worried you'd blurt it out, but I'm glad we agree it'd be better coming from his mum. Coming from anyone else, Owen's bound to be more hurt in the long run.'

Rosie paused, her hand on the boot, ready to close it. 'And you'll make sure she tells him as soon as she's back?'

'I promise. So what is it?' She nodded to the boxes as Rosie shut the boot.

'I bought the village display, like the one in the window.'

Bella whistled.

'I know it's a bit over the top, but it'll look amazing, and I fell in love with it when I saw it.'

'Well I assume this means you're hanging around for Christmas?'

'It does.'

'And will Adam be joining you?'

Rosie shook her head. 'Work, I'm afraid. But Owen and his brother will be there, so I won't be alone.'

'You'll all have fun, I'm sure. Well, I'd better go. I'm coordinating next week's open day at the fire station, and it takes some organising, let me tell you.'

Rosie locked her car. 'I'll walk with you. It's a gorgeous day, and it's about time I saw the fire station that takes up so much of the town's time.'

Pleased at her confidence to take a step into a fire station for the first time since her dad had died, Rosie walked along in the sunshine, chatting to Bella. She took a deep breath when she saw the fire truck outside their destination. She could do this. It was time.

*

Owen dunked a long-handled brush into soapy water and began to clean the paintwork on the truck parked in the fire station driveway. Using a sponge he scrubbed the rear hubcaps and worked his way to the front of the vehicle. He squinted in the sun when he looked up at a figure approaching.

'Hey, Rosie.' He quickly took in the cute denim shorts showing off her legs and the fitted black T-shirt highlighting her copper-coloured hair. 'What brings you here?'

'I thought I'd have a walk and come in to say hi.'

Owen picked up the bucket. He walked over to the trees at the side of the driveway and emptied the grimy water over their roots. 'Can we talk while I work?'

'Sure.'

She leaned against the wall as Owen refilled the bucket with more hot water and added the cleaning agent. He set to work on the front of the truck, filthy with muck and dead flies.

‘So why are you really here?’ He asked as the hot soapy water trickled from the sponge beneath his hand, down to the concrete.

‘I told you, I was out walking.’

He looked at her and smiled, and with a roll of her eyes she said, ‘I thought it’d be a good opportunity to ask you about Christmas decorations. What? Why are you laughing?’

‘You sound like you’re my wife.’ Now there was a thought. He dipped the sponge into the water again.

Defensively, hands on those little hips, she said, ‘I do not!’

‘Oh relax. I’m messing with you.’ He flicked soapy water at her and it landed on her nose. She blushed and swished it away.

He crouched down to scrub the bottom of the front grill, flicking away debris of gravel and twigs.

‘I hope you don’t mind,’ Rosie began, ‘but I bought something Christmassy from Magnolia Gifts.’

‘You’re the official house-sitter. Make yourself at home.’ He continued scrubbing ‘We’ve got a ton of decorations stored in the shed too, so I’ll get them out later.’

‘Thanks.’ She hesitated and then added, ‘I was thinking we should discuss the dinner plans, make sure we’ve got a list of the food everyone likes, that we cater for Tom’s little boy—’

‘Rosie, stop worrying.’ He stood up now. ‘None of us will starve. And we’ve still got more than three weeks till Christmas.’ It was all sounding a bit too domesticated for him, but then he’d always appreciated being a part of the Harrison clan, and now he hoped he could do something towards making this a special Christmas for Rosie. Since the night she’d been attacked and confided in him, she'd lost the hard edges that made her unreachable and so determined not to let him in. What had seemed a life planned out and formulated, he began to realise, was her way of coping, of ensuring she was never taken by surprise again.

Owen waved hello to Gus as his colleague arrived at the station and chatted with Rosie. He didn't miss the nod of approval from the other man either as soon as he was out of Rosie's line of vision. Owen smiled to himself. Carrie always turned heads when they were together: she was blond, tanned, had the high cheekbones and perfectly straight teeth. But the subtlety of Rosie's attractiveness was a whole lot more powerful than that.

'I'll leave you to it, you're busy,' said Rosie.

Gus reappeared and whipped the sponge out of Owen's hand. 'I'll finish off. Why don't you take a break?'

'Are you sure?' Owen knew exactly what Gus was up to, trying to match-make. But he wasn't going to argue. It was a gorgeous day and he'd get to spend time with Rosie. What more could a man ask for?

'Get outta here before I change my mind.' Gus frowned at the flies still stuck to the bumper.

'Finnegan's?' Owen suggested to Rosie.

'Great. We could discuss Christmas.'

'Jeez, I walked right into that one, didn't I?'

*

At the table beside the window, they ordered scones to share, a latte for Owen and a fresh mango juice for Rosie, who decided it was too hot for anything else. She took a corner of scone and spooned on some jam and cream. Even though they'd shared plenty of dinners before now, sharing from the same plate was completely different, especially when Owen's knees, in his navy-blue cargo pants, kept touching hers beneath the wooden table. She watched as he devoured half a scone in record time. It had to be the physical labour making him so hungry, she decided as she read the white Magnolia Creek Fire Brigade logo on his navy-blue T-shirt.

'Well done today,' he said.

'What do you mean?'

'Coming into the fire station.'

'Oh, that.'

'I know it was probably a big step for you, after … well, you know.'

She smiled at him, glad of his understanding, glad she'd been able to do it too.

'I wonder whether your parents will get a white Christmas this year,' she said as they carried on enjoying the scones.

He smiled. 'They might do.'

'Why are you grinning at me?'

'No reason.'

'Come on, there has to be a reason.'

'You're very into Christmas, that's all.'

'Sorry.'

'Don't be sorry, it's great.'

She smoothed more cream onto another piece of fresh scone. 'It was always special when I was little. You Harrisons have got a lot to live up to this year.'

'We'll try our best.' He sipped his latte. 'It was always pretty cool in our house when we were little too. We had these enormous Santa sacks and stockings that Mum made for all three of us. On Christmas Eve we'd hang them up beside the fireplace and leave out a mince pie, a beer for Santa and carrots for the reindeer.'

Rosie grinned. 'I love all the traditions. At our house Dad was always in charge of making the mince pies. He said he couldn't coordinate the main dinner – too many elements – so it was his way of letting me rest up before the big event. I'd help him and he'd always give me the first mince pie of the batch as soon as they were ready. I lost count of how many times I burned my mouth on that first bite.'

'Mince pies are your responsibility this year, then.'

'I'm happy with that.' She finished the pulp in the bottom of her glass.

'So tell me. What other traditions did you have?'

Rosie bit down on her lip, revelling in the sharing. 'Every year, about a fortnight before Christmas, Dad and I used to travel way out to the country and choose a tree ourselves. Of course I'd want the whole lot of trees, from the small fat ones to the tall, towering ones that couldn't possibly have fit in our lounge room or even through the front door.'

'I'd have loved a real tree,' he said. 'But Mum had an artificial one right from early on and she even upgraded it, you know, when they started to get a bit more designer and actually looked like trees rather than plastic doing a pathetic impression of something living.'

'I don't think you can beat the smell of the real thing.'

'Did you celebrate last Christmas with your mum now your dad is no longer around?'

She shook her head. 'I was with Adam and we went to a fancy restaurant in the city.'

'And what was it like?'

'Pretty amazing.'

'But …'

'How do you know there's a "but"?'

'Call it Male Intuition.'

'I'm not sure that even exists.'

'Right, just for that, I'm finishing this last piece of scone.'

She giggled. 'Go ahead, I'm full already.'

'So what's the "but"?'

She met his gaze. 'I had a great time being wined and dined somewhere posh. *But,* it wasn't really Christmas. Not in the sense I remember. I was sad anyway, with Dad gone, and perhaps that's why Adam chose to do something entirely different. But I missed the usual traditions, the simplicities of being at home with family.'

He gave her hand a sympathetic squeeze, then glanced at his watch.

His touch had taken her by surprise. 'Do you have to get back?' she asked.

'I'm due up at the primary school soon with the rest of the crew, to teach fire safety.'

'I'm impressed.'

'We like to start 'em young in these parts, Stevens. We hope that by the time the kids are adults, fire safety will be embedded in their psyche.' He stood up. 'Come on, I'll walk you to your car.'

He paid for their order, refusing any contribution from Rosie, and as he walked her across the road to her pink beetle, she felt a fluttering in her tummy as though she'd been on a real date.

On her drive home, she pulled up at the end of Daisy Lane. She wanted to see the cottage again. It was a dream, a far off one at that, but beneath the glare of the sun, she stood looking at the derelict place she could do so much with. She stood on the tiny veranda, which sat beneath a slim porch, and looked in the window at the front, wondering what it'd be like to come home to this place on a rainy day, lean an umbrella in the corner beside the front door and sit down in front of a roaring fire.

She went round to the back, peering in each window, but it was only when she came back to the front again that she noticed the sign. Except this time, it no longer said For Sale … it read Sold, and her heart sank as much as the churned up earth beneath her feet on the neglected front garden. Her dream was shattered.

*

Rosie took her frustrations out by vacuuming the house top to bottom, dusting every surface she could find and polishing the stainless steel in the kitchen until it shone. Owen returned a couple of hours later as she finished polishing the bannisters in the hallway.

'I don't think even Mum bothers to do that,' he commented. 'What's up?' He must've noticed the scowl.

'Nothing.'

He didn't move.

'The house in Daisy Lane, you know, the one I told you about?'

'The derelict house?'

Rosie slumped down at the foot of the stairs and Owen squeezed onto the step next to her.

'That's the one. It's gone.'

'I'm not sure I follow.'

'Sold,' she said.

'Oh, I see.'

'It was a stupid dream anyway.'

'It wasn't stupid. Your dreams are part of who you are. What, you expect me to say there'll be plenty of other houses?'

'Something like that.' She smiled.

‘Well, I hate to be too predictable.’ He held out a hand and pulled Rosie to standing. ‘Come on, let’s cheer you up. It’s operation Santa time.’

Rosie brought in the boxes containing the Christmas village, and Owen pulled all the Christmas paraphernalia from the shed at the bottom of the garden.

He stood next to the boxes. ‘There’s one other thing we need to do first.’

Rosie looked at the long box open at his feet, the plastic green leaves protruding out enthusiastically. ‘The tree.’ She grinned.

‘Kind of.’ He picked his keys up from the kitchen bench. ‘I think it’s about time I found out what all the fuss is about. We’re having a real tree this year, Stevens.’ He pulled out an extra pair of leather trousers from a cupboard in the laundry and passed them to Rosie. ‘These belonged to Sadie – Tom had a bike before he went into parent-land and traded it for a car and a baby seat – and she’s about your size.’

‘Are you serious?’

‘About the tree or the pants?’

She giggled. ‘Both.’

‘Very serious. Go and get changed.’

The pants looked small but they were a surprisingly good fit. They were soft with stretchy side panels that glided over her hips, and when Rosie reappeared downstairs she didn’t miss Owen checking her out. She shrugged on the spare leather jacket and picked up the spare helmet.

‘Ready?’ Owen called over the din of the engine when Rosie climbed on behind him.

She put a thumb up to show she was ready for the off, glad for now to have nothing but the hum of the engine and the whipping of the air around her as they headed out of Magnolia Creek. She sat rigid at first, scared to relax. Her hands gripped the handrail, and her feet pushed onto the pillion footrests. Her body leaned whichever way the machine took her, but as she relaxed into the ride, she put her arms lightly on Owen's waist and let her body meet his as it had done that first time on the bike.

The scenery was amazing. Trees lined the roads, stretching up to the sky further than Rosie's eyes could see, and the sun bounced off the leaves. They weaved this way and that, and before long pulled in between two gateposts off the main road and into a car park that was a sectioned off part of a field. She held tighter as the Ducati coped with the bumps before they came to a standstill.

She took off her helmet and ruffled her copper locks, hoping she didn't look sweaty from the leathers and headgear worn beneath the summer sun.

'You're a good passenger, Stevens.'

She pulled a face.

'I'm serious. You don't fidget like some girls do. And you were relaxed enough to lean with the bike as we followed the road.'

Rosie wondered how many girls had been on the back of the bike and quickly scolded herself for letting jealousy rear its ugly head over a man who wasn't hers to be jealous about. 'I wanted to survive to tell the tale,' she said.

Families bustled around the farm. Acres of Christmas trees stood in obedient rows: tall, short, medium, wide, narrow. A toddler helped his mum tag a tree and a father and daughter stood by as their tree passed through a contraption to wrap it in netting for transportation home.

‘Come on.’ Owen thought nothing of taking Rosie’s hand and leading her down a row of trees. ‘Let’s get stuck in before they’re all gone.’

‘There are hundreds of them. I don’t think that’ll happen.’

‘Well, when I phoned the owner of the place he explained that most trees are tagged by the start of December.’

Rosie smiled. ‘We’d better get started then, hadn’t we?’

The ground was damp beneath their feet as they went up and down the rows listening to squeals of delight from children and their parents when they located the perfect tree. Rosie stopped next to one that wouldn’t look out of place in a hotel foyer and, shielding her eyes, she gazed up wondering whether any ladder was tall enough to reach the angel’s position at the top.

She jumped at the feel of Owen’s breath against her ear when he said, ‘Not that one,’ and moved past her.

Her fingers reached out and touched the branches of the trees as she made her way further along the row and up the next. The scent of pine needles overpowered and whipped up nostalgia inside of her, each needle she traced beneath her fingers reminiscent of her past.

Owen’s hand squeezed her shoulder. ‘Are you okay?’

She nodded.

‘This was supposed to be a good surprise.’

‘It is, believe me.’

They stepped over a water sprinkler line on the ground and Rosie stopped at a tree halfway down the row. ‘How about this one? It’s a great shape, wide at the bottom, not too pointed at the top.’

'It looks good to me.' He waved over an assistant who measured the tree for pricing and tied a gold ribbon around its widest part to show that it was taken. Rosie watched on, beaming, as the assistant explained the tree would stay right where it was, thriving from the moisture in the soil, until it was dug up and delivered on a day of their choice.

When the tree was paid for and a delivery date arranged, Owen looked up at the black clouds.

'Where did they come from?' Rosie asked.

'I don't know but we'd better get back. We don't want to be caught in the storm.'

A rumble of thunder hastened their walk over to the bike, and the Ducati's engine drowned out any more sounds from the skies as they made their way back to Lakeside Lane.

Rosie already knew in the pit of her stomach that this was going to be a Christmas to remember.

Chapter Twenty-Two

Over the next fortnight Rosie got underway with Christmas preparations, making lists and ensuring that everything was ready. They'd decorated the house after their return from the Christmas tree farm that day and now white fairy lights weaved between bannisters all the way up to the top floor, the Christmas village sat proudly on the sideboard in the lounge room, a garland hung from the knocker on the front door and sprigs of pretend holly – the real thing would struggle to survive the Aussie heat – adorned picture frames and ornaments dotted around the house.

When Rosie had unpacked the Christmas village that same day she'd turned around to see Owen laughing at her.

'What's so funny?' she'd asked.

'Nothing.' He couldn't keep a straight face.

'No, come on!'

'Well I'm just wondering whether there's anything left in Magnolia Gifts after your visit.'

She took out the delicate pieces from their protective bubble wrap. 'Very funny. Just show me where I'm allowed to put it.'

Once they'd found a place and the village was completely assembled, even Owen had to admit it looked pretty classy as well as festive. 'You've done well, Stevens,' he'd told her.

And now, Owen was busy with his latest investment property, spending all day, every day working on it, roaring off on the Ducati bright and early most mornings. When Magnolia House reopened almost two weeks into December, Rosie returned to work and today, with a flurry of organisation and preparation, Magnolia House was almost ready for the first wedding since the fire. In forty-two-degree heat, Rosie coordinated gardeners replanting shrubs and grass at the side of the house where the fire had been, and she kept them well hydrated with plenty of ice-cold water. She arranged a painter to give the discoloured white signpost at the front of the house a fresh lick of paint. And most of all, she kept herself busy to stop her mind from wandering to whose wedding it was. Any minute now, Carrie would be arriving with the bonbonniere for her sister's big day.

In the air conditioned office, Rosie uploaded photographs of the last wedding onto Facebook and responded to comments on previous posts, assuring clients their bookings were still intact following the fire and that Magnolia House looked as spectacular as ever. She'd already sent a mailing to the list of upcoming clients, inviting them to revisit Magnolia House if they had any doubts, and she'd attached photographs she'd taken that morning capturing the early morning glow from the sun coming up over the white wooden roof. In her experience, a picture would reassure clients far more than her words ever could.

'Rosie?' Carrie poked her head round the office door.

'Hello, come in.' She eyed the box in Carrie's arms. 'Have you brought the bonbonniere?'

'I have. All eighty pieces.'

Rosie peaked into the box filled with tiny glass candy jars, each with a thin pink and white spotted bow tied below a silver lid. 'The wedding cake delivery is confirmed for tomorrow morning at nine thirty.'

'Fabulous.'

And then, because this was what they always did with relatives of the wedding party who made deliveries pre-ceremony, Rosie said, 'Can I offer you a tea, coffee, something cold to drink?'

'No thanks.' Carrie's perfect teeth were bright against tanned skin. 'I've got a busy day of pampering with my sister and my mum.'

'That sounds lovely. And I hear you're going away for Christmas.'

Carrie leaned against the doorframe. 'I can't wait. I've enjoyed helping plan Kristy's wedding, but it's been hard work. My sister isn't a girly-girl, but she wanted the kind of wedding she sees in magazines.'

'It'll be a beautiful wedding, and I'm sure she appreciates all the hard work.' It was quite impossible not to like Carrie. 'I've been roped into helping out with the catering. Two staff members jumped ship when we were closed for a few weeks and found themselves jobs elsewhere.'

'Then I look forward to seeing you again tomorrow, Rosie.' And with a shake of her mane of blond hair, Carrie left.

*

'Oh come on, Stevens. Please …'

It was the morning of the wedding and Owen was literally backing Rosie into a corner, the corner of the kitchen.

'I've never used them before,' she pleaded, hands behind her back, refusing to take the clippers from him. 'Believe me when I say you'd be better off leaving your hair as it is.'

'Oh come on, I haven't had time to get my hair cut on account of all the community work I do down at the fire station.'

'Stop trying to make me feel guilty!'

'I'm merely stating facts, Stevens.' He was getting somewhere now – she couldn't stop smiling. 'This hair of mine will spoil the photographs.'

'You're not wrong there.'

'I had two jobs to do for Kristy's wedding: pick up a tux and—'

'Get a haircut,' Rosie finished.

To his delight she frowned but took the clippers anyway. 'You know you can't moan at me if it turns out to be the worst haircut ever.'

Owen pulled a chair to the middle of the kitchen floor. 'I've already fixed on the right clippers for the back. Do upwards to about here.' He indicated the back of his head to around the level of his ears. 'And don't look so nervous.'

'You're going to a wedding, there's pressure.'

'Relax. It's not my wedding, so we're good.' He flung a towel around his shoulders and sat on the chair.

Rosie tucked the towel into the top of his T-shirt. The touch of her fingers against his skin felt comforting, but when the clippers buzzed and she ran them upwards from the base of his neck, he had a much bigger reaction. He shut his eyes when a groan threatened to escape. He cleared his throat as she moved the clippers up the sides above his ears. He'd never realised they were so sensitive until now.

'How's it looking?' he managed to ask.

She ran a nail across the base of his neck and it made him shudder. 'There's some hair the clippers have missed.' She moved closer to finish the job, and when she blew gently against his skin it almost tipped him over the edge.

'Now, do I change clippers?' she asked. 'Owen! Open your eyes.'

'I'm trying to relax in the moment, Stevens.' Really he was doing his best to distract himself from how good it felt when she touched him. 'Change to the yellow clippers, they're slightly longer.'

He closed his eyes again as she moved around him. It was safer that way. The closeness of her body was getting too much.

As her nails gently scraped against his scalp when she checked the clippers had done their job, he was eternally grateful of the extra towel across his lap that hid how much he was enjoying this. When he'd asked her for the favour, this wasn't exactly what he'd anticipated.

'I think we're done,' she announced.

He escaped to the downstairs bathroom to check, grateful of some time to let his physical reaction subside.

'Not bad, Stevens. I may use your services again,' he called to her in the kitchen.

'We'll see about that. Now I have to get ready, so I'll leave you to sweep up.'

*

As Rosie showered and got ready for the day, she tried to make sense of that moment in the kitchen, the moment where she knew she'd crossed a boundary she wasn't sure she could get back from. She'd felt Owen shiver beneath her touch, and she hadn't missed him sigh, either, when she blew the stray hair away from his neck.

She dried her hair and put on a light layer of foundation, some eyeliner and a touch of grey eye shadow. She pulled on a straight, black, knee-length skirt and a white, short-sleeved shirt. She looked at her reflection in the mirror, the open shirt and the place where her cello bridge necklace usually sat. It still looked odd to see bare skin.

By the front door she slipped on black patent heels as she heard Owen come down the stairs behind her, and when she turned she was stunned. The man who usually wore a T-shirt and jeans, or shorts, stood before her in a tux, a crisp white shirt contrasting against tanned skin and a black bow tie hanging teasingly loose around his neck.

She checked her phone was inside her bag – anything to stop staring at him. 'Are you looking forward to the wedding?'

'Not really.' He went into the downstairs bathroom off the hallway and Rosie watched him look in the mirror and take each end of the bow tie. He didn't know what he was doing at all. 'Carrie and I aren't serious, and today I have to meet her entire family.' He leaned around the doorjamb when Rosie giggled. 'I'm glad you think it's funny.'

'I'll be serving Pimm's and Lemonade on the lawn at precisely two o'clock,' she said. 'I suggest you have a few for Dutch courage.'

Owen uttered a few expletives and then emerged from the bathroom, his bow tie still hanging loose. 'I should've got one of those elasticated things. These are impossible.'

'Blimey, I've had to do your hair and now I have to help you get dressed?' Rosie took control and, facing Owen, pulled each end of the bow tie to an appropriate length. 'This isn't really in my job description.'

'How do you know how to do these?' His eyes were fully focused on her.

'Adam has plenty of corporate functions, but he's never had the patience to do a bow tie.' She crossed the two sections over and pushed one through the v-shape. Her hands shook as she formed the loops and finalised the bow.

'There, how's that?' She willed him to go back into the bathroom and look in the mirror instead of at her.

After what felt like forever, he did as she'd hoped and called out, 'I'm impressed.'

Back in the hallway he adjusted the black cummerbund around the top of black trousers and pulled on the jacket he'd hooked over the bannisters.

'The boutonnieres are at Magnolia House,' said Rosie.

'The bou-ton-whats?'

'The boutonnieres: flowers for the lapel on your jacket.' She laughed and picked up her bag. 'I'll see you on the lawn around two o'clock.'

*

Owen sat on the bottom stair when Rosie left the house. She'd been a vision in her smart clothes – the shiny heels, the black skirt and the white shirt that revealed the faint outline of a lace bra. He only snapped out of his daydream when he saw Carrie's sleek black Mercedes take the Hubba's place on the driveway. He opened the door and gave her a wave, then dashed upstairs to grab the finishing touch for his tuxedo.

From the top drawer in his bedside cabinet he took out one of the black velvet boxes. He removed the mother of pearl cufflinks and fixed them through his shirt sleeves with far more prowess than he'd had with the bow tie. He took out the second velvet box containing the gift he'd chosen for Rosie. He'd wanted to give it to her moments ago as she'd tied his bow tie and he'd gazed down at the bare skin of her neck. He'd watched her all the while, her fingers looping the black silk, threading bits through here and there until it looked perfect.

When a toot from the Mercedes snapped him to attention he pocketed the box in his tux and headed downstairs.

*

Rosie hadn't factored in the lawn when she'd chosen her footwear for waitressing at today's wedding. She felt as though she was drunk as her heels sunk into the ground and she tried to keep the tray of drinks level.

'Don't tell me you've been on the Pimm's yourself?' It was Owen.

'Inappropriate shoes,' she explained, moving to the gravel driveway instead. 'That and inexperience with waitressing.'

'You'll be fine.'

'Nice boutonniere by the way.' The silky petals of the deep red rose were a rich contrast to the black of his tux, and he looked even more striking now he was wearing the entire ensemble complete with jacket.

'Boutonniere is a poncy word for a flower, in my opinion. But I have to admit, it's a nice choice. Mum would approve anyway.'

Rosie smiled at three guests who snapped up the remaining glasses of Pimm's from her tray.

'So how's it going, meeting the family?' she whispered to Owen when the guests moved on.

'I've dodged most of them, although I did meet Carrie's parents.'

Rosie leaned past him to where Carrie stood chatting with the mother of the bride. 'Carrie makes a beautiful bridesmaid.'

'She does.' He didn't follow the direction of Rosie's gaze to where Carrie stood looking stunning in her midnight-blue halter-neck dress. His gaze lingered on Rosie instead.

'I'd better go back inside for another tray of these,' she told him. 'Enjoy the ceremony.'

'I'll try.'

*

'Is there a problem?' Owen asked. Carrie's mother looked fraught. So far she'd been pleasant and calm, and there had been no quips of 'Carrie, it'll be your turn next' with nods and winks in Owen's direction. He was grateful for that.

'There aren't enough,' said Bea, the maid of honour.

'Mum, there's nothing we can do about it now.' Carrie tried to calm the situation. 'There aren't enough boutonnieres,' she explained to Owen. 'The florist must've got the numbers wrong.' Turning back to her mother, she said, 'Kristy won't even notice. She's too nervous about her walk down the aisle.'

Owen stepped in. 'May I make a suggestion?'

All eyes were on this newest recruit to their family. Perhaps he should've kept his mouth shut.

‘We have roses like these in our garden,’ he said. ‘Loads of them. They won’t be exactly the same size and the foliage won’t be perfectly arranged, but I think they’ll work. How many do you need?’

Carrie’s relatively normal family meant Owen had only had one drink so far, so he took Carrie’s car back to Lakeside Lane to cut nine more velvet red roses for the male wedding guests. He grabbed the secateurs from the shed and a box to lay the roses in, and with plenty to spare he cut fifteen just in case.

As he chopped the final rose, one of his cufflinks slipped loose from his cuff and landed in the soil beneath. It looked as though he wasn’t any better at fastening those than a bow tie. He went to scoop it up from the dirt, but when he did so he saw a tiny sliver of silver shining beneath the rose bush, away from the roots. He scraped with his fingers and the silver strip became bigger until he realised something was buried there. With a bit of manoeuvring, despite the restrictions of a shirt with white sleeves he didn’t want to muddy, he managed to tug the box out.

Owen prised open the lid and rifled through its contents, expecting it to be something he or one of his brothers had buried in their childhood, during one of their imaginative games which usually involved digging and making a mess.

But it was nothing of the sort.

Here, beneath these beautiful roses in the garden that his mum worshipped, was the ugliest secret of all; the secret he’d been looking to unearth and the reasons behind why he’d never felt good enough for Jane Harrison.

Chapter Twenty-Three

'Where's your cufflink?' Carrie pulled at Owen's shirt sleeve as the dance floor opened up.

He hadn't even thought about it after he'd found that box. It must still be there amongst the filth in the rose bed.

He'd delivered the boutonnieres in a daze, he'd barely touched the wedding breakfast, and now he was going through the motions until he could get the hell out of there, the hell out of Magnolia Creek.

Carrie's body pressed lightly against his as they danced, although Owen felt more like a cardboard figurine than a man with a sexy woman in his arms.

'Do you mind?' Carrie asked as the song came to an end and her father appeared at her side for the next dance.

Glad of the escape, Owen turned to see a harmless but incredibly inebriated best man insisting on a dance with Rosie. He was over there quickly. 'Sorry, mate, she's taken,' he said, and whisked her onto the dance floor before the man fell into her.

'Thank you,' she breathed. 'He was a bit touchy-feely for my liking.'

Owen didn't say anything. He held her close, knowing that after tonight he may not see her again. He had to leave, he had to get out of here, and he wasn't sure whether he'd come back. He felt the weight of the small velvet box in his jacket pocket.

Shorter than Carrie, Rosie's head rested comfortably against his chest and his hand covered the small of her back as he pulled her close to the sounds of an instrumental 'When You Say Nothing At All'. He wanted to remember this girl who'd become a friend, he wanted to whisper his goodbyes into her ear now, tell her everything he'd found in the garden. But he couldn't. He was so ashamed. He had no past. At least not anything that was true. His whole life was a lie. At the moment, he felt as though Rosie was the only solid thing in his life. But she wasn't even his.

As the song came to an end she pulled away, but when he heard the speakers launch into the cello solo of 'Your Song', he pulled her in again. Now it was his turn to hold her up. As they moved to the velvety, wholesome sounds of the strings, he didn't once look at her face. Every sensation came from the feel of her body, the relaxation of her against him.

'You okay?' He asked as the song came to an end.

She nodded.

'Will you come outside with me? I need to give you something.'

'I'm working, I'd better—'

'Rosie, please, this can't wait.' He bit his lip hard, willed her to come with him.

*

Rosie leaned against the railing of the veranda as darkness blanketed Magnolia Creek. Fairy lights hung intermittently through the trees and the frills of the veranda, and lanterns lined either side of the footpath leading up to where Rosie and Owen now stood.

Owen took something from his pocket. 'I was going to give this to you for Christmas, but, well, I decided now was a better time.'

She didn't ask why, and beneath the light of the moon peeping through the branches of a tree, she opened the box to see a silver cello bridge necklace resting on a maroon cushion.

'I know it's not the same,' he said, 'but maybe it'll stop you touching your neck all the time and wondering what's missing.'

She couldn't help the tears that welled up. 'Have you got a tissue?' She sniffed. 'My mascara will start running down my cheeks soon.'

He pulled the pocket square from his tux. 'Sod the decorative purposes of these things, much better to make use of it.'

'Thank you.' Rosie dabbed beneath her eyes.

'Would you like me to put it on for you?' he asked.

Without a word she lifted her hair and Owen's strong and gentle hands looped over her head then brushed against her neck as he fixed the necklace in place. The hairs of her neck prickled. She closed her eyes, imagining the real thing – the maple, deep-brown cello, elegant in its beauty from the scroll at the top of its neck to the strings and its body. She pictured the instrument, its natural wear and tear and the varnish that had worn off behind the neck where it had rested against her dad's chest, against his heart as he'd played so beautifully.

Owen leaned in and kissed her on the cheek before he turned and went back inside, leaving her wondering what she would say to him next.

*

'Where did you get to?' Carrie immediately latched onto Owen's arm when he found his way back to the edge of the small dance floor.

'I needed a bit of fresh air.'

Carrie took a deep breath. 'I think we need to talk, don't you?'

'Not now, Carrie. Today isn't the time.'

'You're wrong. It's the perfect time. Come on.' She ushered him over to the quiet corner where two chairs sat vacant, and she grabbed a glass of champagne from a passing waiter.

'Aren't you driving?' he frowned at the glass, wondering whether she'd assumed she was staying at his place.

'I'm leaving the car here. A few of us have arranged a minibus to take us home.'

'Oh.' So she had no intention of staying with him. 'God, I'm sorry, Carrie. I haven't made much of an impression on you, have I?'

Her hand rested on his arm. 'I don't know about that. We've had fun, but I think I knew from the moment I saw you with Rosie that you and I would never be anything more than friends.'

'Rosie? I—'

'You don't look at me like you look at Rosie.' She knocked back her champagne but she was smiling. 'You look at her like she's another fire to put out, a challenge to overcome.'

God, was it true? And if it was, did it mean that deep down it was the challenge that was the real attraction rather than Rosie herself? He buried his face in his hands, took a deep breath and looked up at Carrie when she spoke again.

‘She’s a nice girl, Owen. Just be sure you really want her before you rock her world.’

He opened his mouth to protest but clamped it shut tightly when he couldn’t think of a defence.

‘You’re a good man.’ Carrie brushed his cheek with the back of her hand and then she was off to the dance floor. She only turned back once, mid dance, to wink at him, and then he left, walking towards Lakeside Lane to contemplate his next move.

Chapter Twenty-Four

Owen stood at the kitchen bench in darkness, the only light spilling out of the lounge from Rosie's Christmas Village. His hand grasped the box until he heard the gentle rumble of the Hubba coming home. The car's headlamps cast a golden glow across the room as the car passed the front door, and Owen was glad he'd waited to see Rosie again before he left Magnolia Creek.

She switched on the light in the hallway and then the one in the kitchen. She jumped when she saw him. 'God, you scared me.' Her hand rested against her chest. 'Why are you lurking here in the dark? Hey, George.' She reached down to stroke the cat who never missed an opportunity to ease his way into her affections.

Owen held Rosie's gaze until hers dropped to the box on the kitchen bench.

'I found it in the garden,' he began. 'And let's just say it explains a few things.'

He pulled open the bag and some mud fell onto the bench top. The only way to explain all this was to show Rosie what was inside, piece by piece.

He held the pile of evidence in his hand. 'My biological father is alive. He's some hot-shot property tycoon. My parents have been lying to me my whole life.'

Rosie stood, open-mouthed, her gaze anywhere but on him.

'Why won't you look at me, Stevens? Did you hear what I said?'

'Yes,' she mumbled to the floor. 'Owen, I've already seen the box and its contents.'

His fingers stilled on the papers.

'I dug it up by mistake, weeks ago.'

He shook his head in disbelief. She stepped towards him but he backed away.

'Owen, ple—'

'No, Rosie!' He pulled his hands away before she could touch him. 'What gave you the right to look? And what gave you the right to keep something like that from me?'

'I wish I'd never, ever found it!'

'But why didn't you say anything?'

'I didn't know how to. And when I thought about your mum's email—'

'What email?'

'Your mum emailed days before I found the box. She told me if there was a fire and we were told to evacuate Magnolia Creek, then I was to call her any time, day or night.'

His fists balled against the kitchen bench as he waited for what she'd say next.

'She said she had some personal items she wanted me to find for her, and that …'

'Oh, don't stop now.' This was almost laughable.

'And that I wasn't to tell you anything,' she finished.

He wanted to punch something – a wall, the sofa, anything. He slumped against the kitchen bench, head in his hands.

Tears began to stream down Rosie's cheeks.

'This is so fucked up, Stevens.'

She hung her head. 'I wrestled with my conscience so many times over this. I didn't know what to say, and then Bella—'

Owen's head shot up. 'Bella's in on this too? My whole life is exploding to shit and I'm the only one who didn't know!'

'I went to Bella because I didn't know what to do. We thought your mum should explain it all, and Bella promised she'd speak to her and get her to do just that.'

'Did you read all this?' Owen picked up the papers and dropped them again as though they were laced with ricin.

'I did. And it's an awful secret to keep from you, but letters, articles and photographs don't mean much on their own. Not without an explanation.'

'Oh, I know the explanation! My biological father is some low life who preyed on my Auntie Natasha, causing a rift between her and my mum. And for all we know she killed herself in what was labelled an *accident* and it would be down to him. Oh, and let's not forget the photograph of daddy-dearest with a girl who looks barely the age of consent!'

'Don't shout at me.'

He didn't respond to that. 'I'm the spitting fucking image of him, too. How do you think that makes me feel? God, no wonder my mum could barely look at me sometimes. I'm slowly turning into him.'

'You're not him.' She put a hand on his arm but he shrugged it off.

'Why did Mum bury it all in the garden? If she didn't want me to know, she should've destroyed everything. God knows I'd be better off not knowing.'

‘Owen, there’s more.’

He shook his head. He didn’t know if he could take any more.

‘Bella told me your mum left your biological father when she found out he’d been having an affair … affairs – we’re not sure – and we know he threatened her.’

‘Did he hurt her?’ The venom he felt for his Mum gave way enough to let sympathy edge its way in.

‘I don’t know all the details. But your mum got to the point where she couldn’t cope, and she left you with Bella when you were eight months old.’

‘Left me?’ When he saw Rosie’s face drop, he knew exactly what she meant. ‘So she didn’t want me, even back then.’

When Rosie reached for him this time, he let her hand grasp his forearm. He had no idea how to process all this: everything his mum had kept from him, the truth behind his feelings of failure for so many years, his inability to measure up.

‘You could’ve come to me earlier, Rosie.’ He sat on a stool at the kitchen bench, long fingers steepled in front of him. ‘I thought we were friends.’

She took a seat next to him. ‘I thought about it, believe me. But I didn’t think it should come from me. I really think you need to talk to your mum about this when she gets back. With secrets this huge, there’s nearly always more to it than there seems on the surface.’

He pulled his arm free of her hand. He had to get out of here, this house, this keeper of secrets he wished he’d never come back to discover.

‘Where are you going?’ Rosie stood back as he stalked out of the kitchen.

He raced up the stairs two at a time. He struggled to extricate himself from the bow tie that felt like a noose around his neck, the jacket and the cummerbund that were as restricting as the BA he wore to go into a structure fire. In his bedroom he threw his remaining cufflink, like a tiny missile, at the window and watched his reflection. Who was the man looking back at him anyway? Who the hell was Owen Harrison?

Dressed in his leathers he flew down the stairs and snatched up his helmet.

'Where are you going?' Rosie clung to the kitchen door frame. 'Don't drive off into the night when you're angry, you'll have an accident.'

'Yeah, well maybe I'll do the world a favour. I'd rather leave this world than become like the man who fathered me.'

'Don't say that, you don't mean it.' She moved in front of the sideboard in the hallway, hands planted on her hips, refusing to budge so he could reach his keys from behind her. 'I'm not moving, Owen. I need to stop you doing something you may regret.'

It was too late for that. Owen closed the gap between them, and with her back pressed against the sideboard there was nowhere for Rosie to go. He grabbed the back of her neck in his palm, their faces centimetres apart, watched as her pupils dilated and drowned the brown eyes he'd never looked this deeply into before. He kissed her forehead, the sides of her face, her cheeks still salty from her tears earlier that evening. And when she gasped and her lips parted, her breathing quickened and he closed the gap completely.

Owen kissed Rosie with the passion he'd held in for so long. His fingers laced around the back of her head, grappling through her poker-straight hair that grazed the top of her waist. Rosie's body relaxed into the kiss, and neither of them came up for air. Her hands held his waist, hesitant to touch, then sneaked beneath his T-shirt, circling his lower back. When Owen's hands moved along her collarbone and his thumbs stroked the skin below, felt the necklace he'd given her, her fingers skimmed up his back, around to his front and down to the hypersensitive spot below his navel.

Owen pulled away. He had to before he couldn't. He touched his forehead to hers, savouring the taste of her still on his lips. He closed his eyes, listened to their heavy breathing until he summoned the strength to reach past her and grab his keys.

He pulled his helmet on and tightened it, shrugged on the leather jacket and fled from the house into the open air. He revved the engine and roared away, the wheels slipping at the end of the driveway before he was off again, into the distance as far from Magnolia Creek as he could go.

Chapter Twenty-Five

Rosie stood there until she couldn't hear the hum of the Ducati any more. When she finally closed the front door and returned to the kitchen, she touched a hand to her lips, remembering a kiss she'd never dared to imagine. She listened to the ticking clock, the cicadas so loud outside that their song carried through the walls.

She stood at the back door and stared into the abyss of roses that had harboured a horrible secret and broken the Owen she'd got to know.

Hours later she reluctantly climbed into bed. She lay staring at the ceiling, watching the shadows created by the moon outside peeping through the gap in the middle of the curtains. And for the first time in a long time, she felt grateful rather than sad about the family she'd once belonged to. She'd always known where she stood, never doubted how proud her parents were of her. There were no secrets, at least none she'd ever known, and she felt blessed for her happy memories.

The house was quiet without him. The cicadas outside continued their evening song as the temperature refused to dip, and the tinkle of a collar accompanied by the gentle pitter-patter of paws on the bedroom carpet announced George's arrival.

'Hey.' Rosie rubbed her fingers beneath the cat's chin when he jumped up onto the bed. He nestled in next to Rosie, purring, and stayed there until her eyelids began to droop and she dozed off.

At nearly four thirty in the morning, Rosie woke to the sound of the Ducati pulling into the driveway. Her movement beneath the duvet caused George to adjust his position, but he soon curled up again and got on with the business of sleeping.

'He's back.' Rosie smiled. Knowing he was safe, she settled down, ready to join George in slumber again, but moments later her bedroom door slowly opened.

'Hi.' Owen stood in the doorway.

She sat up in bed. 'Hi.'

He sat down on the edge of the bed in his leather bike pants and a white T-shirt that showed every contour of his upper body. George opened one eye in greeting as Owen reached out to stroke him.

'I'm sorry I got so angry,' he said.

She chewed the corner of her mouth. 'You had every right to be.'

He smiled at her. 'You're crap at burying stuff, you know.'

She punched him playfully on the arm.

'I'm sorry about the kiss, too,' he added. 'Maybe I'm like my biological father, making a move on a girl who's off limits.' He wasn't smiling now.

'That's a bit dramatic, isn't it?' She wanted to say she wasn't sorry about the kiss. She should be, but she wasn't.

'Well, I shouldn't have kissed you. You're with Adam.'

She wasn't sure whether he was making a statement or asking a question, but after he said it he patted George on the head, smiled at Rosie and said, 'I'll let you get some sleep.'

*

The smell snaking up the stairs tore Owen away from his iPad. He'd been awake for hours, and his stomach growled in protest that it hadn't had so much as a cup of coffee. He grabbed a T-shirt and pulled it over his head and down across his chest as he appeared in the kitchen. He smiled inwardly when he caught Rosie looking at his bare skin, her cheeks colouring.

'What's all this?' He watched as Rosie lifted bacon rashers out of the pan and onto slices of toast, topping them with an egg and adding grilled mushrooms and tomatoes.

'I thought you could use it after yesterday.' She handed him the plate and a glass of fresh orange juice.

Owen was glad to have company after the events of yesterday and the drama of racing off last night. This reminded him of how his mum looked after him and his dad when they came home from a fire call – the CFA's hidden support team was the wives, girlfriends and siblings at home who looked after members of the crew – and he was glad Rosie was here in much the same way.

'Aren't you eating?' He looked up from his plate.

'I already did. I've got to be at work in an hour.' Her iPad sounded on the kitchen bench, but she ignored it.

He mopped egg yolk with a forkful of toast. 'It might be Adam,' he said.

'I'll call him another time.'

Carrie's words about not rocking Rosie's world echoed through his mind. He loaded another forkful of bacon, egg and a small piece of toast and ran it through the HP Sauce on the side of his plate. Over time he and Rosie had got used to one another's preferences, and this morning she hadn't asked him if he wanted sauce, it was just there waiting for him.

Rosie sat down. 'Have you thought about calling your mum?'

Owen shook his head. 'I won't call her.'

'I think you should.'

'Maybe you should call yours once in a while,' he snapped.

When she stayed silent he said, 'Sorry, that was unnecessary.'

'No need to apologise. You're right. I should call her more than I do. And I shouldn't be lecturing you.'

After a while he said, 'I'm going to London, Stevens.' She put down her glass of juice. 'I need to see her, face-to-face.'

'That's probably a good idea.'

'I leave tonight.'

'Wow, you must've been busy after I went to sleep last night.'

Owen swallowed a mouthful. 'Why the long face?'

'What face?'

'You look disappointed.' And she was fiddling with her necklace, a dead giveaway.

'It's just that the tree arrives in a few days, and I was looking forward to decorating it together.'

He didn't miss her voice waver on the word 'together'.

'You'll have to do the tree on your own, but I'll be back on Christmas Eve.' He'd paid over the odds for a ticket to return at that time. 'I wouldn't miss it for the world.'

Chapter Twenty-Six

Outside his hotel in London, his mind still fuggy with jetlag, Owen zipped up the ski jacket he'd had the foresight to bring, glad of the jumper beneath and the jeans. The blanket of winter darkness in London was interrupted by the blue lights bouncing off the London Eye, the giant Ferris wheel standing on the banks of the River Thames; the yellow tinge of streetlamps; the ever moving headlamps of cars.

He flagged down a taxi in amongst the chaos of illuminations. The British cabbie was a chatty one – the drivers in Melbourne were a silent bunch in comparison, needing directions on a major scale as though they'd got their licence from the back of a cereal packet. Their lack of local knowledge was shocking compared to these cabbies, who, according to his mum, were often ranked as number one in the world.

They zigzagged their way in and out of traffic, up and down streets lined with parked cars. The cabbie, Brian, told Owen how he'd been through rigorous training to get his licence. He'd studied for three years, knew thousands of landmarks and streets and hundreds of routes. And as he talked, Owen looked out at a cold, dismal city that was transformed with the twinkling lights of Christmas. A Santa's sleigh pulled by reindeer was strung up in lights high above the shops and office fronts. An iconic red double-decker London bus passed by, its colour just visible beneath the shining lights of the city. Shop fronts were illuminated to entice people in out of the cold.

He wanted to show all this to Rosie, show her how life could be magical. He wanted to show her she didn't have to settle for anything less than extraordinary. Thoughts of Rosie had been a welcome distraction on the long flight from Australia, a way to block out the confrontation he was about to have now that they'd pulled up outside the pillar-box red front door in Camden where his Auntie Sarah had lived for almost two decades.

Puffs of grey air came from his mouth as he stood outside the house, the toes of his feet numb as they lingered on the doorstep and the tips of his ears cold enough to remind him of how Rosie had cut his hair before the wedding.

A warm glow came from the downstairs window, and it took him a while to extricate his hand from the warm embrace of his coat pocket and knock on the wooden front door.

He held his breath while a figure shuffled down the hallway.

This was it. It was truth time.

*

Jane Harrison stood at the front door of the townhouse, the cold billowing its way through the open door as she stared, unblinking at her son.

Owen had thought about this moment a lot since he'd found the box of secrets lurking beneath the rose bush. He'd thought about the hatred he could feel, the spite for the secrets she'd kept from him and the begging he could do to find out who he really was. But now he was here, he had no idea how to react. It felt as though he was part of a game of dizzy astronauts, and sooner or later he'd stop whizzing round and have to stagger in one direction and hope it got him to where he needed to go.

His mum ushered him inside, out of the cold. 'What are you doing here?'

He turned to her in the hallway, still bundled up in his coat. 'I found the box.'

The colour drained from her face, and Owen moved past her to shut the front door. He stared at it long after it clicked into place, and when he turned Jane had slumped down onto the bottom stair.

'I'd like to say I know everything,' he said, 'but I don't. I've got no idea what the real truth is, and that's why I'm here.'

'I see.'

'Is that all you've got to say?'

'It's a shock.'

'I'll say!' The house was silent apart from their voices filling the hallway. 'Where's Dad?'

'He's meeting a doctor friend who he was at University with and he'll stop for takeaway on his way home.'

Owen was glad. He needed this explanation to come from her. He shrugged off his coat and hung it on the rack behind the front door before he followed her through to the dining room.

An oak table dominated the space in front of a characterful fireplace with a tiled surround. His mum motioned him to sit down.

'I don't want to,' he answered.

'Owen, for goodness sake …'

'I said I don't want to!'

Her composure threatened to send him over the edge, even though common sense told him that inside she was anything but calm. He'd expected a little more panic, more fear in her than this.

'Can I get you a cup of tea?'

Owen harrumphed. 'The truth is all I'm here for.'

If it was possible, her shoulders sagged further south. 'I wanted to tell you everything, when I was ready, when I thought you could handle it.'

'When I could handle it?' His voice bounced off the walls. 'Did you ever really think that moment would come?'

'I guess not. Maybe I was kidding myself. Maybe I was scared of what would happen when you knew.'

'Rosie found the box you know, not me.' He wasn't sure why he told her that part, but it felt important. 'Out of some misguided sense of loyalty to you, she didn't tell me about it. But then when I was cutting some roses, I found it for myself.'

Jane looked towards the bay window. Owen assumed there must be a garden out there, but for now, all they could see were the two reflections staring back at each other, searching for answers.

She rubbed her arms even though the heating was working overtime in the place. 'Let's go into the lounge, it's too cold in here.'

Owen followed her. She could run from room to room for all he cared, as long as she gave him answers in the end. He had nowhere he needed to be.

'I guess I'd better start from the beginning.' She sat in the small, square lounge with floral sofas and plain walls. Her hands nervously clinched her knees in her black corduroy trousers as Owen sank into an armchair opposite. ‘Let me tell the whole story before you jump in.’

‘Okay.’ He didn’t see why he had to promise her anything, but he’d do his best if it meant he got answers. ‘Go on,’ he urged when it seemed she was never going to continue.

‘I met Gregory – Gregory Falmer was his name then – when I was eighteen. He was all charm, good-looking and successful, qualities that left him with no problem attracting attention from women, including me.’ She met Owen’s eyes briefly but then looked away. ‘Gregory was seven years older than I was, and when I found out I was pregnant with you, he didn’t hesitate in asking me to marry him. I thought my life was all mapped out for me, I was so happy. My sister …’ Her voice faltered.

‘Auntie Natasha?’

She nodded.

‘You never talk about her,’ said Owen.

‘No, I don’t.’ She took a deep breath. ‘Natasha was younger than me and idolised me, her big sister. She was forever trying on my clothes, borrowing make-up and never returning it, begging me to take her out for the evening with my friends if we were going into the city.

‘Natasha said something to me, shortly after I got married. She told me Gregory had forced himself on her.’

‘You mean he raped her?’ Owen didn’t want any misunderstandings, not any more. He wanted nothing but the truth.

Jane’s fingers curled into her palms. ‘Yes.’

‘And you stayed with him?’

‘When she told me what had happened, I didn’t believe her.’

Stunned, Owen said nothing and let her continue.

'I'd seen the way Natasha looked at Gregory, like he was something else of mine she wanted to borrow. She'd flirt around him, giggle at his jokes. When I confronted Gregory he said she'd come on to him, and under no circumstances did he force himself on her.'

'Did you believe him?'

'I had no reason not to. My God, he was convincing. He actually looked upset when I asked him about it. He told me she'd been flinging herself at him from the moment we started dating, and he hadn't wanted to tell me because he knew I'd be upset. It was her word against his, and I'm ashamed to say I believed him and not her.'

Tears appeared at the corners of her eyes and she swiped them away with the back of her hand. 'Natasha stopped speaking to me after that, and I was busy looking after you. I was sleep deprived and assumed I had a husband I could trust.'

'So what happened then?' Owen leaned forwards, arms resting on his thighs as Jane fell silent. 'Mum, tell me everything, please.'

She pulled a tissue from her sleeve, wiped her eyes, scared away the quivering lip and carried on.

'Natasha went travelling with friends after I refused to listen to her. She went bungee jumping in New Zealand, white water rafting, even worked in America for a while. I hoped that when she eventually came home, we'd move on from what had happened and be sisters again, friends.'

She stood and walked over to the window, staring out at the night sky, at the headlamps of cars filled with people heading out for the evening or bringing people home to their families. 'Natasha was the quietest out of all three of us girls. She loved to paint and draw, but after our confrontation she never picked up a brush again, she never sat at the easel with a blank canvas and turned it into something beautiful.'

Jane stared into the darkness some more before she came back to the sofa. 'What I loved about Gregory was how he didn't just sit around waiting for life to happen to him. He went out and grabbed what he wanted. He told me he'd worked crappy jobs over the years, but with every position he'd kept his eyes and ears open, learning from the bottom up. Not too unlike someone else I know.' She smiled at her son.

Owen wasn't sure whether he liked the comparison. 'I get the feeling that what Gregory Falmer wanted he got, and stuff everyone else?'

'I got swept along with Gregory and the holiday home business. His career was going well, we had a bouncing baby boy, and apart from the fallout with Natasha, I was content with my life. Gregory encouraged me to take an accountancy course and work from home, which I did, and that meant we could keep the business a "family business", which he hoped one day you would be able to run.'

A car outside beeped and another answered back with its own horn.

'One day I questioned an item on a bank statement,' Jane went on. 'It was a simple item that read "roof repairs" but it was repeated three times, for the exact same amount. Anyway, Gregory told me he was perfectly capable of running a business and that I should concentrate on doing the accounts as he'd asked rather than worrying about minor details.

'A few more items appeared on the next bank statement, but this time I didn't mention it because I wanted to find out what was going on. I was panicking that Gregory was in financial trouble, trying to syphon off money for a loan shark or something equally as terrifying. I was scared we'd lose everything.'

Owen almost reached his hand out to cover hers, but he couldn't, not yet. 'Who were the payments really going to?'

'C. Gilbertson,' she breathed. 'I looked into roofing companies with the same name, I viewed the customer database, but nothing came up. Then the phone calls started.'

'Phone calls?'

'You were three months old and sometimes the phone would ring in the day – I'd curse if you were asleep, it took such an effort to get you to sleep sometimes – or else it was in the middle of the night when Gregory was out of town. There was always silence at the other end, and the calls never happened when Gregory was around. I mentioned it to him and he wasn't rattled, but he changed our number anyway.

'Tamsin Fielding turned up at the house one day when Gregory was up in Cairns on business, and that was the day my world began to fall apart, bit by bit.'

Owen passed her a tissue, keeping the box in his hand, afraid to put it down and miss the story that could help him understand the complexities of this whole mess.

'Tamsin worked for Gregory, designing and maintaining the interiors of the holiday properties and adding the finishing touches. Well, she certainly did that.'

'They had an affair?'

‘They’d had a brief fling. Tamsin said it was over before it really even started, but she came to me when she found something else out about Gregory.’

‘Was Tamsin the girl in the photograph?’ Owen cringed at the memory of the photo lying with all the other bumf in the box, the picture of his father half naked with a girl even more scantily clad than him.

Jane shook her head. ‘That was Carly.’ Her hands pulled apart the sodden tissue in her hands.

‘Carly?’

‘Carly Gilbertson.’

Owen’s eyebrows knitted together. ‘C. Gilbertson.’

‘She was fifteen.’

He exhaled long and hard. ‘Did he know she was underage?’

‘Who knows, but a quick check of the personnel records could’ve told him she was a minor. Anyway, Tamsin caught Gregory and Carly on camera – she’s the one who took the photograph and made a copy of the personnel records to prove Carly’s age – and the only reason she didn’t go to the police was because she felt guilty about me. She felt it should be my decision.’

‘And what did you do?’

‘I told Tamsin to get that girl away from Gregory. Tamsin wheedled the truth out of her in the end. I couldn’t bear to go near her. Anyway, Gregory got bored of Carly once he’d overcome the challenge and she’d given him what he wanted. She threatened to go to the police and claim the sex wasn’t consensual. She got a hundred thousand dollars out of him in the end.’

Owen stared out into the darkness beyond the lounge window. Strike two – not only was he ambitious like his biological father, but he liked a challenge.

'Our lives were a total mess, Owen. I didn't want your father to go to jail, but I told Carly the police should be told. She refused to go to them and said she'd deny it if anyone else tried to file a report. I think she was terrified she'd have to pay back the money, and by that time she'd spent a lot of it. She rented her own apartment – she didn't get on with her parents at all – she bought clothes, went out all the time, all the extras she would never have been able to afford on her salary. I think she was one mixed up kid. I've often thought of her over the years, wondering whether she regrets what happened.'

'Did you confront my father about it?'

'I didn't breathe a word. I wanted to bide my time, put everything together. I had the bank statements and the photograph …' Jane looked at her son and this time she didn't look away. 'And two days later, just when I thought I couldn't break any more, Natasha died.'

Owen scraped a hand across his jaw. His throat was dry and his jumper was making him itch around his neck. He left the room and came back with two large measures of gin and tonic from the drinks cabinet in the dining room.

Jane took the gin and swigged it as though it were water.

'I saw the article about Auntie Natasha in the box,' Owen told her. He welcomed the burning feeling of the gin in his throat.

'A sailing accident.' Jane shook her head and glugged back more of her drink.

'You sound as though you doubt that.'

'Nobody knows for sure what happened, and nobody will ever know. Maybe it's my guilt making me think it wasn't an accident. I always wondered if sailing, like abseiling and jumping off bridges, was another way for Natasha to obliterate what had happened with Gregory and how I'd refused to believe her. I've never forgiven myself for that, Owen. I was her older sister. I was supposed to look out for her just like you look out for Tom and Ben, and part of me thinks … part of me thinks she killed herself out there in the water.'

'I don't believe this.' Owen shook his head, downed his drink and went back to the dining room. He returned with the entire bottle of gin this time.

Jane looked into the clear liquid when he'd topped up her glass. 'She died never knowing that eventually I found out what a son of a bitch I'd married.'

The chime of the carriage clock on the mantelpiece silenced them as it sounded seven times. Owen's flesh crawled at the thought of his biological father playing any part in ruining other people's lives, at the thought of him taking advantage of a young girl, his duplicity within his own family and attack on his sister-in-law.

Jane's eyes were red-rimmed, tired from her revelations. 'After the funeral I told Gregory I had all the evidence I needed to see him imprisoned and lose everything. But the worst … the worst was when I confronted him again about Natasha and he didn't even bother to try to deny it. He said she'd been all over him for months and she wanted it as much as he did. I saw red that night, flew at him scratching his face, kicking him. I slammed the door and I never wanted to see him again.'

Maybe it was selfish to ask, but Owen had to know. 'Did he care that he'd lost me?'

Jane's voice and face softened. 'I'm sorry if this is hard to hear, Owen—'

‘I don’t care how much it’ll hurt.’ He did care, but he cared about the truth more.

‘Gregory was proud to have a son, a son who could one day follow in his footsteps and carry on his successful business, but I needed time to think about how to involve him in his son’s life without involving him in mine, and I wasn’t sorry when he upped and disappeared.

‘My dad died soon after. Natasha had always been a daddy’s girl, and I think a piece of him broke when she died. Amid the funeral arrangements and thoughts of family, I knew it was unfair to keep Gregory from you, so when Gregory turned up at the flat, I let him in, ready to talk. What a mistake that was.’ She shuddered. ‘Goodness only knows how he’d heard, but he knew Dad had passed away, and he must’ve remembered Dad was worth a bit of money. Split two ways it amounted to almost a million dollars for me and the same for Sarah. It would’ve been split three ways had Natasha still been alive.

‘Gregory’s business was suffering – something else he’d kept from me so well – and he threatened me. It was as though the past few years with him had never happened, as if the baby lying on the blanket in the corner of the room didn’t exist. I’m sorry, Owen.’

Owen bit down on his bottom lip, hard. ‘Don’t stop now.’

‘He shoved me against the wall, made his demands again and each time I said no. Then he went for you. He grabbed you, bundled you in the blanket and held you against his chest. Oh, I was so afraid he’d hurt you, that he’d squeeze you too hard.’ Her voice caught. ‘He said he’d take you away if I didn’t give him that money and the evidence I had against him. He’d called my bluff and he knew it. When he started making his way to the door, I screamed. I wanted you … I wanted you, Owen, in my arms, safe against me. I'm sorry.'

She left the room and Owen sat staring at the dip in the sofa cushion from where she'd been sitting. By the time she came back, the foam of the chair had reshaped itself.

'That day was the worst day of my life, but also the best,' she told him, a fresh tissue in her hand. 'It was the first day I really spoke to Michael and we started to get to know one another.' She smiled at the mention of Michael Harrison, the only dad Owen had ever known. 'We'd met a handful of times. He lived upstairs and we'd pass in the corridor and say hello when I was on my way home or he was on his way to a shift at the hospital where he worked as a junior doctor.

'When Michael heard me screaming, he flew in the door, snatched you away from Gregory and put you in my arms. He had Gregory against the wall before Gregory even knew what was happening. I remember screaming that I had all the evidence I needed to bury him: he'd lose his business, he'd never see you again and worse, he'd go to jail for what he'd done to Carly and Natasha. He pointed a finger at me and told me I hadn't heard the last of it. Your dad stepped in then and saw him off, but Gregory's face appeared in my nightmares for a long time afterwards.'

Owen thought about the two men, how one had put him first, how the other had used him as a pawn in his financial game. Biological ties meant very little to him right now.

'Why didn't you go to the police?' he asked. 'They would never have taken me away from you.'

‘I was scared, Owen. I knew what Gregory was capable of. He’d lied his way through life to get what he wanted and I couldn’t take the risk. We never even divorced. I knew it would be so messy and I’d had enough.’

‘So you and Dad…’

‘We’re not married.’ She looked away. ‘After that night Michael and I became closer and slowly our friendship blossomed into something more. At the start he’d come over after a shift, spend time with us both. Sometimes we would cook together, discuss his job, my dreams of a career. It was Michael who persuaded me to go into nursing and without his offer to babysit whenever he wasn’t working, I’m not sure I’d have ever been able to do it.

‘One night, when he was looking after you, I came home to find him asleep on the sofa. I covered him with a blanket and he woke up as I was tucking it around his neck so he wouldn’t get cold. We looked at each other and that was the moment I knew. I knew I wanted to spend the rest of my life with him.’

‘But you were married to someone else?’

‘Only on paper. And your Dad knew my reasons why I couldn’t make contact with Gregory to ask for a divorce. Your Dad and I agreed to wear rings because to us we’re married together for life in more ways than could ever be expressed on a piece of paper.’

Owen paused, tried to take in what he was hearing. Eventually he spoke. ‘That’s not the end of the story though, is it?’

‘No, it’s not.’ Her lips pressed together, against her teeth. ‘Michael was offering me the world, but after we moved out of the city, everything that had happened hit me all over again. I felt wretched some days, worried

Gregory would come back and take you from me, worried Carly's life and perhaps others had been ruined by Gregory. I felt guilty about Natasha and how I'd dismissed her accusations, and I thought Michael deserved a hell of a lot more than the mess I was offering. I fell apart. One day, when Michael was at work, it was as though the walls were closing in all around me.' Her face was pained as though she were back there now, unable to get free. 'I took you to Bella and Rodney's and I left you there. I left my baby. I couldn't cope. I've felt guilty every day since, even after I came to my senses and returned home to Magnolia Creek.'

'Where did you go, when you left?'

'I went to Western Australia, back to the suburb where I grew up. I rented an apartment short-term using the money from my inheritance and every day I visited Natasha's grave and my parents' too.'

'Did Dad know where you were?'

She nodded. 'I called Bella every day and she passed him messages so he'd know I was safe. He took you back home and took leave of absence from work, and he only left you with Bella again when he flew to Perth to get me. When I saw him standing there outside the apartment I'd rented, he wrapped his arms around me without saying a word, and I knew I was going home.'

Owen raked a hand through his hair. 'Bella's always felt like a second mum to me.' He shook his head. 'She always looked out for me. She was never too busy to stop what she was doing and ask me how I was, what I was up to.'

'She's got a soft spot for you. Even after you were back with me, she loved to mind you if I needed to go shopping or run errands.' Her words brought tears to his eyes as they sat staring across the room at one another. 'She used to say you were—'

'Bella's little sweetheart,' they said at the same time.

Jane smiled. 'She's my best friend, always will be.'

'What I don't understand is why you kept the box. Why didn't you destroy it?'

'It was my insurance policy. If Gregory came crawling back wanting his share of Mum and Dad's inheritance, then I could use everything in the box to chase him away again.

'When we renovated the house in Magnolia Creek, I threw myself into landscaping the garden. I hated having the box in the house, so I buried it outside. I wanted to bury that man as deep as I could, with Natasha getting the final say by piling her favourite flowers on top of him. The flowers were beautiful, just like her, with prickly thorns underneath, just like him.'

Owen thought about how, over the years, she'd spent so much time tending to those flowers, sometimes watching them as if she expected them to suddenly do anything different other than waver in the breeze.

'When you said you were going into the property business, Owen, my heart constricted. I hated the reminder of your biological father, but it didn't take long for me to realise that you are your own person. You're twice the man he ever was, and I didn't ever want you to know what your biological father was really like. I thought I could keep the secret and feel the pain for both of us, but I see now how that was wrong of me.'

'You made me feel as though I was never good enough,' said Owen as Jane refused to look at him.

'I never meant to make you feel that way. It's certainly not what I thought.'

‘But you let your fears come between us.’

Her voice shook when she said, ‘I can’t even begin to tell you how sorry I am.’

‘Is that why you wanted me to go into the medical profession, so I wouldn’t follow in Gregory Falmer’s footsteps?’

She let out a deep breath. ‘In some way I suppose it was. You know, you do get some of your genetic make-up from me. You never let me push you into anything, you were independent from a very early age and you’ve always followed your heart. I couldn’t be more proud.’

Owen paused for a moment. ‘My property business is, and always will be, above board. I’m nothing like him in business.’

Jane took Owen’s hand. ‘I decided very early on that I didn’t want you to know what kind of a man Gregory was. I didn’t want you to be confused, to feel ashamed, embarrassed. I wanted you to feel proud, and the way you looked up to Michael was all I’d ever wanted.’ She sat back again. ‘That article, the one you found hidden beneath the books in the lounge room, knocked the life out of me. I’d seen it that morning and shoved it there when I heard you come down the stairs. There he was with a new family. He’d changed his name to Declan Roberts, no doubt to cover his tracks, but even though I’d told him to keep the hell away from us, it hurt that he’d replaced you.’

‘I had a right to know.’

She nodded, unable to deny it. ‘I feared that if we told you, you’d try to contact him and he’d reject you, hurting you all over again. I felt there was no end to how much he could ruin our lives.’

Owen knocked back another glug of gin. 'You know, sometimes I felt as though you loved those roses more than me.'

Tears glistened in her eyes. 'You know, your dad never got angry at me, he was always so kind, but the day you came home with your tattoo, he was almost at the end of his tether. Oh, it wasn't that he really minded, you were a grown man after all, but he wondered whether you'd got the tattoo to get my attention.'

'I'm not sure why I got it really.'

'You said I paid a lot of attention to the roses and you're right, I was obsessed by them, losing myself in memories of Natasha and how much I was to blame for losing her. Your dad said the same and saw the rose tattoo as a cry for attention. But I wouldn't listen.' She looked down at her lap.

Owen supposed it made sense, although if that was why he'd done it, it had certainly been subconsciously.

'I'd watch you sometimes,' he said after a while. 'I'd see you sitting on the edge of the pool, your legs dangling, and your mind a million miles away. This secret even stopped you from going into the water. You let us enjoy it but somehow you never seemed to want to. And …'

'And what?' she asked when he hesitated.

'I remember, it was my thirteenth birthday and I came racing out the back of the house. I couldn't wait to tell you that the entire class had had popcorn in my honour. But there you were, trailing a single red rose across the surface of the water. I called to you, you didn't hear me.'

'I don't remember.'

'I do,' he said sombrely.

‘I was always afraid something would happen to you, Owen, and it’d serve me right for lying. Ever since the day Gregory tried to snatch you, the fear never left me. I’d watch you jump into the pool and panic you’d never resurface. I’d watch you run around with your brothers and imagine one day you’d just keep running and I’d never see you again. It was as though I was always waiting for something bad to happen.’

She drew in her breath. ‘I never once stopped loving you, from the moment I knew I was carrying you in my tummy, to the moment you knocked on the door tonight, and it’ll never change. I’m proud of your achievements, Owen. You always excelled in everything you did and overcame anything that stood in your way, but I’m most proud of the man you’ve turned out to be. You’re always so in tune with other people’s feelings. Oh, you have this bikie look with your leathers and your height and your stature and the tattoo, but underneath you always did have the kindest heart.’

Her shoulders finally gave way to sobs, and Owen took her in his arms as she clung tightly to him, the same way she would’ve held him to her the night his biological father tried to take him away.

They stayed that way, talking and comforting one another, until the clock chimed eight o’clock and the man who’d always been his dad came home for dinner.

Chapter Twenty-Seven

The pine aroma filled the room at twenty-seven Lakeside Lane, and Rosie admired the conical-shaped tree from as many angles as she could now that she'd managed to make it stand up straight. She touched the deep-green pine needles that left scent on her fingers and paused to think about her dad. He'd have hugged her and said, 'It's a great tree, Rosie.' They'd have giggled as they hid presents beneath it, tempted to shake them or feel them to work out what they could possibly be.

Rosie almost reached out for the phone to call her mum but decided it could wait until closer to Christmas. It was time to tackle the next and worst job of the season: unravelling the lights. It would help her work away the frustration that Adam hadn't even sent her anything yet for Christmas. Surely he hadn't forgotten?

Once the lights were laid out in a trail across the floor, she pulled the set of kitchen steps to the side of the tree, climbed up and, starting at the top, wound the lights round and round, getting a face full of branches pinging back each time. Owen had found three sets of lights – good job as the tree looked a lot bigger now it was inside instead of standing amongst its friends on the farm – all white with a master switch to enable the lights to alternate between constant, twinkling, or a setting that made the lights gradually fade in and out. By the time she'd finished, she felt as though she smelt as much of tree as the tree itself. Next, it was time for the baubles: silver, red and gold. She'd never subscribed to the idea of 'theme' with a tree and preferred the haphazard, natural look. Christmas, to Rosie, wasn't about perfection. It was about the fun and childishness of it all, and part of that was hanging a whole array of decorations.

She smiled when she pulled out the next two decorations. Three snowflakes, kept between two pieces of cardboard to keep them flat, had been decorated with balled-up tissue paper and glitter, and each had a gold ribbon looped out of the top, ready to hang on the tree. On the back of one it said 'Owen', another said 'Ben' and the third, 'Tom'. Whatever had happened in the past, Jane Harrison must love her boys to keep these so pristine for so many years.

When Rosie's iPad sounded to announce a FaceTime call, she tutted and waded through the tissue paper tossed across the lounge room. She tiptoed gingerly in case any ornaments lingered beneath. Adam certainly knew how to pick his moment.

'This is a surprise!' she said when she answered the call, because looking back at her was Owen, and she was desperate to know how things were going in London.

'I wanted to check you hadn't trashed the house.' He grinned into the camera.

She turned the iPad round and heard him laugh as he saw the mess for himself. Then she turned the focus on the tree.

'Wow, looks even better than it did out at the farm,' he said.

Rosie moved the camera to the handmade snowflakes and a Santa made out of an old toilet roll with cotton wool for its beard and pipe cleaners for his arms.

‘I’d forgotten about that gem.’ Owen laughed. ‘I made toilet-Santa at school in year two.’

‘It’s brilliant.’ Rosie turned the camera back on her.

‘Miss Aves, my teacher, loved me,’ he said. ‘There should be a stylish reindeer there somewhere too.’

‘Ah yes, I wasn’t sure where to put that.’ She stepped over the tissue paper and focused the camera on the decoration sitting beside the television, a crazy-looking reindeer made out of a polystyrene cup turned upside-down and coloured in brown felt tip pen with a smiling face drawn on. It had a red, slightly squashed pom-pom for a nose and twigs as antlers.

She moved away from the mess and propped the iPad up against her bag on the kitchen bench. ‘So how’s it going? Have you seen your mum?’

‘I have. And believe me when I say it’s a long story.’

Rosie sat back on a stool. ‘The tree can wait. I’ve got time.’

*

The story of Owen’s past exhausted Rosie as though she’d been a part of it. But he was talking to his mum at least. They were even going out for dinner that evening, and Rosie was glad they were starting to mend a relationship that seemed worth saving.

She finished the tree, cleaned the house from top to bottom and, satisfied that she was Christmas-ready, she had lunch out on the deck and then lazed on the sofa, wishing away the hours until it was dark so she could switch on the Christmas lights.

Her iPad sounded from the coffee table next to her and Rosie reached over lazily and pulled it onto her lap.

‘I thought you were at dinner.’ She smiled when she saw Owen for a second time.

‘Dinner was hours ago, Stevens.’ Surrounded by darkness, he was all bundled up with a grey scarf wrapped around his neck and tucked inside the collar of his coat. ‘It’s almost ten o’clock now.’

‘How did it go?’

‘It was fine. Dad was there too and for tonight we agreed not to go over old ground. I think that’s what made the evening.’

‘I’m really pleased, Owen.’

‘Nature versus nurture, Stevens.’

‘Huh?’

‘Nurture is just as powerful in my opinion. This visit has been a real starting point, like starting afresh. And at least now I know everything.’

Rosie knew that if the sparkle in his eyes was anything to go by, the whole family would be able to move forwards from this, together.

‘I’ve got something to show you.’ He flipped his iPad round to show the lights of a London Street.’

She gasped. ‘Where are you?’

‘Standing on the famous Oxford Street.’

‘Show me everything.’ She couldn’t get close enough to her screen, her excitement bubbling as he moved the camera round. ‘I can see the big red bus,’ she squealed. ‘A double-decker!’

He moved the iPad to look up at the Christmas lights. A giant lit-up cube with bows in lights depicted a present. A 3D star shone in yellow and silver-blue. Strands of fairy lights were woven through a tree at the side of the road, standing out against the night sky.

He brought the camera’s focus down to street level and a man standing on a bench snapping away on a camera, a Union Jack rucksack on his back. 'Please don't tell me I look like him,' he whispered.

'I doubt you'd be able to carry off the bag.'

Owen turned the iPad on himself. 'It's bloody freezing, Stevens – I'm wearing thermal socks.'

'Now that's cold.'

'I won't tell you what I'm wearing under my jeans.'

She giggled as he moved away from the swarm of last-minute Christmas shoppers. 'You should come and see London for yourself.'

'Adam talked about taking a trip to Europe one day.' The words were out before she could stop them. Maybe his name had fallen into the conversation as a way of exonerating herself from this repartee that felt too comfortable.

'Well, when you come, come in the winter, there's nothing like it. You could ice skate at the Tower of London, hit the markets for your Christmas shopping, soak up the over-the-top festive spirit. You'd love it.'

Glad he'd ignored the reference to Adam, she asked, 'Does that mean you're not coming home?'

'I'll be home on Christmas Eve as planned, ready for the Harrison family Christmas.'

Her heart warmed at the thought of being included in the arrangements this year. 'Does Tom know anything?'

'About the sordid family secret?' Owen shook his head. 'Once my parents are back in Australia, we'll deal with it, but for now all he needs to know is that everything is fine. Everything is going to be fine, Stevens.' He blew on his fingers to warm them up and then swapped hands with the iPad and blew onto his other hand. 'I need to thank you, Rosie.'

'It must be serious. You're using my first name.'

‘It is a serious “thank you”. If you weren’t so incredibly crap at burying something, I wouldn’t have found the box and I may never have had this conversation with my parents. And thank you for being there that night when I stormed out of Magnolia Creek after the wedding. Thank you for being the voice in my head when I roared away on the bike, the voice that brought me to my senses and made me turn round.’

Rosie gulped as they looked at one another through FaceTime, and despite a separation of thousands of miles, she’d never felt this close to anyone.

Chapter Twenty-Eight

Owen had had a better time in London than he'd anticipated, but he was glad to get some distance at the end of the visit, to let the dust settle for a while until his parents returned to Australia themselves. They'd insisted on driving him to the airport as though he were a kid unable to make his way across the big city alone. But he'd loved every minute of the attention and concern, especially from his mum.

'You are nothing like Gregory,' she'd told him as they said their goodbyes at London's Heathrow. She touched his cheek tenderly. 'You treat women with respect, he never did. You go after what you want but not if it means hurting people along the way. Owen Harrison, you are your dad's son.' She'd looked up at Michael then and Michael had pulled them both into his warm embrace.

At Melbourne airport some twenty-eight hours later, Owen climbed into the familiar yellow taxi, irritated that he had to use his navigation skills rather than lazily listening to a London cabbie who knew his way around. His identity had been in tatters when he'd left the country ten days ago, but as they passed by the concrete and high-rises in the city, he felt as though he'd found a part of himself. He'd never get those days of his childhood back, those days his mum had been so distant, but at least now he was beginning to understand her reasons why.

When the taxi pulled into the driveway of his parents' home, he pulled out the colourful dollars hiding at the back of his wallet behind the UK currency and paid the driver. His heart lifted at the sight of the Hubba out front. It was a strange sensation to be so happy that someone would be inside, waiting for him to come home.

He pushed open the front door. If he got on with the job quick smart, he could string the fairy lights around it and the outside windows by tonight.

'Stevens?' he called out as he dumped his holdall in the hallway, but she was nowhere to be seen. He smiled when he saw the tree in the lounge, finished with an angel on top. He could imagine her stretching up to put it in place.

At the sound of splashes in the pool, Owen headed out back. Rosie was in the water, laughing, and he grinned. But when he walked to the edge of the deck he saw she had company. His insides plummeted because there was Adam, sitting in the spa, head tipped back as the bubbles leapt up around him. He was a Christmas gift Owen definitely hadn't anticipated.

Rosie emerged from the pool and grabbed a towel, muttered something to Adam and then joined Owen on the deck.

'You should've called me to come and get you from the airport.' Water dripped from the tip of her button nose.

'You look busy,' he replied coolly.

'He turned up first thing this morning as a surprise.' Rosie's eyes never left his.

So the guy did have the decency to spend Christmas with his girlfriend. Clearly he hadn't given Adam enough credit.

'Do you mind an extra one for Christmas dinner?' Rosie's brown eyes searched his as her breathing settled into a steadier pace.

'It's fine. I'm going to take a shower and then have a kip.'

He felt her eyes watching him as he wearily climbed the stairs to bed.

*

Owen slept for less than two hours but stayed in his room as long as he could before he felt he had to emerge and see the happy couple. He went straight outside and strung the lights around the doorway. He couldn't be bothered with the windows. Maybe next year.

Rosie caught him in the hallway as he came back inside. 'I've hidden the box in the shed for you.' Her voice fell on him softly. 'I didn't know what to do with it.'

'Thanks, I'd hate for Tom to come across it before my parents have a chance to talk to him first.'

'Owen, I—'

'Please don't apologise about your boyfriend turning up for Christmas, it's hardly a crime.' Her eyes were downcast to the floor. 'Seriously, Stevens.' He lifted her chin with his fingers so she had no choice but to look at him. 'Don't worry about it.'

He left her standing in the hallway, still looking up, lips slightly parted, and went through the kitchen and outside to do the decent thing and make the guy feel welcome. Ever since he'd learnt what an arsehole his biological father was, he was determined to be the complete opposite.

'How are you at carol singing, Adam?' he asked after they'd skated over the preliminaries. He crossed one foot across his other knee as he sat out on the deck.

'Terrible,' Adam replied.

'Great, that makes a few of us, then.'

'Why do you ask?'

Rosie hovered between both men as though she didn't know quite where to sit.

'It's the annual Christmas Carol concert tonight at Magnolia Tavern. It's fun and a bit of a laugh but best enjoyed with a few beers.'

'I'll bear that in mind.' Adam pulled Rosie in close.

Owen couldn't stand by and watch. 'Another tradition is to have a Christmas Eve swim, and I think I need it after the flight.'

Adam yawned. 'I'm going for a lie down. I only flew in this morning myself.' And with that he took Rosie by the hand and headed upstairs, leaving Owen with only George for company.

*

'Rosie?' Owen called upstairs for the fourth time that evening, impatience growing. Or was it the apprehension of spending the evening as a gooseberry?

She trotted down the stairs in a black dress fitted to the waist and swinging out from her hips in little folds. She slipped on the pair of black satin flat shoes in her hand.

'Where's Adam?' He cleared his throat and tried not to stare at her effortless elegance, hair piled up and fixed in place with a sparkling clip that would be sure to catch the Christmas lights of the pub and dazzle anyone who came near her. Not that she needed any help in that respect.

‘He’s been working long hours over the last week. Says he’s got a bit of a cold,’ she explained.

‘Or maybe he’s afraid he’ll show us all up with his choir-boy voice.’

Rosie put a finger to her lips. ‘He’s sleeping, let’s go.’

‘You do realise this isn’t *quite* as big as Carols by Candlelight, don’t you?’ He nodded to her dress.

‘I’m not daft. I just wanted to make an effort, feel nice for a change.’

When did she ever look anything but good?

‘I feel underdressed now.’ He patted his black cotton shirt and looked down at his dark wash jeans.

‘Now who’s being daft?’

*

The beer garden at Magnolia Tavern was already bustling when they arrived, and it wasn’t even nine o’clock yet.

‘The singing won’t start till it’s dark,’ Owen explained, ‘so plenty of time to get sloshed first.’ He pulled a face as he pushed open the door to the pub. ‘Come to think of it, maybe that’s why the singing is so appalling each year.’

They grabbed a couple of beers, and on their way outside again Bella made a beeline for Owen. He pulled her into a tight hug and they held it until someone needed to go through the door they were standing in front of.

‘Owen, I—’

‘No, Bella, not tonight. We’ll talk, but for tonight let’s show this one a real Magnolia Creek Christmas.’ He indicated Rosie beside him and Bella nodded, giving Rosie’s arm a squeeze.

Owen and Rosie talked until it was dark – about the tree Owen said was taking over the lounge; the food Rosie had stuffed into the fridge and was enough to feed the entire town; the preparation list Rosie had pinned next to the bushfire emergency plan.

As darkness descended Rosie shivered. It wasn't cold, not in the slightest, but with the magical lights shining from the trees and the smiles on faces as song sheets were handed out, the atmosphere was charged. They started with 'Jingle Bells', followed by 'Away in A Manger', 'Santa Claus is Coming to Town', and 'Silent Night'. And when they launched into the chorus of 'All I Want for Christmas Is You', Rosie felt the warmth of Owen's body behind her right shoulder and the words struggled to form on her lips. She was further away from Adam this year than she had ever been before, even though he was only a few hundred metres away, asleep in her bed.

The crowds dispersed after the carols for more Christmas Eve drinking. Families took their children home to tuck in, older couples bid goodnight to other residents, and Rosie leaned against a tree as the coolness of her beer trickled through her insides.

'Have you thought about whether you want to contact your biological father?' she asked.

'Now I know he's alive you mean? I don't know. I mean, I've always thought he was dead, that getting in contact wasn't an option – unless I developed psychic powers of course. What do you think I should do?'

She smiled now. 'Since when have you listened to anyone else, let alone me?'

'Good point, Stevens.'

They took their empty beer bottles inside and passed through the lit-up archway in the direction of home.

'I feel like I've just found my mum, after all this time.' Owen stared straight ahead. 'And it's bad enough digesting what my biological father did in the past, let alone finding out there's more. I'm starting to think it's better to let things go than fight to understand them completely.'

As they walked Rosie thought about what Owen had said. Maybe all this time with Adam she'd been fighting her own battle in search of the perfect dream. Had she pushed aside real life to look for a happiness she was never going to find?

Chapter Twenty-Nine

Tom, Sadie and Ryan descended on the house before lunchtime on Christmas day, and Tom was instantly charmed by Rosie; less so by Adam, who couldn't seem to get it through his head that Tom *chose* to be a stay-at-home dad. Owen handed the man a beer and tried to remember he was way out of his comfort zone being here with all of them.

It was a warm summer's day, but with a storm lingering overhead in the form of weighty grey clouds, Rosie and Owen elected to eat indoors at the table that stretched along the kitchen near to the double doors at the back of the house.

'Rosie's great,' Tom whispered when he and Owen moved away from the girls in the kitchen as Sadie told Rosie how great the tree looked, how amazing the table settings were.

Owen held Ryan in his arms, close to the tree but far enough to stop Ryan grabbing the baubles or the lights that made him grin and gurgle. 'She's worked really hard today. She was like a whirlwind in the kitchen, wouldn't hear of accepting any help.'

Tom leant closer to his brother. 'That's not exactly what I meant.'

'I know it wasn't.' Owen handed Ryan back to Tom without meeting his gaze.

‘So?’

Owen watched Rosie lay a sprig of something-or-other on top of the turkey before Sadie lifted the platter over to the table. ‘There’s nothing to tell. As you can see for yourself, she’s already spoken for.’ Owen’s brows knitted together as Adam passed Rosie and grazed his hand across her lower back.

He skulled the rest of his beer, and as Adam swapped the kitchen area for the armchair nearest the Christmas tree, Owen joined Rosie.

‘Anything I can do for the dinner, Stevens?’ He rested a hand on her shoulder but removed it when Adam looked up from his iPad. Actually, it was pretty good Christmas entertainment to wind the guy up; he was easy bait, and Owen wasn’t a complete saint.

‘It’s all sorted in here.’ With a ruby red oven mitt protecting her hand from the steam, Rosie strained the vegetables. ‘I’m enjoying myself.’

He leaned closer. ‘Did you call your mum to wish her a Merry Christmas?’

She smiled. ‘I did, and she’s going to call over New Year’s too.’

‘I’m glad.’ He loved how easily she slotted in here and wondered whether, after this house-sit, she’d want to keep in touch. He wondered whether he’d ever see her again.

*

‘Well that tasted even better than it looked, Rosie.’ Following lunch, Tom sat back and patted his stomach. ‘I just wish I had a drawstring waist on these jeans.’

Smiling, Rosie stood to clear the plates. ‘I’ll take that as a compliment.’

Owen whisked the plate out of her hands. ‘Oh no you don’t, you’re not clearing up.’

'He's right,' said Adam, collecting dishes from the centre of the table.

'And don't even think of telling me you enjoy it as much as the cooking,' Owen called from the kitchen.

Rosie moved round the table next to Sadie. 'You'll get no arguments from me. The clearing up is all yours!'

'I love the Christmas village.' Sadie was still trying to persuade Ryan to try the mashed up cauliflower, long after the adults had finished their food. She gave up and let him chew on the roast potato he held in his fist. 'Where's it from?'

'Magnolia Gifts.'

'Oh, I love that place. You wait till Easter when they have the cutest Easter baskets. I can't wait until Ryan is old enough to do a big Easter egg hunt.'

'There's a chocolate shop opening up next year too,' said Rosie mischievously. 'You could buy your basket and then go and fill it with your own selection.'

'Now that sounds like a great idea,' Sadie smiled.

The women chatted as the men cleared up and finally it was present time. They congregated in the lounge area as storm clouds hovered ominously outside.

'You men were the picture of domesticity up there,' said Rosie. She sipped her wine. 'Aren't you drinking today?' She'd noticed Owen sipping on orange juice.

'I'd better not. Plenty of guys have family commitments today, so I want to be available in case I'm called.'

'But you've got family commitments,' she said.

'I know, but I don't have kids of my own and many of the others do. And Christmas is all about the kids. You guys are big enough and ugly enough to cope without me for a while if I have to go.'

Rosie bent down to the bottom of the tree and pulled out a box wrapped in shiny silver paper with white snowflakes. She handed it straight to Ryan. 'Master Ryan, Merry Christmas.' She planted a kiss of top of his downy head.

'You didn't have to do that.' Sadie grinned as Ryan's hands smacked against the box having no idea how this present opening worked.

'I wanted to.'

'Wowzers!' Tom was straight into ripping off the paper for his son and pulled out a bright yellow and orange plastic bulldozer. 'Look, Ryan, the driver lights up.' He pressed one button and then another for the sound effects. Ryan was fascinated by the wrapping paper scrunched between his fists while his dad was having a great time playing with the truck and sussing out its functions.

Adam sat forwards on the sofa and rubbed Rosie's shoulders as she sat on the floor. She reached her hand up and covered his. It was nice to have him here; weird, but nice.

Tom and Sadie gave Owen a new pair of biker gloves, they gave Rosie a silver bracelet with delicate flowers which she loved, and Owen bought his brother and Sadie a day out at Domaine Chandon in the Yarra Valley.

'Is babysitting included?' asked Tom.

'I guess so.'

'Overnight?'

Owen laughed. 'I walked right into that one, didn't I?'

Owen pulled another gift from beneath the tree and handed it to Rosie. 'It's just a little something.'

Rosie took the flat package wrapped in gold paper and tied with a green bow. Adam hovered behind her and she gulped as she released the ribbon and found a square, black envelope beneath the wrapping.

'What is it?' Adam urged.

She smiled at the gift certificate inside.

'It's to ensure she gets her dream Christmas next year,' Owen explained as Rosie showed everyone the gift certificate for the tree farm they'd visited weeks before.

Rosie regaled the story of choosing the real tree that stood in the corner now, omitting details of her journey up there on Owen's bike.

'Thank you, Owen. I got something for you, too.' She found his gift and watched him tug away paper to reveal an intercom kit for his motorbike. To mask her embarrassment she grabbed Adam's present next, his favourite aftershave, Armani Acqua di Gio. She'd bought it for him and posted it a couple of weeks ago and he'd put it beneath the tree earlier today.

'Thank you, Rosie.' He kissed her cheek. 'My turn,' he said excitedly. He crouched down and pulled a small parcel from the back of the tree.

'When did you hide that?' She smiled up at him.

'Moments after I arrived – what, did you think I'd forgotten?'

Rosie loosened the white satin bow and peeled away the silver wrapping to reveal a grey velvet box, and for a moment she couldn't breathe. She opened the velvet box, but instead of the ring she had expected to see sitting on a bed of plush velvet, it was a key.

'I don't understand,' she said.

Adam knelt down beside her. 'It's not just any key, Rosie. It's a key to our new place.'

‘What?’

‘I’ve bought us an apartment in the city, in the heart of the Docklands: three bedrooms and three bathrooms. Friends welcome,’ he directed to the rest of the room. ‘There’s a gym in the complex, a sauna and pool, barbecue area, the works.’

‘Adam, I don’t know what to say.’ Her mind leapt to the cottage on Daisy Lane, but of course, she’d never even told him about it. And even if she had, she doubted Adam had, for one single minute, stopped to think about what she wanted. He called the shots in this relationship, always had. But then again, here he was, offering her what she’d always wanted: stability, security, permanence.

A buzzing from the kitchen bench stole Rosie’s attention away from the key. Owen leapt up, checked his pager and made a phone call as Sadie asked Adam all about the new pad.

Owen reappeared. ‘I have to go. Fire call.’

‘Stay safe,’ said Rosie, the memory of her dad more on her mind as she shared another family’s Christmas.

Their gazes met briefly before he left, and when Rosie heard the familiar rumble of the Ducati, she wished she could jump onto the back of the bike too and get far away from here so she didn’t have to think about what her future held now.

Chapter Thirty

The fire call was to a structure fire, a residential property just outside Magnolia Creek, and Owen pulled on his gear before joining the rest of the crew. Sirens blaring, the fire engine made its way to the scene.

When they arrived the family were outside, watching on as flames took hold. The youngest child was screaming and clinging to his older sister's leg, the mother was crying and the dad looked on at the devastation with utter disbelief.

The crew confirmed nobody was inside the house – even the family dog had got out in time. The crew hosed the front windows of the house where the flames were belting out and threatening to reach for the tree in the front yard. A paved area separated the house from the grass, and with any luck they could extinguish the worst before the fire spread. The last thing they wanted was flames or embers to reach the grass and start a major bushfire. The house was in a remote location with the nearest neighbour well over a hundred metres away, and all that separated them was fields and grass, fuel for the fire.

Once the worst of the flames had been extinguished, Owen entered the building behind a colleague, using hand signals and yelling at the top of his voice as they made their way through an unfamiliar structure. This was a challenge Owen could tackle, one he wanted to overcome. But as he watched his colleague's back and directed the hose to the flames that almost lit their way like lighting on the floor of an airplane cabin, Owen knew he'd lost the challenge of Rosie.

She wasn't his. She never would be.

*

By the time Owen arrived back at the house, Tom, Sadie and Ryan had already left.

Rosie poured a glass of red wine. When Owen shook his head at the offer, she said, 'Come on, you look as though you need it and it's only one.'

'Thank you.' He took the glass gratefully. 'I bet Ryan fell asleep on the way home. The kid must be exhausted, I know I am.' He took a generous gulp of red. 'Where's Adam?'

'He overdid the beer this afternoon. He's sleeping it off upstairs.' She sat down next to him. 'Was the fire really bad?'

'The family were lucky. From what we know, the Christmas tree was too close to a floor lamp and the lower branches caught on fire. The whole tree was alight in less than thirty seconds. It was lucky they were all in the room and saw it happen so they could escape. If those two kids had been asleep in bed, and the adults had been at the back of the house in the kitchen, then …'

'But they weren't, Owen, they weren't.' Her dad had been through the same emotions too, and she knew that caring was part of the job, the part that drove firefighters to acts of heroism without a second thought. 'And you came home safely too,' she said. To break the stare between them both, she asked, 'Are you hungry?'

He shook his head but when she frowned he admitted, 'Actually, I am a bit.' He laughed as her frown deepened. 'Okay, a lot.'

She opened a plastic container. 'Can I interest you in a homemade mince pie? They're my speciality.'

'Sounds great. In fact,' he grinned, 'make it two, with cream.'

'Thank you for my voucher,' she said as she warmed the mince pies in the microwave and then drizzled a generous helping of cream over them.

'I wanted to be sure you didn't bow out of Christmas. And now you have a new apartment, it'll be perfect. I just hope some poor bugger doesn't have to carry the tree up too many flights of stairs.'

'I'm sure there's a lift,' she said.

His gaze locked with hers. 'That was some Christmas present. When do you get to see the place for yourself?'

'I'll go over next week.' She busied herself wiping up the blob of cream she'd spilt on the kitchen bench.

When Owen had finished eating, she watched him go over to the bookcase and pull something out from behind the travel books. He handed her a flat red and gold parcel. There was a label attached which read, 'Merry Christmas Rosie, Love your Secret Santa.'

'It's something I wanted you to have, but I didn't want to give it to you in front of everyone else,' he explained.

By 'everyone else' she assumed he meant Adam.

Inside the wrapping was a CD. She turned it over to see the cover.

Owen spoke first. 'She's a cello diva, she's—'

'I know.' Tears stung Rosie's eyes as she clutched the CD by a modern cellist Rosie had listened to many a time. 'Your Song', 'What a Wonderful World', and 'Heaven', were just some of the tracks. 'I don't know what to say.'

'I got you this, too.' He produced a thin, flat envelope from his back pocket.

Her hands shook as she opened what she'd assumed was a Christmas card. But inside was much more than the previous gifts. It was a voucher, written on embossed paper.

'It's a day with the lady herself,' he explained.

Rosie stared at the voucher for a day playing cello with one of the best cellists in the world, one who had played with the Sydney Symphony Orchestra and to members of the royal family.

'I want you to experience a little piece of wonderful, Rosie. You might think you're not ready yet, but you will be. Trust me.' He took her hands in his.

'Rosie …' He stepped closer. But when his fingers wrapped around her left hand he froze, because beneath his grasp was the rock that hadn't been there before he left for the fire station. Adam had given her a second present, cleverly hidden within the branches of the tree, and one he'd only given her when they were alone. And when Adam uttered the words 'Will you marry me?' she'd said 'Yes'; of course she had. It was the right thing to do, what she'd wanted for so long.

Looking at Owen now, Rosie questioned whether doing the right thing was always the right thing to do.

Owen stared down at the princess-cut diamond engagement ring. He didn't say anything. He didn't have to. Rosie could read it all in his eyes: disappointment, regret, sadness, loss. He dropped her hand, nodded and accepted the reality for what it was, and then turned and headed upstairs without looking back.

Chapter Thirty-One

The weather rocketed to forty degrees two days later, and Rosie dropped Adam at the airport in a cloud of confusion. She had everything she'd ever wanted: the ring, the key to an apartment, the promise of a secure future. Adam had seen her through the darkest days after her dad died. He'd held her up when she'd almost fallen apart with the loneliness that nobody else understood, and he'd been the one constant in her life. To alter that was unimaginable for her, the girl who feared not knowing what was around the next corner.

'There's high fire danger today.' Owen was in the kitchen when she arrived home from the airport. 'I've looked at the FireReady app, and there's a total fire ban with a grassfire sixty kilometres away.'

The FireReady app usually made her feel in control and stopped her getting into a tizzy when she saw the bushfire plan. Usually it helped keep her thoughts organised, ready to take action if necessary. But that was before a day of high fire danger.

She must've looked concerned because Owen said, 'I've watered the garden and hosed down the trees, the gutters are clear and I've given the shrubs, rockery and the eaves a decent soaking. I don't think Magnolia Creek is in danger.' He kept his distance as though the ring on her finger repelled him. 'If you're worried, Tom is happy to put you up for the night. Or you could head to your mum's.'

Her chest tightened. 'I'll be fine staying here.'

Perhaps she should never have come to Magnolia Creek. If she'd found a job in the city instead, she'd never have met Owen and his family. And if that had been the case, she'd be happy with Adam. She wouldn't be questioning the future laid out before her now, represented by a ring and a key.

'Rosie, it's a safety precaution, that's all.'

What had happened to calling her Stevens?

Everything had changed.

'Is anyone else evacuating in Magnolia Creek?' she asked.

'Not that I know of.' His refusal to look at her hurt more than anything.

'Then what makes you think I need to? I'm fine here. I'll keep checking the FireReady app, I'll be careful.'

Desperate to quench her thirst in this heat, Rosie took the orange juice from the fridge, and when she closed the door she saw what was pinned to the front. 'What's this?' An e-ticket lay beneath an owl fridge magnet.

'I'm going back to London,' said Owen. 'For six months.'

She tried to stop her hand shaking as she poured the juice.

'I leave in three days,' he added.

The bitterness of the juice lingered on her tongue. Was this for the best? Would this help her to do the right thing, to take her life in the safe direction she'd always hoped for?

Instead of her hand reaching for the cello bridge on her necklace, her fingers went to the ring on her fourth finger. Her fingers had swollen in the heat and the ring wouldn't move. It felt as though it was getting even tighter.

Owen said nothing more about London, and when he left for the fire station, Rosie sat on the sofa as the Ducati rumbled away. She drew her knees up to her chin. The Christmas tree lights were switched off, the air conditioner hummed gently and George jumped up to keep her company. The love and attention from the feline nuzzling against her hand and fighting for attention was enough to make the tears fall. The problem with mapping your life out so carefully was that when goalposts moved, the entire game changed.

She lay on the sofa and George curled up beside her. A murky sky rolling over Magnolia Creek mesmerised her as she thought about Adam, her engagement and her new place to live. She thought about Owen, too. And after she'd checked the FireReady app to ensure the grassfires were still some distance away, she allowed herself to drift off to sleep, knowing exactly what she had to do.

*

Rosie's iPhone trilled beside her on the coffee table, and with George still heavily ensconced against her on the sofa, she tried to reach out without disturbing him.

'Did I wake you?' It was Owen.

'I dozed off on the sofa.' A faint whiff of smoke hung in the air and when she looked outside the sky was a deeper, spookier grey than before. 'Where are you? I can barely hear you.' George jumped off the sofa when she sat up. She pushed one finger into the ear without the phone so she could hear him better.

'Rosie, there's a big fire front ten kilometres away from Magnolia Creek.' He spoke concisely, not wasting a second. 'I'm on the scene now. I was instructed to take a break, grab water and rehydrate, so thought I'd call.'

'Is it coming this way?'

'It's holding for now, but we're close to sounding the siren in Magnolia Creek.'

Rosie's nails dug into her bare leg. The siren only sounded if the town needed to evacuate. There hadn't been an incident here for years. This couldn't be happening.

Her dad's face flashed in her mind, the sound of a bow being pulled across cello strings rung in her ears.

'Rosie? Rosie?' Owen shouted at her down the phone.

Her voice came out small. 'I'm still here.'

'Rosie, the siren is the last stage before the town evacuates.'

'I know.'

'You need to leave sooner rather than later. Fire can take hold quickly and the last thing you want to be doing is getting caught in it, or unable to leave. Please, go to Tom and Sadie's – their address is on the post-it beside the bushfire plan. Or go to your mum's, wherever you'd be more comfortable.' She heard him exhale. 'Rosie, just get out of there.'

'But—'

He ignored her pleas. 'Turn right at the end of Lakeside Lane and you'll be driving away from it. That road will take you towards the city.'

The sky outside was filled with a haunting grey. Paralysed by fear, it was as though someone had dropped a great weight on each of her legs, rendering it impossible to move.

‘Rosie!’ Owen yelled again.

‘I’m here.’

‘I’ve got to go. We’re hoping the fire won’t reach Magnolia Creek, but this is the worst I’ve ever seen it. Get out now, Rosie.’ When she said nothing, he said, ‘Not in ten minutes time. Get out now!’

She heard him breathe down the phone, reluctant to hang up until he knew she’d heard him right. She snapped to attention, her legs hoisting her upwards. ‘Do you have a pet carrier for George?’

He told her where to find one and thankfully George didn’t bolt at the sight of it. She ran upstairs and shoved valuables and a few clothes into an overnight bag. She grabbed her keys from the hook beside the door, and with the bag slung over her shoulder and the pet carrier in the other arm, she pulled open the front door.

The air was thicker with smoke than she’d realised as she ran to the car. The fires seemed to be trying to wrap the entire town in a suffocating blanket, and she coughed as she climbed into the back seat to fix the pet carrier in place by threading the seat belt through the plastic handle. She squeezed out of the car again and leapt into the front seat, started the engine of the Hubba and turned on the lights to find her way through smoke billowing all around. Her dad’s voice rang in her ears. It told her to stay calm, drive carefully, to stay safe.

But Rosie wasn’t ready. She was far from it. She burst into tears, just as she’d done once when she’d been stuck on a zip wire at the park, too scared to drop as the gap felt too high off the ground. She’d cried until her dad had come and rescued her. The other kids had been jeering, telling her she was a scaredy cat, a chicken; her dad had wrapped his arms around her legs and lifted her out of harm's way.

She looked out at the steel sky, quiet in its threat, and at the orange glow in the distance that shocked her so much she almost couldn't breathe. She heard Adam's voice on Christmas day, his excitement over the apartment he'd bought for them and the proposal on his lips when he'd asked her to marry him. He was going to be so hurt when she told him she'd changed her mind, when she told him he wasn't the man for her.

She slumped against the steering wheel and shut her eyes. Fire had robbed her of her father, and she wasn't about to let it take anything else away. Her fist thumped the leather once, twice, three times, four times. 'No, no, no, no!' Her voice grew louder with every shout until she looked up, revved the engine into life and prepared to fight. This couldn't be her time. All the playing it safe couldn't ultimately lead to this, could it?

The evacuation siren was sounding now, over and over, the noise whirring round and round in her head as she drove away. Away from danger, away from Owen Harrison.

Chapter Thirty-Two

The oppressive heat beneath Owen's yellows came from the radiant heat of the fires and the heavy clothing. His feet felt swollen and smoke stung at his eyes. The incident controller already had an understanding of the combined effects of fuel, weather and topography, and his voice rumbled on air thick with smoke and flying embers. The fire was spreading fast with plenty of hectares of unburnt land remaining. The meagre rainfall of the season had done a poor job at dampening down the dry grasses beneath the punishing Australian sun, and with temperatures well into the forties today, the threat to Magnolia Creek was imminent.

Despite fuel breaks dug into the edges of the surrounding fields, the flames were leaping those with the help of the wind speed and putting the town in jeopardy. His strike team was instructed to head to the eastern flank as another crew took the western flank. They were to launch a direct attack on the fire to try to stop it reaching the town.

Wearing goggles, gloves and a dust mask, memories of Black Saturday were very much in the forefront of Owen's mind as he met thick black ash that blocked the sun and the eerie orange glow as the flames beat down so close to him and the rest of the crew. He thought about Rosie. Had she listened to him and left the house? He hoped she wasn't one of those people who intrepidly stayed on at their property, convinced the danger would pass. He wondered whether George was with her too or whether she was still standing out on the back deck trying to coax the bloody cat inside. He'd done that plenty of times himself.

Fighting away the terror at the thought of her being so damned determined not to let an animal perish that she'd sacrifice her own safety, he boarded the second tanker as three lined up and headed down to the eastern flank of the fire. The sky that greeted them there was as bad as his memories of Black Saturday. The driver yelled at the crew to destroy the fencing around the land they needed to access in order to get the trucks through. Owen jumped down as they slowed, and using wire cutters he tore the fence apart bit by bit, helped by Sonia, a fellow CFA volunteer.

Visibility was atrocious as the truck ploughed on. Adrenalin pumped through every crevice in Owen's body and all of his senses were on high alert, ready for instruction, ready to take the initiative as he and every member of the crew constantly regauged the seriousness of the fire. Owen's eyes darted left, right, up, down, watching for dangerous embers to catch before they were carried on the wind and out of his control. As the truck moved he blasted the flames with the hose, determined not to let the fire that ravaged with the finer fuel of grass beat them. This sort of fire was capable of travelling up to sixty kilometres per hour in open grassland, and any change to the wind speed would increase the threat, carrying the fire over to nearby towns.

Owen's fear escalated when the team got the call that the fire had reached Magnolia Creek. The siren had been sounded long ago.

The truck headed that way, and as they came into Magnolia Creek he felt as though he was about to pass out. The roads were clear all the way to town, but flying embers had started a new attack here, starting with Finnegan's café.

Bella.

*

Rosie drove some twenty kilometres out of Magnolia Creek and pulled in at a petrol station where she glugged back a bottle of water and sat in the back seat with George, stroking him when she opened the carrier and he immediately leapt onto her lap as though he understood the mutual need for comfort.

She knew then that she was safe, but as she sat there talking to the cat like some crazy lady, she snapped. Owen wasn't out of danger, not at all, and she'd left him up there. And no matter how much she heard his voice telling her 'Stevens, I'm man enough to look after myself', she couldn't just sit here and do nothing.

And so an hour after she'd realised she was going to be just fine, she started up the Hubba and drove back. Back to Magnolia Creek.

*

Owen barely let the fire truck come to a standstill before he leapt out and ran straight towards the café. The sound of glass exploding from the force of the flames had him ducking for cover. He'd not heard Bella on the radio waves from the fire station or heard her name mentioned by any crew tonight. Did that mean she was still upstairs in the café? Rodney wasn't on the team tonight, he was out of town, but had Bella done the sensible thing and left?

Owen lifted a foot and booted open the front door to the café, using the TIC to detect any movement inside. Along with Gus and two other colleagues, he entered the café. He headed towards the stairs in case the woman who had been there for him his entire life was trapped on the floor above, but a flaming part of the ceiling came crashing down in front of him, blocking his path. And then it was like a Jenga game as bit by bit the entire ceiling gave way. Gus pulled Owen from the café as the other firefighters ran for their lives, and he held Owen back when he tried to go back in there.

Owen yelled Bella's name at the top of his voice, shouting towards the top window as the flames took hold and the sides of the café folded inwards like a collapsed cardboard box.

'Fuck! No!' Owen's face jerked away from the fierce flames and his body was starting to wilt under the intense heat and pressure. He yanked off his BA gear and then turned and vomited in the gutter.

It was a scene of devastation and he watched on, helpless as other members of the crew fought the flames until all that remained was a black, charcoal shell full of debris. Tears stung at his eyes. The rest of the crew were fighting the flames that attacked the bush framing the road towards Lakeside Lane. Embers must've jumped and picked their victims, grabbing them quickly and taking hold.

Owen's mind was anywhere but the job. His mind was on Bella and whether she'd made it out on time. His mind was on Rosie and whether she'd driven away from danger before she'd been overcome with smoke or trapped by the fire.

Two helicopters rose in the air and dumped water on the edge of the fire to get a lead on beating the flames, and Owen tried to stifle the persistent cough as bile rose and he vomited again.

'Owen, you're no use to anyone if you cook yourself.' It was Bella.

He threw his arms around her and she clung onto him.

'Oh God, Bella. I thought …'

Tears filled her eyes when she spoke. 'I only came back today – spent Christmas at my in-laws – and I went straight to the fire station but Niamh had everything under control there.'

'I didn't hear you on the radio.'

'Like I said, Niamh had everything under control. I'm sorry to have worried you.'

'I'm sorry about the café.' They both looked at the hopeless scene before them. 'Thank God you weren't there when the embers attacked.'

'I'm feeling very lucky right now.' She managed a smile. 'And it's bricks and mortar, Owen. We'll rebuild. We're all safe, that's the main thing.'

She handed him a drink containing electrolytes. It was revolting but necessary. She passed him another bottle of water that he poured over his head, saturating his hair and cooling the throbbing sensation in his temples.

Owen knew he couldn't go anywhere to check on Rosie while the fire still raged. He had to put others first before he could get to her. He pulled on his head gear yet again and took over from Gus, who had been pulled out due to his body temperature being too high.

It took another hour and a half to bring the fire in town under control. Sometimes it felt as though all they were doing was stopping the fire from spreading, making no headway at all with the bulk of it. Flames had spread right to the entrance of Lakeside Lane, and had Owen's team reached the scene minutes later, the fire could've travelled down the roadside and taken his parents' house with it. Magnolia Creek had escaped danger for now, but there was still a risk over the next day or so that flying embers could start spot fires. They'd need to be vigilant, but he prayed the worst was over.

Right now his concern was Rosie. As he'd fought the fire, he'd made a deal with himself that as soon as they beat this thing, he'd tell her everything. He'd tell her everything before he left for the UK. He had to tell her before she went off and married Adam, before she felt she was in so deep that she couldn't change anything. And if she walked away, then he would just have to accept that.

*

As Rosie neared Magnolia Creek, the car started to smell of smoke which found its way through any tiny gap it could. She couldn't see any violent orange in the air, which had to be a good sign, right?

She peered over the steering wheel like an old age pensioner terrified of driving, winding her way along the roads that lead to the main street. Her phone bleeped next to her to indicate an incoming text message and she snatched it up, anxious to know whether Owen was okay, whether Magnolia Creek would survive this.

Her heart sank when she read a message from Adam to say his flight was cancelled and he was holed up in a hotel. She stared at the phone, gutted it hadn't been a message from Owen. When she looked up she saw a bend in the road. A bend she hadn't expected. And she was heading straight for the bushes and trees in front of her.

She slammed on the brakes and yanked the wheel, but the only sound for miles was no longer the evacuation siren. It was the sound of metal crunching, glass smashing.

And her world went black.

Chapter Thirty-Three

Owen dumped his gear and yellows at the fire station. He phoned Rosie's mobile but no answer. He phoned Tom, but Tom hadn't heard from her. He jumped onto the Ducati and made the short journey back to the house, blackness framing the road instead of the lush green beauty of the bush. Smoke hung in the air and clung to every part of him.

When Owen neared the turn-off for Lakeside Lane, that was when he saw it. The Hubba.

He almost lost control of the Ducati in his efforts to stop. Running towards the Hubba he called out her name. He could see Rosie, her hair unmistakable, the air bag deployed in front of her. He pulled at the door handle, but it wouldn't budge. He looked around and found the biggest rock he could at the side of the road and smashed the passenger window. Pulling his leather jacket over his hand he pushed away the glass and reached through to open it from the inside.

'Rosie, Rosie … can you hear me?'

She couldn't.

He leant close to her and felt her breath on his face. 'Oh, Rosie. Please be okay, please.' He daren't move her.

George mewed from the backseat, still intact in his carrier. 'She'll be okay, George, you'll see.'

She was breathing, but he didn't know how bad this was. Her internal injuries could be massive. Blood was trickling down the side of her face, coagulating in her hair. He called the ambulance and held her hand as they waited. He'd never forgive himself for not being there for her. Never.

In the ambulance Rosie slipped in and out of consciousness. Owen coughed and spluttered for most of the journey from the smoke inhalation and the panic he'd felt. Rosie wrapped her fingers around his when he touched her hand, she said his name. But then she also said Adam's. She was confused, out of it, and he was desperate to talk to her.

He leaned closer when she tried to speak again. 'Don't talk, not now,' he said.

She tried again and he made out the words 'came back'.

Came back where?

At the hospital the doctors insisted they examine him, but he'd refused to let them until he knew the situation with Rosie. She was stable, they told him, and he'd relented. And when they were giving him the once over, he realised what Rosie had meant in the ambulance. 'Came back', she'd said. She must've left Magnolia Creek and come back. Had she come back for him?

He looked at her, sleeping now right there in front of him. He desperately wanted her to wake up. He wanted to tell her how he felt, find out if he'd imagined the feelings were reciprocated.

He stroked her copper hair now, dishevelled against the pillow, spattered and tangled with dried blood, as she lay in the middle of the room on a bed that made her look tiny. Her eyelashes caressed the tops of her cheekbones as she slept. She had bruising down one side of her face, white strips of plaster held bloody skin together and she had an oxygen cannula inserted. A needle protruded from her hand with a drip attached, and a funny white clip sat on the tip of her finger. She'd sustained a head injury when her head had smacked against her window, but she'd been lucky. Apart from severe concussion and a hell of a lot of bruising, numerous x-rays confirmed she was in one piece.

He only looked away from her face when the door to her room opened. In walked a woman cradling an enormous bouquet of camellias, roses and lilies.

The woman rushed to Rosie's side immediately. Owen dropped Rosie's hand, took the bouquet and laid it on the chair by the door.

'Who are you?' The woman asked.

'I'm Owen. Rosie was house-sitting for my parents in Magnolia Creek.'

'Right.' She didn't take her eyes away from Rosie. 'I'm Sasha, Rosie's mum.'

He'd figured, given the remarkable likeness in skin and hair colouring. 'She's going to be fine,' he assured Sasha. He covered his mouth when he coughed.

'That's a nasty cough you've got there.' Sasha turned to him now, keeping a hold of her daughter's hand. 'Were you with Rosie?'

'No. I'm a firefighter.' He coughed again and this time Sasha stood and poured him a glass of water from the jug beside the bed. 'I found her in the car,' he explained.

Owen remembered what Rosie had said about her mum never coping with being married to a fireman. He wasn't sure how this woman was going to react to him.

'Then you're a hero,' she told him, patting his upper arm. 'And I need to thank you.' Tears welled at the corners of her eyes, but she turned back to Rosie before they could escape. 'I must call Adam,' said Sasha. 'I couldn't get an answer when I tried earlier, and he'll want to be here with her.'

Of course.

'I'd better go outside to call.' She seemed reluctant to leave Rosie's side.

'Don't worry, I'll stay with her.'

'Would you?' She pulled her phone out of her bag. 'I won't be long.'

He sat beside the bed gently stroking the back of Rosie's hand. He willed her to wake up. He wanted to be the first person she saw so she'd know he would be there for her. He'd never wanted to settle down, but spending time with Rosie made him want a change of pace. Somehow being with her just felt right.

'He's on his way.' Sasha smiled when she came back into the room. 'His flight was cancelled, so he was in a hotel at the airport waiting for another one.'

'That's good.' Not for him though.

'Adam's good for her, Owen.'

Oh God, had he made his own feelings that obvious?

'He's steady, stable,' Sasha went on. 'He's someone she'll be able to rely on.'

Yes, but did she really love him the way she should love someone? Or was she playing it too safe?

Owen noticed Rosie's eyelashes flutter and her eyes opened a fraction before shutting again. She shifted in the bed.

'Rosie, it's Mum. I'm here, darling. You're going to be fine.'

He opened his mouth to speak but nothing came out.

'Adam's on his way. He'll be here for you soon.' Sasha looked over at Owen and he hated to admit it, but he was intimidated. Was he really about to ruin what Rosie had fought for her entire life? Was he about to take away any part of her happiness?

He stepped towards the bed but her eyes stayed shut. Sasha stroked her daughter's head.

'Adam …' Rosie spoke but she was still disorientated.

'He's on his way,' said Sasha.

'Mum?'

'It's me, yes.'

'I need to …' Rosie coughed and Owen backed away towards the door. He needed some air, a few minutes to compose himself.

He hovered in the doorway for a minute and heard Rosie ask for Adam again. 'I need to see him,' she said.

And with that he gently shut the door behind him.

Rosie deserved the world, and he'd done his best to make her see she shouldn't settle for anything less than wonderful. But she'd got everything she'd always wanted – the guy, the home, the security – and hadn't been able to imagine life any other way. He had to walk away now.

Owen took a taxi back to Magnolia Creek and picked up the Ducati from where he'd left it, near the trees Rosie had crashed side-on into. He'd called Bella, who had come and taken the cat before the ambulance arrived, and the Hubba had been taken away, the roads quiet in the aftermath of the fires.

Bella must've let his parents know about the fire because there was a message on the answer machine when he got home. They were taking an earlier flight and would be home within thirty-six hours. Owen took the stairs to his room as the sun set at the close of another day. He paused at Rosie's bedroom, many of her things still as they'd been before.

In the shower it took two big dollops of shampoo to finally lather the smell out of his hair and what felt like a gallon of soap to clean his body. He stood under the jets until the hot water began to run cold, and when his head hit the pillow that night, he knew it was time to let Rosie go. And it was time for him to move on.

Chapter Thirty-Four

Rosie closed the book she was reading when her mum poked her head around the door to the spare room at her house in Geelong.

'Cup of tea?' Her mum handed her a polka-dot mug.

'Thanks. What time is it?'

'Nine thirty.'

'I'm improving.' Rosie smiled. The wounds on the side of her face had long gone and the bruising had faded, and she hoped in time she'd feel completely back to normal.

She'd thought of Owen a lot since the fires and the accident a month ago. The biggest surprise of all had been finding him and learning through him that she must allow herself to be truly happy.

'You're almost back to your normal self.' Her mum handed her a plate with three cookies on it. 'I made oatmeal and raisin cookies.'

Rosie grinned. 'You've only got a couple of hours left to fuss over me before the next house-sit, so I'll humour you.' Rosie's name was still on the house-sitting register and they'd contacted her a few days ago to say there was a month-long house-sit in Magnolia Creek that they couldn't interest anybody with. Rosie presumed it was too far from the city for most people. When she'd called Magnolia House to see if her part-time position had been filled and they'd said 'of course not', all the pieces had fitted together perfectly. This was a fresh start for her, and for once, she didn't mind the thought of not having mapped out plans beyond the next few weeks. And when the agency had given her the address of the house as the cottage in Daisy Lane, she knew it was meant to be.

'Have you heard from Adam lately?' her mum asked her now.

Rosie shook her head. 'We're still friends, but I think it's best we're not in contact for a while.'

'I guess you both need to move on.'

Adam had come straight to the hospital, and as soon as she was up to a lengthy conversation, Rosie had talked to him. She'd finally told him exactly the way she felt. She told him how she'd longed to feel settled, to feel safe, ever since her mum left when she was little. She told him how she'd thought their relationship was everything she'd ever wanted or needed, but that it wasn't fair to him anymore. Adam had nodded, said he understood. The sadness in his eyes had said otherwise and Rosie had hated hurting him, but he didn't deserve someone who didn't love him properly. Years ago she'd fallen into his arms thinking he could make her life complete, and he had for a while. But it was time now, time to go their separate ways and time for her to take a risk on the unknown.

'Everything okay?' Rosie asked as her mum fidgeted as though she wanted to say something but couldn't.

'I haven't told you everything.'

'About what?' Rosie put the plate of cookies down beside her bed.

'About Owen.'

'Owen?'

'He was the one who found you, after the accident.'

'I know. I talked to him in the ambulance.' Confused she asked, 'Is there something else?'

'He was holding your hand when I arrived.'

Rosie looked down at the cookies.

'I have to ask, Rosie. Was there something between you two? Is that why you finished with Adam?'

Since the split with Adam and the recuperation from her accident, Rosie and her mum had grown closer. They'd talked a lot about Adam and why she'd stayed with him for so long, and it had helped Rosie to know she'd definitely made the right decision. But she hadn't shared much about Owen. He'd come up in conversation as Rosie talked about the house-sit and Magnolia Creek, but perhaps she hadn't been as great at disguising her feelings as she'd thought.

'Meeting Owen helped me see that I was with Adam for all the wrong reasons,' Rosie explained. 'Owen's moved on now, but I'm not sorry I ended things with Adam.'

She looked over at her house-sitting boxes, still filled with her belongings from Magnolia Creek. Her mum had contacted Jane Harrison and driven up there to get all her things when Rosie was first out of hospital. When her mum returned to Geelong, she'd filled Rosie in on the fire damage to Finnegan's café and the narrow escape for many businesses and all the residents of the town. Rosie had longed for news of Owen, but all she knew was that he'd headed over to the UK to take the property market by storm. It was probably for the best too. It would give Rosie time to get her head together and maybe, when he came back, she'd be able to tell him how she really felt.

Chapter Thirty-Five

With the car packed, Rosie drove the same roads she'd taken three months ago. She drove along sedately – it would take time to relax behind the wheel again – but as the trees formed a canopy overhead and her hired Volkswagen Beetle wound its way through Victoria's Dandenong Ranges, she began to relax. She thought about the Harrisons as she drove. They were a nice family, and though they had plenty to deal with, she'd like to see them after she settled in again. It was a small town so they were bound to run into one another, and Rosie wanted a chance to clear the air after finding herself unwittingly involved in keeping the family secret.

She followed the road's twists and turns, the roof down and the wind toying with her hair as the sun dared to peek through the trees in intervals. She was looking forward to catching up with Bella, who was staying with Rodney in one of the cottages at Magnolia House while the café was gutted and rebuilt. They'd spoken on the phone a few days after Rosie came out of hospital and Rosie had told her all about Adam too. She'd bake some scones today or tomorrow and take them to Bella, it was the least she could do.

She drove through Fernybrooke, following the bend round to the right, past the yellow triangle warning sign with the chunky, black wombat silhouette she remembered from the last time she'd driven this way. And when the sign reading 'Welcome to Magnolia Creek' in fancy, loopy letters came into view, she couldn't stop smiling.

Her grin faded when she saw the blackened edges of bush where there had once been nothing but green, and she realised how close she'd come to not being here at all. She passed another wooden sign announcing a new chocolate shop that'd be opening up in late autumn and promised original handmade chocolates, ice-creams of all flavours and a café to relax in and enjoy views of the surrounding Aussie bushland. And as the sun rose into the sky and she pulled up outside the cottage, the smile was back. The property looked better than she could've ever imagined. Whoever had bought it had done an admirable job. Her heart sagged a little that it wasn't hers, but then again, she knew herself better than ever now, and it wouldn't be long before she could save a deposit, secure a full-time job and find the perfect home, exactly where she wanted it to be.

Rosie hauled her bags out of the boot and walked up the short path to the front veranda, passing through the little white gate in the middle of the white picket fence she'd imagined putting in at the cottage. Hidden on the veranda, behind a terracotta pot filled with cream roses, was a key safe. She put in the code she'd been sent via email and took out the key to let herself in to a small hallway with a stream of sunlight coming from the door in the kitchen at the opposite end of the cottage.

Inside was perfect. She followed the short hallway past two rooms, one set up as a formal lounge and the other as a dining room. She passed the bathroom and sighed at the sight of the most beautiful claw foot bath – exactly the sort she'd have chosen had it been her cottage. At the rear of the house was a large open plan oak-fitted kitchen-diner. A vase of dancing pink roses stood tall and proud in the centre of a round wooden table, and at the other end of the room was a spiral staircase with an ornate wrought-iron bannister.

Rosie leaned in to smell the flowers, closing her eyes and letting her mind drift back to long summer nights in the garden at Lakeside Lane.

'Oh, hello boy.' She reached out to stroke the cat winding its way down the spiral staircase. The agency had explained this house-sit would involve pet-sitting duties and Rosie had been more than happy to oblige, if only for the company.

'You're gorgeous,' she said. 'In fact …' She didn't say anything else because her heart skipped a beat when she heard footsteps on the staircase.

She looked up at the man dressed in dark jeans and a black shirt, his hand gliding down the bannister.

'Owen.'

'Hi, Rosie.'

He held up a key and smiled, and then she understood. 'This is your house,' she said.

'Do you like it?'

She couldn't speak.

'It took a bit of sneaking around to do the place up without you knowing I'd bought it. I dumped all my tools here under the cover of night as soon as the sale went through, and every time I came here I hid the bike in case you wandered past.'

George brushed against her legs as Owen moved closer. He looped her hair behind her ears, delicately moving it behind her shoulders, away from her face, so as not to touch the scars.

She gulped. 'I don't believe it.'

He stood facing her now.

'I thought you were overseas,' she said.

'I was. But then I spoke to Bella and she told me what had happened between you and Adam. Out of curiosity I looked up the house-sitting agency and there was your profile. I had to take the chance on you and organised this house to be put on the books, requested you as my sitter.' He held his hands out in a fait accompli gesture.

She felt his breath in her hair, on her face, as his hands rested on the back on her neck, pulling her closer still.

'So I was your plan all along?' she asked. 'I was your latest challenge?'

He shook his head and then met her gaze. 'I admit I bought the house because of you. I thought of you when I painted the fence, the veranda, sanded the floors inside and installed the ornate fireplace. But I swear, Stevens, I wasn't trying to win you. If you'd moved in with Adam, been happy, I would've respected that, and this place … well I would've had to let it go too.'

She looked around her at the freshly painted walls, the gingham curtains hanging at the kitchen window. 'Why didn't you wait for me to wake in hospital?'

'You seemed to have everything you'd ever wanted. And your mum didn't look too happy about the possibility of me wrecking that.'

'She's fine. She just wants what's best for me.'

'Of course she does. But I had to walk away.'

'Owen Harrison, walk away?'

He grinned. 'I know.'

She took a deep breath, let it out. ‘I thought I was happy before I met you.’

He lowered his lips to hers and kissed her gently. ‘I thought I was too.’

He took her hand and led her into the dining room. Next to a second ornate fireplace was a cello, lying on its side. But as she took a step closer she realised it wasn’t just any cello. She swallowed hard and slowly knelt down beside the walnut instrument. Her fingers traced along the worn fingerboard she’d seen her dad touch a thousand times. Her hand brushed the tiny scratches next to the bridge, her eyes followed the curves of the f-holes on either side of the strings. She still had the voucher for the cello lesson Owen had given her for Christmas, and for the first time since, she actually thought she might use it.

Owen’s hand rested on her shoulder. ‘I went to extraordinary lengths to get the thing here without your knowledge. I think your mum might be warming to me.’

‘She was in on this?’ Rosie stood and looked into his eyes.

‘I contacted her a couple of days ago, and yesterday I drove the pickup to Geelong in the early hours of the morning. There wasn’t much time to chat, but I think she realises I’m not going to hurt you or let you down.’

Rosie reached for his hand, but instead of taking it, Owen crouched down and grabbed her lower legs, hoisting her up over his shoulder in a fireman’s lift. He turned and went through to the lounge and started up the spiral staircase.

‘Don’t you dare drop me!’ She couldn’t stop giggling. ‘I’ve spent enough time in hospital.’

‘Relax, I’m a professional. I could do this in my sleep.’

He set her down at the top of the staircase and kissed her again, his mouth warm and exciting in its unfamiliarity. He pulled her in to the house's second bedroom.

'What's this?' Before her was a bed draped in delicate white linen and in the middle were rose petals arranged in the shape of a heart.

He wrapped his arms around her waist, nuzzled her neck. 'Don't you dare broadcast this at the fire station, it's not a side of Owen Harrison I want made public.'

In the corner of her eye, Rosie noticed the tartan seat running along the length of the window.

'I put that in,' said Owen. 'I thought you'd like it.'

Rosie held her breath as he trailed kisses across her collar bone, up her neck.

'And what's that?' In the middle of the bed, in the centre of the roses forming the heart, was a letter.

'It's the house-sitting contract.'

She pulled away from him. 'You're really going to make me sign one of those?'

He unbuttoned her cotton dress and trailed kisses lower still. 'You bet I am. I'm not letting you get away from me again.' And he sealed the deal with a kiss that felt as though it would never end.

House-sitter Required – Magnolia Creek

House Owner: Owen Harrison
Start Date: Now
End Date: Indefinitely
Location: Rosie Cottage, Daisy Lane, Magnolia Creek

When I saw Rosie Cottage, I knew I'd found hidden beauty behind its mere existence. However, after restoring the cottage to its former glory, it still needs one final touch. I challenge you, Rosie Stevens, to turn it into a home filled with happiness, laughter and dreams that are nothing short of wonderful. If you agree to the following terms, then please sign below. And welcome home …

I, Rosie Stevens, promise to be the woman I want to be, not the woman anyone else expects me to be.

I will embrace life and take a chance on a little piece of wonderful.

I will embrace my past, rather than fear it, through beautiful music by playing the cello that has stayed quiet for too long.

And I promise to never, ever make Owen Harrison drive a pink car again!

Signed: *Rosie Stevens*

Acknowledgments

I'd like to thank Elissa Jans, volunteer firefighter and Community Safety Coordinator with Olinda Fire Brigade, Victoria, Australia, who answered my many research questions. Thank you too, to other members of the CFA who read passages of my story to enable me to make it realistic and technically accurate.

Thank you to my blog group, The Write Romantics, for being there to bounce ideas off, discuss characters and plot, and share in the ups and downs of the writing life. All ten of us have formed a lifelong friendship that is incredibly special to me. My thanks goes to my editor, Rachel Daven-Skinner, and to my proofreader, Stephanie Box. Thank you to Debbie Clement for designing a cover that I love.

Thank you to both my beta readers, Sharon and Alison. It's always scary passing a manuscript over to people who love reading books in the same genre, so I was glad that both of you really enjoyed reading What Rosie Found Next.

And finally, as always, thank you to my husband and my children for giving me the support and encouragement to keep writing. I couldn't do it without you.

Handle Me with Care

Does true love come along more than once in a lifetime?

Maddie Kershaw doesn't think so. She lost the love of her life in the 9/11 attacks, and since then has hopped from one casual fling to the next. But when she delivers an erotic cake to a one-hundredth birthday party by mistake, she meets Evan and starts to believe in second chances … until she realises there's a risk of getting hurt all over again.

Evan Quinn is serially single, yet when he meets Maddie he feels an instant connection, so much so that he confesses on their first date that he may have testicular cancer. Was it a mistake to tell her? He wants Maddie more than he has ever wanted any other woman. But he doesn't want her pity.

With the odds stacked against them both, finding love won't be easy. But beneath the Australian sun, a Happy Ever After could be worth fighting for.

The Friendship Tree

Is running away ever the answer?

Tamara Harding left the UK to join family in Australia, but more importantly, to put ten thousand miles between her and her ex, Bradley Cox. She is soon drawn in to the small community of Brewer Creek where she becomes the coordinator for an old fashioned Friendship Tree – a chart telling people who they can call on in times of trouble.

As she vows to start over, she meets Jake Manning – and life gets more complicated than she could ever have imagined. Jake is the direct competitor for the family business, and a man with a dark secret, and Tamara struggles to fight her attraction to him as she deals with secrets of her own and an ex who refuses to give up.

When danger descends on Brewer Creek in the form of Jake's own past, Tamara soon realises the Friendship Tree does a lot more than organise fundraising events and working bees; it has the power to unite an entire town. But will Tamara see past the complications and allow herself a happy ending with Jake? Or will she run away again?

Printed in Great Britain
by Amazon

61054475R00182